RHYTHM
of Us

FATED
HEARTS
SERIES
2

INTERNATIONAL BESTSELLING AUTHOR
AIMEE NICOLE WALKER

RHYTHM
of Us

CHAPTER
One

Xavier Cruz

I STOOD OUTSIDE THE BOWLING ALLEY STARING AT THE ENTRANCE DOOR like hell was waiting for me on the other side. In reality, I'd been living in my own personal hell for over a year and deserved whatever reception I got once I walked through that door. I'd left after Ava's wedding in June without an explanation to anyone, and I hadn't looked back. I'd missed every holiday and birthday, becoming more sullen and depressed with every lost visit home. Lost because I couldn't ever get the time back.

It was June again, nearly one year later, and I had returned for my best friend Chase's wedding to Grayson Wright. Chase was the brother of my heart, and we were just as close as any biological brothers would be. Chase's grandmother, Agnes Simmons, had become my guardian when I was five years old. Gram rescued me from a life of abuse and misery when I'd moved in with her and Chase.

At the age of five, I had already known I was different. I wanted to wear silky, shiny shirts and play with dolls, which had infuriated my father. I used to sneak some of my sister's things into my backpack to take to preschool with me. My teacher, Miss Annette, would always let me wear whatever I'd brought, and she always let me play with dolls whenever I wanted. Miss Annette never told me the clothes I wore were for girls or that playing with dolls made me a sissy. That was my father's job. Miss Annette loved me as I was, and I thanked God for her every single day.

I don't remember a lot about my childhood, but I remember the straw that broke my father's back. I asked him for a princess party for my sixth birthday. He lost all control and hit me with his belt until I could barely sit. The whole time he shouted that he was going to beat the devil out of me. At some point, I tuned him out and drifted off to a dreamland where people loved me for who I was and didn't hate me because I was different.

What happened the next day was permanently etched into my mind and was easily my most cherished memory. I'll never forget Chase holding my hand beneath the monkey bars while I cried and told him what happened. I begged him to keep my secret, and he kept his promise, even though he wanted to tell Miss Annette so badly. It was only when my oldest sister, Ellie, showed up at preschool to pick me up that I broke down and told Miss Annette, Gram, and Ellie what had happened to me. Chase had held my hand through that too.

I was scared when I'd talked to the police officers and the children's protective services social workers, but Gram had promised me that I'd get to live with her and Chase soon and that she'd never let anyone hurt me ever again. Like Chase, she'd been true to her word. But the heartache and horror I had suffered of late was all on my shoulders and no one else's.

Would Gram, Chase, and Ellie still love me if they found out what I'd done, who I had become in LA? I was stronger now and could see a little clearer, but had too much time passed since I'd left with barely a phone call back home for them to forgive me? Would they understand? There was only one way to find out.

I began to shake and tremble as I reached for the door. I dropped my hand and breathed deeply through my nose, urging my body to relax and ignore the craving for a small little pill that would make all of my fears and worries temporarily disappear. The driving need to lose myself in chemicals was the strongest I had felt since quitting a few months ago. *No!* I wouldn't give in. I'd fought too damn hard to get sober, and I refused to go back.

"I can do this. I can do this," I chanted to myself.

"Hey, stranger, are you really that worried about your bowling game?" a warm masculine voice asked from behind me.

Startled, I turned around so fast I lost my balance on the steps. Ben St. Claire, my sister's sexy-as-fuck, straight best friend and coworker at Wright Creations tried to grab me to keep me from falling, but I still crashed against his chest. I wasn't sure how Ellie could just be friends with the sexy guy, but she swore that's all they were.

The spicy smell of his cologne filled my nostrils, and I nearly embarrassed myself by taking a few extra whiffs. His strong arms were wrapped around me, holding me securely to his chest. Either Ben had really been working out since I'd last seen him or his business suits hid a delightfully strong body beneath all that fabric. I longed to stay in his arms, lay my head against his firm chest, and let my worries melt away. It occurred to me that Ben could be just as potent and addictive as any drug, and I'd need to keep my distance or find myself in jeopardy of screwing up my recovery. *Who was I kidding?* Ben was straight as an arrow and not interested in me at all.

I'd first met Ben the previous year when I'd returned home from LA. Chase had invited me to have lunch with him and Ellie one afternoon but hadn't told me he had also invited Ben. His looks got my attention, but his personality was what had captivated me and held my interest long after the lunch was over. If only he were gay and my head wasn't so screwed up right now.

"Sorry." My voice sounded strangled as I looked up into Ben's face. It was too dark outside to see his eyes, but I vividly remembered the gray color. They might have starred in a fantasy—or twenty—of mine. I stood up straight and ignored the tingling awareness that shot through my body. "I suck at bowling, and everyone knows it," I admitted.

"Then why the hesitation and pep talk?" Ben's brow furrowed with concern.

I could easily see why Ellie liked Ben so much. He had this strong presence about him that made a person want to lean on him in bad times. He gave off a vibe that nothing fazed him. It was all calm confidence and an I've-got-this kind of thing. When he spoke to you, you knew you had his complete attention and that he was totally focused on the conversation. He was trustworthy, and people like that had been sorely lacking in my life in Los Angeles.

"Cruz." Ben's compassionate voice interrupted my thoughts when I took too long to answer his simple question.

"Can you just call me Xavier?" I asked softly. What no one inside the bowling alley knew was that I had permanently severed all ties with my life in LA. I would not be going back there for any reason. I came home to start all over again, and I could only hope the people I loved would forgive my neglect.

"Xavier." Ben repeated my name softly, almost tenderly, but that must have been wishful thinking on my part. "I like it a lot. So, why are you out here making us both late?"

"I haven't been a very good friend, brother, or grandson, and I'm afraid I won't be wanted." There it was, the ugly truth that had been stuck in my throat for the past ten minutes. Oddly, just confessing my fears to Ben made me feel ten times better.

"Nonsense," Ben said firmly and without pause. "Your sister, grandmother, and friends are crazy about you, Xavier. Sure, they were hurt when you didn't come back for the holidays, but they also knew something was going on with you. If you're worried about anything at all, worry about getting smothered in hugs and kisses." I must've made a face that matched my doubtful thoughts. "I guess we'll just have to find out then, won't we?" Ben reached around me and opened the door to the bowling alley, grabbed my arm, and pulled me inside behind him. "Hey, everybody," he shouted, "look who I found loitering outside."

All heads swiveled in our direction. "Jerk," I hissed for his ears only. I held my breath while waiting for their reactions. The surprise quickly turned into happiness, and I was wrapped up in so many arms it was hard to tell who had me and who didn't. The relief I felt was immeasurable. Then they all began talking at once.

"I'm so glad you made it," Chase told me. "It wouldn't have been the same without you by my side." Amazingly, he still wanted me to be his best man.

"No way I'd miss your big day, Chase."

"We've missed you, jackass," Grayson said. "Try not to pull a disappearing act on us again. This one"—he aimed a thumb in Chase's direction—"worries about you constantly."

"I'm sorry I worried you, Chase. I'm home for good now," I told him.

"I've missed you so much, baby brother." Ellie began to cry.

"I've missed you too." It broke my heart to see her so upset. "I won't ever disappear like that again." She pulled back from the hug and searched my eyes for signs that I wasn't telling the truth. She must have liked what she saw because she nodded.

"Get the hell out of my way," Gram yelled, pushing her way to the front of the crowd. "Xavier Miguel Cruz, you're lucky I don't kick your ass up one side of this bowling alley and down the other. Where the hell have you been?"

"I missed you so much, Gram." I pulled her into a hug and didn't let go for several long minutes. I'd missed her seventieth birthday, and I regretted it more than I could ever express to her with words. This was the woman who took me in and gave me a beautiful life beyond my wildest dreams. "I'm so sorry." I whispered the words in her ear. "I'm home for good now."

"Shh, Xavier." She pulled back and placed a loving hand on the side of my face. "You've always been such a good boy. Everyone falls down and needs a hand up. Don't think you're taking this journey through life on your own. Okay, my sweet boy?"

"Yes, Gram." She wouldn't be so proud of me if she learned the things I'd done. I couldn't change any of it, but I could make sure history didn't repeat itself. She patted my cheeks and stepped away.

"Let's get this party started," she whooped.

"Good to see you, son," Lennie, Gram's hotter-than-hell boyfriend, said. Even Gram referred to him as a DILF. He shook my hand and then wrapped his arm around Gram.

"Thanks, Lennie. It's great to be home." Truer words had never been spoken.

"So, here's what we're going to do." Chase thankfully pulled everyone's attention away from me. I'd have to thank him for it later. "We're going to play groom versus groom. My people versus Gray's people."

"They'll be *our* people in a few weeks," Gray reminded him. He blew air kisses at Chase that made me smile. The newness clearly had not worn off for those two. If anything, they'd only grown closer over the past year.

"Well, until then, we're pitting them against one another," Chase said. His competitive streak hadn't lessened over the years. "The only exception being Ava. She isn't allowed to bowl."

"Said who? Not my doctor." Ava pouted as she joined the group. I turned and saw her very prominent baby bump. She turned to me and smiled brightly. "I go to the bathroom and miss all the excitement." Ava threw her arms around my neck.

"You look beautiful," I said into her blonde curls. "Congratulations on the baby."

"Thank you." She stepped back and looked into my eyes, searching just like Gram had. "I want Uncle Cruz to be a big part of the tadpole's life."

"Uncle *Xavier* won't miss a thing." Her shrewd eyes narrowed when I corrected my name. I had started going by only my last name the moment I'd landed in California almost seven years ago. Ava knew there was more to me going by my first name again, but she didn't ask.

I was grateful everyone had welcomed me back without question. I was relieved that I didn't see any of the resentment and disappointment in their expressions that I had feared. My stomach had been a tangled knot these last few weeks as I made the final leg of my journey home. A sense of calm and peace descended on me as I was surrounded by the people I loved most in the world. I was well and truly home where I belonged.

"Welcome home, Uncle Xavier."

"Can we get teamed up and get started?" Chase asked impatiently.

"God, someone should have hired strippers for us for putting up with his tyrannical shit," someone called out. I looked over and found a handsome guy standing next to Gray with an arm slung around his shoulders. I'd met him once but couldn't remember his name. It started with an *M* or something.

"Shut up, Miller," Chase tossed back at him.

That was it. Miller. He was a handsome devil with twinkling blue eyes that were currently roaming all over me. It would be no hardship getting to know Gray's best friend better. I glanced over in Ben's direction and saw him talking to Ellie. The two of them looked to be in their own little world, and I wondered again what was really going on between them. Ben pulled Ellie into a hug and held her head gently against his chest. The tenderness in his touch caused my chest to ache out of pure longing. The realization that I might never find someone to care about me like that sucked all the happiness out of my return home. The jealousy that burned through me as I watched them share an intimate moment was followed quickly by shame. So Ben wasn't for me, but couldn't I at least drum up a little happiness that my sister had found someone like him?

Ben looked up at me and caught me staring. I quickly averted my gaze but not before I missed the softness in his expression as he revealed the feelings he had for my sister. I also didn't miss that his gray eyes had transformed to a lighter shade. He was one of those unlucky souls whose eye color gave away their moods. Too bad I wouldn't be learning what those colors meant.

We were quickly divided into two teams and given lanes according to our relationships with the grooms. Some of the guests were coworkers of both Gray and Chase, and they argued good-naturedly over them. As luck would have it, attainable Miller with the twinkling eyes was on Gray's team, and Ben, whom I wanted but would never have, was on my team.

We introduced ourselves to our opponents, and I didn't miss the way Miller's hand lingered in mine when we shook hands. The spark I felt for him wasn't as intense as with Ben, but I could probably make it work. I turned away to enter my name into the computer when Miller moved on to speak to Ben.

"It's good to see you again," Ben said to Miller. There was a tone in his voice I couldn't quite place.

"Ben, it's always a pleasure." Miller's voice was friendly but not gooey warm like it was when he spoke to me.

There was something between them, but I couldn't put my finger on it. They weren't awkward around each other or unfriendly, but there was something odd about the way they spoke to one another. It was stiff and very formal like you'd expect at a dinner meeting with a client. I wondered what the story was between them.

"Are you happy to be home?"

Once again, Ben's voice spoken so close behind me gave me a start, but I didn't let it show. It made me think of him pressing his chest to my back as he entered my body, saying my name once he was buried to the hilt. Would his voice get deeper during sex? Would he fuck me hard or tender or both? Would he like the way I reached back and fisted my hands in his silky, black hair while he made me his? I loved that he was half a foot taller than me and must've been pushing two hundred and ten pounds to my one hundred and fifty. I'd love to feel his weight pressing down on me.

"Yep," I said casually, pretending I hadn't just thought about having sex with my sister's straight, almost boyfriend. I took a deep, relaxing breath. I entered my name into the computer and stepped aside so the other guys on my team could do the same.

"I'm happy too," Ben said.

I'd been in the man's presence for less than thirty minutes, and I had already been jealous over the fact that he wasn't gay and had feelings for my sister, fantasized about having sex with him, and got all fuzzy inside when he said he was happy I was home. It was more than a little scary all the things he made me feel, none of which were good for my recovery. Ben would never be mine. Even if he was gay, he'd never want someone with my baggage, and the sooner I accepted those facts the better. I had no room in my life for re-lationships at the moment anyway.

"Thank you." I offered him a small smile and then picked up my bowling ball to take my first turn. I wished I had paid attention and not entered my name first. I took a deep breath, lined up the ball with the arrows on the lane, and let it fly. I'm not sure who was more surprised when I knocked all the pins down—Chase, Ben, or myself.

"I thought you said you sucked at bowling?" Ben asked with a suspicious scowl as he picked up his ball for his turn.

"I do," I replied.

"He does," Chase said at the same time.

"Maybe I bring you good luck." My mind heard *good fuck*, but before I could say anything, Ben turned and rolled the ball down the lane. He threw up his hands and whooped as he too bowled a strike. He held his hand up in the air for a high five, and I smacked his hand with mine. I ignored the electric jolt that singed my hand where our skin touched.

Gray and Chase began to playfully trash talk. I would normally have found the moment extremely entertaining and even joined in, but I was too busy building a fort around my heart out of self-preservation. I could not—no, would not—allow myself to think about Ben as anything other than my sister's maybe boyfriend.

CHAPTER
Two

Bennett St. Claire

THERE WAS NOTHING ABOUT XAVIER CRUZ THAT DIDN'T DRIVE ME wild. He hit every single one of my hot buttons—some I hadn't even known existed. For instance, that tiny hoop at the corner of his luscious bottom lip drove me wild with the urge to tug it with my teeth. It made me wonder where else he might be pierced. God, I'd give Chase's right nut to find out. After all, it was all Chase's damn fault I found myself in this predicament. He's the one who had invited Xavier to lunch last year in an attempt at matchmaking, which had failed miserably. It didn't appear Xavier saw me as anything other than Ellie's friend.

Xavier was exactly the opposite of who I normally found myself attracted to. I was usually drawn to professional guys like myself. Xavier was an edgy musician and so damn beautiful I could barely take my eyes off him. Too bad he didn't seem to notice or perhaps he just didn't care.

I remembered the day we met so vividly. It was the first time I had met a man and wanted to take the time to get to know him better. His shy smile and the sparkle in his eyes took my breath away. It went beyond just his physical good looks too. There was something about him that had grabbed me and wouldn't let go, but Xavier had gone back to LA after a few months, and I had never had the chance to figure out what that *something* was. All I knew right then was that the sparkle in his eyes that had captivated me last year had dimmed, and I wanted to be the one who put it back.

I stood off to the side where I could keep my eyes on my prize while the other guys took their turns bowling. I memorized every detail of Xavier so I could replay them later when I got home. I loved his messy, dark brown hair that was probably a month or two past a haircut, but that sexy bedhead made my fingers itch to run through it. His skin was golden brown and reminded me of the color of my favorite caramel candy. My mouth watered wanting to taste him. His dreamy, light brown eyes stood out in contrast to his long-as-fuck, black eyelashes. I could've written a poem about Xavier's lush, pillowy lips. The thoughts they conjured up were probably still illegal in some states.

I let my eyes travel down his lean frame and imagined the beautifully toned body beneath his casual clothes. He was quite a bit shorter than me, probably five eight to my six three, but the thought of tucking his head beneath my chin made me feel warm and fuzzy. I realized he wasn't dressed like a rocker but had chosen to wear basic dark denim and a Nationals T-shirt. He had changed the way he dressed and had gone back to using his first name rather than his stage name. Ellie was right that something was wrong with him, and damned if I didn't want to find out what it was so I could help fix it.

I was a fixer. I fixed things for the people that I cared about. I didn't know Xavier well enough to categorize him as a person I cared about, but his sister was at the top of my list of favorite people. We had clicked the minute I'd met her on my first day at Wright Creations. Our relationship reminded me a lot of Chase's friendship with Ava. I looked around and saw them sitting next to each other. Ava was pouting because her giant of a husband and Chase had talked her into sitting it out.

I had once asked Ellie why Ava seemed so much closer to Chase than Xavier. She told me Ava hadn't moved to DC until her freshman year of high school, and by that time, Xavier was already attending Saint Cecilia's, a prestigious private school for performing arts instead of the public high school Ava and Chase attended. It had impressed me when I'd learned Xavier was a very accomplished, classically trained musician. I think his prestigious education explained why he didn't come across as a rocker. He dressed the part, and he sang the part, but Xavier was soft spoken and lacked the swagger I expected from a rocker. He was a great example of why you shouldn't label people or try to cram them into preconceived boxes and categories.

He had shocked everyone when he'd boarded a plane bound for LA to pursue a career as a rock star instead of continuing his training and playing in a symphony. He had applied for and been accepted to Julliard but had decided not to go a few weeks before he was due to leave for New York. I was dying to know the story behind his decision.

"So, are you just home for the wedding, or are you staying for a while?" Miller asked Xavier.

"I'm home for good." Xavier's voice was calm and emotionless.

"Can I buy you a beer?" Miller moved a little closer, cocking his head to the side.

I recognized that coy move from when Miller had used it on me, and damn, had it worked. We spent one long, hot night together shortly after I'd started working for Gray. We both knew it was a one-time thing and our run-ins hadn't been awkward until tonight at the bowling alley when he'd flirted with the man I wanted.

"Thank you, but I don't drink." Xavier smiled shyly.

"A soda, perhaps?"

I'd never been a jealous man. I'd never met a man I wanted to commit myself to, so jealousy would have been a ridiculous waste of energy. Even if I had wanted a commitment, the amount of time I had spent traveling for my job over the past few years probably would have destroyed any attempt at a relationship. But I'd learned something new and totally unexpected about myself tonight, and it had me feeling off-balance.

When it came to Xavier Cruz, there was an ugly green monster living inside me that was burning an acidic hole in my stomach. I stood there quietly, but in my mind, I had punched Miller in his flirty, fucking mouth and staked my claim by pulling Xavier into my arms and planting a big kiss on his lips. Tongues and roaming hands were definitely involved. The vision was so real I could almost taste him. I took a step forward but was saved from making a fool of myself when Gray intervened.

"Hell no," Gray told Miller, furiously shaking his head. "Xavier isn't going to be one of your toys, Miller. Go find someone else to screw around with and leave him alone."

"Yes, Dad," Miller whined and turned away to get a beer from the bar.

"Thanks for saving me from big bad Miller." Xavier said with a playful smile that didn't quite reach his eyes. "But I am perfectly capable of saying no for myself."

I stood quietly and watched the interaction between Xavier and Gray. It surprised me to see how protective Gray was of him, and I figured it had to stem from the time Xavier had come back from LA with Chase and Gray. I found myself wanting to shield him from all the ugliness in the world. The protectiveness I felt toward Xavier went above and beyond anything I had experienced before, and I found it to be a little unnerving.

"I know that, X," Gray said affectionately. "I didn't mean to insult you, but I know Miller's track record. He's more suited to someone like him," Gray clipped, pointing over my shoulder.

I turned to see who had irritated Gray so much on such a happy night. Chase's good friend and former lover, JJ, had just entered the bowling alley. He stood just inside the door, looking uncomfortable, until his eyes landed on Chase, then a slow smile spread across his handsome face, and he made his way over to our group. I heard a low growl emanate from Gray's throat.

I'd had the displeasure of accidentally overhearing arguments between Chase and Gray over JJ on a few different occasions. I tried not to eavesdrop, but I had gotten pinned in the hallway or bathroom a time or two, not knowing whether I should make my presence known or wait until they were done talking. My curiosity had always gotten the best of me.

It all boiled down to Gray being jealous that JJ was Chase's former lover and Chase's insistence on JJ remaining in his life. Chase was adamant JJ only wanted friendship, and Gray was more adamant that JJ was in love with Chase and always had been. Chase would blow out a frustrated breath and tell Gray that wasn't true, and that it didn't matter even if it was because Chase loved Gray and only Gray. That little speech was always given with absolute sincerity and won Gray over every single time.

I would stand smugly in the hallway or bathroom, thankful I wasn't a jealous man and that I wasn't involved in a relationship. It seemed so much cleaner to hook up then go home to the peacefulness of my own house.

But tonight, at the bachelor party, I learned another surprising thing about myself. I wanted Xavier Cruz with a fervor I'd never known, and I didn't want anyone else to look at him, let alone touch him. I wasn't in love with him. I wasn't even sure I liked him, but I sure as hell wanted to find out. I saw in his eyes that something or someone was haunting him. Maybe others wouldn't recognize it, but I sure as hell did. I had seen that same haunted look in my own eyes growing up. I knew it wasn't going to be easy and would require a lot of patience on my part, but I also felt in my heart that Xavier would be worth the wait.

"Hey, cutie." JJ pulled Xavier into a one-armed hug, then proceeded to ruffle his hair. "It's good you came home. Permanently, I hope."

Xavier jabbed him in the ribs with his elbow a few times, and JJ finally stopped. "You're still so freaking annoying," Xavier groused while he tried to straighten his messy hair.

I didn't miss the smile that clung to his lips over JJ's antics, and I was ready to join Team Gray where JJ was concerned. A snarl began to rumble in my chest. Gray looked over at me as if he could sense my inner thoughts. He raised a questioning brow at me, but I only shrugged in response. I couldn't put a label on anything I felt that night, other than irritation that other men wanted Xavier. I wanted him to myself, but for how long, I couldn't say.

"Let's bowl," Gram said, coming up behind us. "Lennie wants to go home soon so I can tuck him in." This was said with an exaggerated, lecherous wink that had all of us groaning at the implied mental images. "Oh, shut up," Gram snapped at us. "I may be old, but I'm not dead, and I'm going to enjoy sexy time with my man while I still can."

"Please stop, Gram," Chase begged.

Beers got passed around, and I found myself relaxing and enjoying the night with my friends. At one point, Miller and JJ, being the consummate bachelors, started giving Chase and Gray a hard time about committing to one sex partner for the rest of their lives.

"I mean, don't you get sick of having sex with him?" Miller drunkenly asked Chase while pointing at Gray. "I'm not saying you suck in the bedroom," he quickly explained to Gray, "well I'm sure you suck there, and other places too, but what I meant was don't you get worried about just having sex with each other. Forever!"

"I'm the luckiest man in the world," Chase said sweetly. "It just gets better and better every time."

"Baby, I'm the lucky one." Gray pulled his fiancé into his arms for a heated kiss.

"I might puke," JJ stated flatly, but I didn't miss the look he cast in Chase's direction. I figured Gray was probably right and JJ was in love with Chase.

While JJ and Miller made gagging noises like ten-year-olds, I focused on Gray and Chase's interactions. They were so in tune with each other that I found myself wondering for the first time if I was possibly missing out on something in my life. What would it feel like to have someone special waiting for me at home, ready to offer me a hug and kiss after a hard day? What if sleeping with the same man night after night felt like a sacred bond and not a noose? The more I questioned the more I drank. The next thing I knew, the party was over, and I was too far gone to drive. I'd never been much of a drinker, and it was embarrassing that I had to ask someone to drive me home. I looked around for Ellie but couldn't find her anywhere.

"She's not here," a soft voice said from behind me. "But I'll give you a ride, Ben."

I spun around and found Xavier standing close behind me, so close I could smell him. God, how I wanted him to take me for a ride, but my idea of a ride and the kind Xavier was offering were a lot different. At least I wasn't so far gone that I blurted out what I was thinking.

"Thanks," I answered with a sloppy smile. "Where'd my best girl go?"

"She wasn't feeling good and left about six beers ago." Xavier's voice held a slight hint of derision. "Do you need help getting to my car?"

"Nah, I'm okay." I walked a few steps behind him so I could look at his tight ass in his dark jeans. I also noticed how long his legs looked as they gobbled up the pavement on the way to his... "Oh my fucking God."

"Yeah, I get that a lot," Xavier replied smugly.

I stood still, barely breathing, and stared at the magnificent piece of American history in the parking lot. It was one of the finest pieces of metal to come out of Detroit. How had I not noticed it when I arrived? "Is that a '68 or '69?" I asked when I found my voice. The parking lot lights shined their approving beams on top of her shiny black paint. I expected to hear angels singing at any moment. "What a beauty. What's her name?"

"Midnight Mistress is a '69 Camaro SS," Xavier said in a loving voice. He turned around and looked at me. I peeled my eyes from Mistress when I heard him laugh softly. "Are you just going to stand there and stare or get in and go for a ride?"

I snapped out of my trance and walked over to the passenger side and waited while Xavier unlocked the door for me. I slid onto the soft leather seat and leaned across to unlock his door for him. We shut our doors at the same time and exchanged an easy smile when he put the key in the ignition. My dick and Mistress's engine roared to life simultaneously. I whimpered slightly when Xavier gave her some gas and drove toward the parking lot exit. He chuckled letting me know he'd heard me, but I wasn't embarrassed. I was pretty sure he understood how I felt.

I looked out over the long, sleek hood and all I could imagine was bending Xavier over it while I drove long and hard inside him. I would have one hand fisted in his hair and the other holding him down against the metal. I closed my eyes and could even hear the animalistic sounds I made as I fucked him. This man affected me in ways I'd never experienced before.

"You'll need to tell me where I'm going," Xavier said.

"Oh," I said, not realizing he'd come to a complete stop. *How long had we been sitting there while I had indecent thoughts about what I wanted to do to him on the hood of his own car?* I was thankful the interior of the car was dark enough to hide my raging hard-on. "Turn left," I instructed, forcing my mind to focus on giving him directions so I could go home and replay my car fantasy when I was alone and could do something about it.

"This is a nice neighborhood," Xavier casually said when he pulled into my driveway.

"I like it a lot," I replied. "My neighbor, Mrs. Hernandez, is also the property owner. She's a really sweet lady, and I've been happy here, but I want to buy my own home someday so I can have a bit more privacy." I thought about Mrs. Hernandez's attempts to fix me up with her granddaughter and laughed.

"What's so funny?" Xavier sounded confused.

"Mrs. Hernandez is always trying to fix me up with her granddaughter, Marisol." I looked over at Xavier and saw the confusion on his face matched his voice.

"That's a bad thing?"

"Marisol is a beautiful young woman, but she's not the one for me," I answered honestly. "If Mrs. Hernandez knew my track record, she wouldn't be trying to fix me up with her precious Marisol."

Xavier shrugged and turned to look out the windshield, but I could tell his mind was working something out from the scowl on his face. I wished he'd say what he was thinking or ask me whatever it was he wanted to know. Instead, we sat in awkward silence for a few minutes.

"Thanks for the ride, Xavier." My voice broke into his musings, and he looked at me with a small smile on his face. "I rarely drink, and I'm sorry you were inconvenienced. Well, not really since you drove me home in Mistress." I ran my hands lovingly over the dashboard for a minute before I realized I was making a complete ass of myself. Again. "Goodnight." I opened the door and started to climb out.

"What time do you want to pick up your car tomorrow?"

Had I heard him right? Was he offering to take me back to the bowling alley? I kept my body moving before I was tempted to pull him over the console and into my arms. "Anytime is fine for me," I replied casually.

"How about Mistress and I pick you up around ten?"

I leaned down and peered into the car. Xavier wasn't looking at me and continued to stare out the windshield. He had a white-knuckled grip on the steering wheel, and his posture was rigid. His offer to help me didn't match his body language, and I knew I should decline.

"Sounds great," I said instead, not willing to pass up the opportunity to spend more time with him. "See you tomorrow." I stood up straight, closed the door, and walked away without looking back.

CHAPTER
Three

Xavier

S LAP. *SLAP. SLAP.* MY SNEAKERS POUNDED THE PAVEMENT AS I TRIED to outrun my nightmares and demons. I pushed myself harder and longer, trading one addiction for another—drugs for exercise. The impact ricocheted in my knees, and my chest burned from the exertion of moving air in and out of my lungs, but I couldn't stop. Not yet.

The bad dreams the night before had been the worst ones I'd had in weeks, maybe months as I'd worked to get the drugs I'd gotten hooked on while trying to cope with the abusive relationship I had with my band manager, Damien Diamond, out of my system. I wasn't positive what had triggered the nightmares this time, but I suspected it was being around alcohol while trying to fight my attraction to Ben St. Claire.

Ben's gorgeous image immediately popped up in my head, and I pushed it away, choosing to concentrate on getting myself healthy. Fantasizing about my sister's sorta boyfriend wasn't good for me. Even if Ben was gay and interested, I'd avoid a relationship with him. The last thing I needed was to get involved with a guy, no matter how great he was. I had my recovery to focus on, and I had lost faith in my own judgment after my last relationship. Besides, it was pretty arrogant to think someone like him would want a fuckup like me.

I'd come a long way in a few short months, I knew that, but I still had a long way to go. I didn't find myself craving Ecstasy or weed as much anymore, but I still hadn't forgiven myself for my role in my own downfall. I battled self-hatred far more than I fought the temptation to use, and I needed to find a way to come to peace with myself. If I didn't, I'd be stuck stagnant in my dark past forever.

What hurt the most was losing my ability to write music. My brain was completely silent. No new lyrics or melodies. There had been nothing since I'd returned to LA last year. Gray and Chase had come to my rescue when they were in LA on a business trip last April. I had been a hot freaking mess at that point, and I hadn't even been taking drugs then. The drug use hadn't started until I'd foolishly let my bandmates guilt me into coming back on top of the threats Damien made if I didn't return. I boarded a flight to LA last June but landed in hell instead. I let the drugs numb my pain and misery, but I only ended up hurting myself even more in the long run. I hated the out of control way I felt when I was high, and I hated myself even more for being weak and allowing Damien to mistreat me.

Damien watched my every goddamned move, so going to therapy to get sober wasn't an option. I found an online counseling site and connected with a sponsor who agreed to chat with me online and exchange emails. I started cutting back on the Ecstasy a little at a time until I stopped using altogether. I would fake being high around my bandmates, and they'd been too fucked up to notice.

When I rejoined the band, I swore to myself that I wouldn't allow anything sexual to happen between me and Damien again, but I gave in to him the first night I took Ecstasy. I knew better than to start taking that shit, but

I just wanted to get lost and I thought getting high was the best way to do it. I had started to spiral into depression once I returned to LA, and E gave me a break from the darkness. Damien promised he'd ease up on his jealousy and possessiveness, but his verbal abuse only got worse as soon as I gave in to him again.

He had been consumed by thoughts of me with other men for the entire two months I'd been away from him and the band. There were some nights after my return when he went on such violent rants that I actually feared for my life, but he never physically abused me until the night he learned about my sponsor, Kevin Smithson, after going through my phone and email while I performed onstage. That was the night Damien Diamond went too far, and I left the band for good.

Thump. Thump. Thump. My heart pounded in my chest but more from the painful memories than the exertion of running. I needed to get my mind on healthier things and people instead of drugs and Damien. But try as I might, I couldn't keep Ben's image out of my head. The sounds he'd made when he'd lovingly caressed Midnight Mistress had made my dick hard enough to drill through concrete. I was so turned on by the time I got to his house that I couldn't even look at him. *Why the hell had I offered to drive him to his car?*

Physically, I felt better than I had in years. I'd started working out every time I craved a high. All the exercise and healthy living had a side effect I hadn't anticipated, though—it made me horny as hell, and all I wanted to do was fuck. I'd always had a healthy sex drive, but this went beyond anything I was used to. Throw in being closed inside a car with Ben for fifteen minutes, and I'd nearly jerked my dick raw after I got home from his house. Just like that, my hard-on was back in full force. *Damn it!* My dick didn't care if Ben was straight or gay, and it definitely didn't care about my no relationships until I felt stronger rule. It was a selfish bastard and just wanted relief.

Jogging back to my sister's house with an erection was awkward to say the least. What was even more awkward was rushing into the bathroom to do something about my unwelcome stiffy to find my sister kneeling over the toilet while she vomited and retched until there couldn't have been anything left inside her. Her vomiting worked wonders to deflate my erection. I didn't know what to do for her except to hold her hair back and wipe her face with a cool rag once she flushed the toilet and sat up.

"El." I crouched down in front of her and cupped her face in my hands. "What's wrong? You left the bachelor party early, and now you're vomiting. Is there a virus going around?"

"It's nothing. Maybe something I ate at the party." Ellie tried to brush my hands away so she could avert her eyes.

"Not so fast," I told her, searching her face. "I didn't see you eat anything at the party. So what's really going on?"

"Then it was something I ate before I got there," she replied weakly as she tried to stand up. I offered her my hand and helped her rise to her feet. "Please don't worry about me, Xavier. I'm going to be okay." She wrapped her arms around my waist and laid her head against my chest. "I could probably use some saltines and Sprite, though. Could you get those for me while I brush my teeth?"

"Sure." I dropped a kiss on the top of her head and went to the kitchen to get what she'd asked for. I poured a glass of the lemon-lime soda Gram used to give me every time I had an upset stomach and grabbed a packet of crackers from the cabinet.

Something more was going on with Ellie; I felt it in my bones. But what? How long had she been sick, and why wouldn't she tell me the truth? My mind raced with worrisome thoughts of cancer or something equally scary. I had three constants in my life—Gram, Ellie, and Chase. The thought of losing one of them was enough to bring me to my knees, but I stood strong in the small kitchen of the house Ellie loved so damn much. I closed my eyes and prayed to God, hoping he would still listen to a fuckup like me.

"Are you meditating?" Ellie's voice broke into my thoughts. She sounded normal and not weak like she had been minutes before.

"Praying," I retorted. "I'm worried about you."

"Aww, Xavier. I promise there's nothing wrong with me. I'm fine. What do you have planned for today?" Ellie asked, changing the subject.

"I need to take a shower and pick Ben up at ten," I responded. "He had a little too much to drink last night, so I gave him a ride home."

"I've known Ben for a few years now, and I've never seen him drunk. I wonder what happened to make him lose his well-crafted control. Did he say anything on the ride home?"

He'd moaned and groaned as he'd felt up Mistress and had given me the hardest erection I'd had in years, but I didn't think that was what Ellie meant. "Not really," I answered honestly. "We talked about my car and how sweet she is, but that's about it." I studied her as she took a small sip of Sprite. "So what is going on between you and Ben?" I asked, recalling what he'd said about Mrs. Hernandez's granddaughter not being right for him. Was Ellie right for him? He'd mentioned his track record being less than impressive, and I didn't want my sister to be one of his casualties.

Ellie shrugged nonchalantly but wouldn't make eye contact. "We're just friends, Xavier. That's all we'll ever be. People make a big deal out of us spending a lot of time together, but he's honestly just my best friend."

"But…"

"You better hit the shower so you don't keep Ben waiting," El said, interrupting me. "He's a real stickler for punctuality." She snickered a little bit. "Unlike others I know." She raised her head and aimed a teasing wink in my direction.

"I've grown out of that," I said defensively, "Except when I have to hold my sister's hair back while she spews. That might make me late."

"Smart ass," Ellie called after me when I left the kitchen. "I used to change your dirty diapers. I guess we're even now."

I was still smiling when I climbed into the shower a few minutes later. I let the hot water beat down on my body, soothing away the aches in my muscles and washing away the sweat and dirt from my skin. I closed my eyes and pretended the water also washed my soul clean like a baptism.

I spent the entire trip to Ben's house reminding myself he was straight, possibly a little slutty by his own admission, and not for me. Falling for straight men was a total waste of energy and destined to end in heartbreak, and it had never happened to me. I'd watched many gay guys fall for their straight coworkers or friends too many times to count, and I was glad that wasn't a club or team I had joined. I had never even been in real jeopardy of falling for a straight guy until I'd met Ben. *It was just lust.* I was sure it would pass as soon as I met a gay man I was equally attracted to who returned my interest. *Forget about men and relationships. Focus on getting stronger one day at a time.*

That theory lasted as long as it took for Ben to walk out his front door. Damn, he was beautiful. I had seen him in business suits and casual looks, but this might be my new favorite for reasons unknown to me. He was wearing a simple T-shirt and navy-blue track pants. The pants made his legs look five miles long as they ate up the pavement, bringing temptation closer and closer to me.

I sucked in a breath when I noticed the unfettered bounce of his cock and balls beneath the smooth fabric. *Holy shit. Ben St. Claire was about to get into my car wearing no underwear. Commando. Free balling.* I feared I wouldn't survive it.

Our eyes locked when he climbed inside my car and closed the door. His moody gray eyes were a shade I hadn't seen before. It made me want to learn the meaning behind that particular shade and all the others I'd seen the few times I'd been around him. That morning his eyes were so light they were nearly transparent. The color was more noticeable because the outer rim of his irises remained a dark gray. I sat there staring at him like a complete idiot for God knew how long, unable to find words.

"Hey," he spoke casually, breaking the silence. "What are your plans this afternoon?"

"Uh." *Climbing onto your lap, ripping that ball cap off your head, and running my fingers through your inky black hair while I grind my ass against your package until it hardens for me. Rubbing my cheek against the dark stubble on your jaw before I press my lips to yours. Sliding down to my knees, pulling your pants down with me, and sucking your dick into my mouth.* Of course, I didn't say any of those things. "I have some errands to run. Besides, Ellie isn't feeling well, and I don't want to leave her alone."

"Okay. No problem. I was just going to invite you to my softball game this afternoon. Gray and his brother, Preston, are on my team. I thought you might like to watch us make complete fools of ourselves."

"Maybe next time." I heard myself answer and wished I could stab myself with a sharp object. No good would come from me spending a lot of time around Ben.

"Cool," he replied, but then his expression turned serious, and his eyes turned darker, almost stormy. "What's wrong with Ellie?" There was no mistaking the tenderness and concern he had for my sister and her well-being.

"I was about to ask you the same question."

"Me?"

"You're around her a lot more than I am, and I was hoping you could tell me what's going on." I blew out a frustrated breath and looked out Mistress's windshield. I needed to be able to focus on my words and thoughts, which wasn't possible when I was looking into Ben's eyes. "She said it was something she ate before the party, but I don't believe her. She's hiding something." I put Mistress in gear and backed out of Ben's driveway. "Have you noticed anything?"

"Not really," Ben said after a long pause. "I'll pay closer attention if you want me to."

"Please," I replied softly. "I'll give you my number, and you can text me or call me anytime."

Ben agreed, and we spent the rest of the short trip to the bowling alley in silence. It seemed like both our minds were someplace else, but I was sure our brains weren't traveling down the same track. Mine was still trying to undress him to find every pleasure point on his long, lean body. I don't know where his mind was at the moment, but it probably didn't include getting naked and sweaty with me.

"Thanks for the ride." Ben's soft voice sent chills of lust down my spine when I pulled up beside his car. "I'll keep an eye on Ellie for you, okay?" His words washed over me and brought a smidgeon of peace to my ravaged mind for the first time in days. I could easily become more addicted to him than any drug. "It's going to be okay."

We exchanged phone numbers before Ben got out of my car. He waved as he drove past me and headed toward the parking lot exit. I sat in the lot for a few more minutes before I ran my errands, and my mind stayed on Ben the entire time. The only time he left my thoughts was when I returned home and found Ellie sound asleep on the couch. She'd only been awake for a few hours, but she was already sleeping again. I wanted to believe everything was okay, but I knew in my heart something more serious was going on. I just hoped I was strong enough to help Ellie through whatever challenge she was facing.

CHAPTER
Four

Ben

THE FOLLOWING MONDAY I FOUND MYSELF IN ELLIE'S OFFICE BRIGHT and early. I could tell by Xavier's tone the day before that he was really worried about his sister, and I wanted to be able to put both of us at ease. Okay, I also wanted any excuse to text or call him.

I wanted so badly to ask him out, but I couldn't actually do it. My lack of confidence didn't have to do with my looks or my ability to attract another man. I didn't know how to flirt and date, which was a sad state of affairs for a thirty-year-old man. My idea of flirting was a head nod in the direction of the exit of the bar or toward the bathroom for a quick and dirty hookup. I knew I needed to step up my game with Xavier, which was another reason I was in Ellie's office first thing that morning.

"Good morning, gorgeous." I crossed into her office with extra pep in my step, but I nearly gasped when I saw how tired she looked and noticed the dark circles under her eyes and the complete lack of spark in her gaze.

"Hello to you too," she responded, but her smile didn't reach her eyes like it normally did. "Did you enjoy your ride in Midnight Mistress?"

"Yes." My eyes searched her face for clues about what was ailing her while my heart ached that she hadn't confided in me. "Ellie," I began, but a quick wave of her hand cut me off.

"I'm fine, Ben." She narrowed her eyes and studied me suspiciously. "Did my brother send you in here to spy on me?"

Busted. "No." My breezy dismissal might have been too quick if her raised brow was any indication. "I *am* here about Xavier but not on his behalf." I blew out a frustrated breath and flopped down in the chair in front of her desk. "I don't know how to say this delicately, El. I'm way out of my comfort zone here."

"You want him bad, don't you?"

"Is it that obvious?" I whined. "He doesn't seem to notice me, and I'm horrible at dating. I can pick up one-night stands left and right, but I shut down when it comes to asking a dude to dinner."

Ellie tilted her head while she contemplated the situation. "I think your attraction to him is noticeable only to people who know you, like myself, Gray, and Chase. Xavier doesn't know you well enough, and I'm not sure his brain is capable of picking up how attracted you are to him right now." She started to giggle and quickly covered her mouth. She regained her composure after several seconds and said, "I'm pretty sure he thinks you're…" She launched into another giggling fit.

"He thinks…" I waved my hand around in exasperation, trying to encourage her to finish her sentence.

Ellie sat up straight and dropped the bomb on me. "He thinks you're straight." Her lips twitched with mirth as if she hadn't just blown my universe apart.

"Are you fucking serious?" I stood up and paced in front of her desk. "How is that even possible? Why does he think that?" I asked, stopping abruptly in front of her.

Ellie shrugged casually. "Like I said, I don't think his head is in the right place, and we spend so much time together people assume we're a couple."

"El, please tell me I've never misled you or made you believe that…"

"You haven't," she interrupted. "I've always known exactly who you are, and I'm so very thankful for your friendship, Bennett." She stood up slowly, braced her hands on her desk, and closed her eyes a second as if she were feeling dizzy. I started to go to her, but she waved me off once again. "I'm fine, Ben."

"You're not fine, and I need you to tell me what's wrong," I pleaded.

"Ben, please respect my need for privacy. I *am* fine, and there is nothing to worry about." She slowly walked to me, and I automatically reached for Ellie, pulling her into a hug.

She was slimmer than the last time I'd hugged her just a few days prior, and it scared me to death, but I'd do as she asked. "I'm here for you, Ellie. Please tell me you know I'd do anything in the world for you."

"I do know that, and I love you for it. I also want to tell you I think you'd be the best thing to ever happen to Xavier. I don't know what the hell happened to him in LA, but it's taken a huge toll on him. I lost my smiling, happy brother, Ben. I want him back, and I think you're the one who can make that happen, but I'm afraid it will be a lot of work. I see such hollowness in his eyes, and it scares me to death," Ellie whispered against my chest.

"I'm not afraid of hard work, Ellie. I've never really dated before, and I've never wanted to until I met him. The spark ignited when he was here for a few months last year, but he was gone before I could do anything about it. I saw him at the bachelor party, and the spark morphed into a blaze. I hear what you're saying, though. I can and will be patient. But I'm not willing to let him leave again without letting him know how I feel." I chuckled lightly before adding, "And, it seems like I have a pretty big task on my hands since he thinks I'm straight."

Ellie and I laughed together for a few minutes before I gave her a soft, reassuring kiss on her brow and left to go to my office. I walked into my sanctuary and found it already occupied by Chase Rivers, who was leaning against my desk, facing the door. He studied me through squinted eyes.

"About last Saturday night..." he started.

"Nothing happened, Chase," I interrupted before he could continue. I knew he loved Xavier with all his heart, but I wasn't ready to have a heart-to-heart with him about his friend. Everything I felt for Xavier was new and confusing but still so freaking exciting. For once in my life, I wanted to be distracted from work and have plans for the evening that didn't include a random hookup and meaningless sex. It was all Chase's and Gray's fault I changed, and a small part of me was angry that I'd started questioning my simple lifestyle. "Besides, he's a grown man."

"I am well aware he's a grown man, Ben. I grew up with him, and we're the exact same age. What's with the defensive tone? Did you think I wanted to bust your balls? That isn't why I'm here."

I blew out a frustrated breath as I flopped down in my comfy desk chair. "I'm sorry if I was rude just now. It's just really complicated, and I'm not sure I want to talk about it." I began toying with a pen on my desk, rolling it back and forth. I finally looked up at Chase and asked, "Did you know Xavier thinks I'm straight? I just learned that from Ellie."

"To be honest, your sexuality hasn't been brought up in conversation." Chase grinned wickedly but wisely held back his laughter when he saw the look on my face. "How can he *not* see how interested you are in him?" Chase pondered out loud. "It's so damn obvious a blind person could see it. You should've seen your face when Miller started flirting with him. Gray didn't intervene to save Xavier from slutty Miller. He was saving Miller from the beat down you were about to hand him."

"I'm not sure I like that I've been so obvious, but he's the only one who hasn't noticed. I don't think he's into me at all." I sounded like a whiny teenage girl.

"That's because you don't know him well enough to know the signs. He's definitely into you, but since he apparently thinks you're straight, he's doing his best to fight his feelings. What good ever comes from letting yourself fall for a straight guy?"

"True, but then what should I do?" It seemed I did want to talk to Chase about the situation after all. "I know he's not in a good place right now, and I don't want to push him away, but I can't let him go on thinking I'm straight."

"Just let things fall into place. You'll have plenty of opportunity to get to know each other better. I'm sure you'll find a subtle way to show him you're into dudes," Chase said.

Suddenly, I had a vision of me not-so-subtly showing Xavier how badly I wanted him. I wouldn't be delicate when I pushed him against a wall and kissed him with every ounce of pent-up frustration I'd felt since I'd met him. I wouldn't be refined when I let my hands roam all over his lean body. I wouldn't be restrained when I dropped to my knees and…

"Where'd you go just now?" Chase's question interrupted my vivid daydream.

Having a creative imagination was a wonderful thing until you got sucked so far into your fantasy that you forgot your surroundings and got embarrassingly aroused at work. I opened my mouth to offer some sort of answer that would be a total lie, but Chase held up his hand.

"Forget I asked," Chase amended with a smirk, then rose quickly to his feet. "I'm pretty sure I know where your mind went. I'm getting out of here so you can get to work. I'd hate for the bosses to catch their new creative director being lazy."

"And," I said, "as *your* immediate supervisor, I suggest you get back to your office and create something magical for that delicatessen client. I'm not sure how you're going to make cold cuts and cheese look sexy, but I have faith in you."

Chase saluted me saucily and left my office, leaving me to grin at his retreating back. We'd come a long way since we'd first met when he'd come to work at Wright Creations last March. Admittedly, all the issues between us had been my fault. I'd done absolutely nothing to make him feel welcome and had even gone out of my way to be a douche to him. I saw Chase as the competition and had been insecure about my career for the first time in my young life. I had behaved like a complete jackass until Chase had had enough and called me out for it.

We'd formed a truce and have since become really good friends. In fact, the day he slammed into my office to confront me about my behavior was the very same day he introduced me to Xavier at lunch. *Hmmm, coincidence or another example of his Cupid skills?* Well, it certainly felt like someone had shot me with something. I leaned my head back against my chair and closed my eyes in contemplation. I needed an action plan because waiting patiently wasn't an option, so I filled the rest of the day with work and brainstorming ideas for how I could make Xavier mine.

CHAPTER
Five

Xavier

I HAD ANOTHER NIGHTMARE ABOUT DAMIEN AND THE NIGHT HE AT-tacked me, and I woke up mad at the world. I was tired of remembering how helpless and defenseless I'd felt when he'd held me down and nearly choked the life out of me. He had never taken things that far before that night. He usually chose to throw things and yell, so I was completely unprepared for his attack. I would've died that night if my bandmates hadn't overheard the scuffle and the threats he'd screamed at me and come to my rescue.

"You were a nobody until I came along. I created you, and only I get to fuck you, Cruz. You belong to ME!"

Damien had me pinned to the floor of my dressing room with his knees on my chest. He'd cuffed my hands to the base of a metal shelving unit that was bolted to the floor and was immovable no matter how much I tried.

The harder I fought him the tighter he squeezed my neck with his strong hands. My lungs burned with a lack of oxygen, and my ribs felt like they were going to cave in from the pressure of Damien's weight on my chest. Black dots had appeared in my vision, and I started to welcome the darkness, but nothing could block the evil sound of his voice and his words from penetrating my soul.

"You thought you could sneak around behind my back and meet another man? I found all of your emails to Kevin Smithson, Cruz. Were you planning on fucking him behind my back? Were all those sweet little exchanges about helping you get clean so he could have what belonged to me? I will be the last man you ever fuck. Do you hear me? I'd rather kill you than let someone touch what is mine."

I had accepted that I was going to die that night, but then my bandmates kicked down the dressing room door and pulled Damien off me. By that point, my once tight-knit relationship with my bandmates had deteriorated until they became virtual strangers to me. I had harbored a lot of resentment toward them because at times I blamed them for my predicament. It was my band who had talked me into coming back to LA by promising me that things would change and telling me that Damien had promised to accept that things were over between us.

I had been stupid to believe any of them and quickly realized my mistake when I arrived the first night to find them all stoned out of their minds. It was easier to blame my bandmates than myself for falling back into Damien's arms. Not a single one of them had made me take Ecstasy that first time or any of the times after. None of them forced me to smoke weed to bring myself down from my high. Even though things were strained between us, I had never been so glad to look up and see Pax and Stix pulling Damien off me. But, in my most recent nightmare they didn't pull him off. Instead, they stood over me and laughed with him while the life faded from my body.

I was determined to do something about my fear, to beat it down like I had my addiction to E. So I signed up for kickboxing classes at the local gym, and just that made me feel so much better. It cleared the lingering cobwebs of the nightmare from my brain and let me focus on the here and now rather than the then and there.

I decided to go to the store and pick up a few things for Ellie because she hadn't looked very good that morning. I begged her not to go to work, but she insisted she was fine and didn't need to stay home. I remembered Gram giving me chicken noodle soup, Sprite, and crackers as a child when I didn't feel good. I figured Ellie's stomach wouldn't be able to handle much, but she should surely be able to keep that down.

I was walking toward the checkout lanes when I saw a familiar dark-haired lady scanning the paperback novels. Some kids had heroes who were larger than life, cape-wearing men who had secret powers they used to try and save the world. My hero was a tiny angel with curly dark hair and cornflower-blue eyes. Her superpower wasn't laser-beam eyes or the ability to climb the side of a building. No, her superpower was unconditional love and the ability to give hugs that took away a kid's pain. My hero was Miss Annette, and she was the preschool teacher who, along with Gram, had saved my life.

"Miss Annette," I said softly behind her, not wanting to scare her.

She spun around at the sound of my voice, a huge smile on her face. "Xavier," she said in pure delight. Time had been very kind to Miss Annette, who I suspected was in her late forties. Her skin was as flawless as I remembered, and her smile still lit up my heart. Miss Annette threw her tiny arms up around my neck and pulled me down for a hug. I had forgotten how little she was until she stood on her tiptoes to give me a kiss on my cheek. "I'm so excited to see you, and my goodness, you appeared at just the right time."

"I did?"

"You did, sweet angel." Miss Annette clasped her tiny hands to her chest and looked at me with earnest joy. "I have a student this year who reminds me so much of you at his age. He's really confused about the way he's feeling, and his sweet mother could really use your guidance."

"Miss Annette, I'm not sure I'm the one this kid needs to talk to. I mean, my life hasn't been exactly role-model worthy, and…"

"Xavier," Miss Annette said seriously, "I'm not asking you to be Max's life coach or father figure, but maybe you could just listen to him and share the things you felt when you were his age."

"I don't know, Miss Annette." I didn't see how I could offer the kid or his mother any help in my current screwed-up state.

"Here," Miss Annette said, pulling her phone out of her purse and pushing a few buttons. "Look at his sweet face and tell me if you can refuse him." She turned the phone around, and I saw a sweet little boy sitting in a circle of girls playing with dolls and a playhouse. He was wearing a tiara, a pink feather boa, and lacy gloves up to his elbows. It was like looking at a picture of me at his age, except this sweet kid had blond hair and blue eyes. "Tell me Max doesn't look familiar to you, Xavier. That you don't see and know how confused he is right now. Tell me you can't offer his mom an encouraging word or maybe a hug."

I caved. After all, Miss Annette was one of my real-life heroes, and I couldn't let her or little Max down. "What day and time would work best?"

"Lindsey picks him up at four thirty, so maybe you could come one day this week to meet her and talk to Max."

"I'll be there, Miss Annette."

She dropped her phone back into her purse and cupped my face with both tiny hands. "I love you, Xavier. I always have, and I always will. You have the purest heart of anyone I've ever known, and if anyone can help little Max, it's you."

"I love you too, Miss Annette." I gave her a big hug, feeling lighter than I had in a long time. I was loved by a lot of people, and it was time I focused on them and my future, not the hateful people from my past. "I will see you sometime this week."

The clock ticked to five thirty while I warmed up the soup on the stove. I knew Ellie would be home any minute, and I wanted to surprise her. My mind was still stuck on the conversation I had had with Miss Annette as I lazily stirred the soup in the pot.

What could I really offer Max and his mom? My life had become a hot mess, and it seemed like I was the last person who should be giving advice

to a confused kid and his mother. On the other hand, my early years wearing feminine clothes had nothing to do with my current predicament. All
I really needed to do was sit and listen to the little guy and maybe offer an
encouraging word or two to him and his mom. I was overthinking things
and stressing myself out for no good reason.

I had bigger fish to fry anyway. I hadn't heard from Ben all damn day,
and I was getting more and more agitated with every minute that passed. I
expected him to check up on Ellie this morning or at lunch and text or call
me, but nothing. He wasn't much of a *friend* to her if he couldn't be bothered to do a simple thing like make sure she felt better.

I heard the front door fly open followed by a loud thud and the sound
of someone running down the hallway toward the bedrooms and bathrooms.
I turned the burner down and scrambled out of the kitchen to see what was
going on. I saw Ellie's purse and briefcase lying on the floor just inside the
door. I picked them up and set them on the couch, then shut the front door.
I went in search of my sister and found her in the master bathroom leaning
over the toilet, her body shaking as it heaved repeatedly.

"Morning sickness my ass," she growled, not realizing I was standing
in the doorway.

"El," I said softly, coming into the room and kneeling beside her. I tried
not to scare her, but I did anyway. Her big brown eyes were huge and fright-
ened against her ashen complexion. "You're pregnant?" I asked quietly while
I kneeled down beside her.

"I fucked up, Xavier," she said tearfully and leaned her head against my
chest. "I'm so damn stupid."

"No, you're not," I said while stroking her hair. "You're brilliant, but
even intelligent people get pregnant unexpectedly." I tried to be supportive
and happy for my sister, but all I could think about was my own misery over
the fact Ben had had sex with her. I'd always known he wasn't meant to be
mine, but there was this tiny part of me that had hoped it could work out.
That same jealousy I had felt at the bowling alley burned through my body,
but I pushed away my feelings and focused on Ellie.

"I was so stupid, Xavier." She began crying in earnest now, her tears quickly soaking through my T-shirt. I sat down on the floor beside her so I could be more comfortable and rocked her back and forth, whispering words of love and encouragement. "I thought he loved me, but I should have known I was just like the rest of them. He used me for sex just like his other conquests."

The fire that raged through my veins completely obliterated the longing I'd experienced just seconds earlier. I knew Ben was a player by his own admission, but I thought his feelings for my sister were special, tender even. I saw the way he looked at her, touched her, and held her like he cherished Ellie above anyone else. Why would he treat someone he obviously cared about that way? There was only one way to find out, and I planned to talk to him as soon as I got my sister settled.

"El, I warmed up some chicken soup for you and bought you some more Sprite and crackers. How about you get cleaned up and I'll bring you a tray so you can eat in bed. I know you probably don't feel like eating, but you should try for yourself and the baby."

Ellie cried even harder. "You are so good, Xavier, and I am such a fuckup."

"I'm not good, El. I was really messed up this past year, and I'm in no position to sit in judgment of anyone, even if I wanted to, and I don't. I'll tell you about it sometime when things have settled down. It will cheer you right up when you learn how stupid I was."

"I'll never be cheerful over your misery, X." She sat up and looked into my eyes. "I'm here to listen to you whenever you're ready to talk, and I promise I will love you just as much after you tell me what happened in LA. There is nothing you could do to lose me, Xavier. You're the only family I've got, and I won't let anything or anyone come between us."

Ellie was right about it being just the two of us left. Our parents had fled in the middle of the night with my other brothers and sisters when they realized abuse charges were going to be filed against my father. I've never missed my parents one single day since I went to live with Gram, but I often thought about my brothers and sisters, wondering how they turned out.

"Don't forget Gram and Chase," I reminded her sweetly. "They're our family even if we don't have a single strand of matching DNA."

"Of course," Ellie playfully chastised me. "I can't believe I'm about to say this, but I'm ravenous right now. Chicken noodle soup has never sounded so good."

I held out my hand for her and pulled us both up off the tiled bathroom floor. "Do you want to shower first? You might feel better."

"That sounds like heaven," she said blissfully. "I won't be long."

I returned to the kitchen and focused on the task at hand. I couldn't let Ellie know how angry I was at Ben. I'd deal with his ass as soon as I could. Ranting about his cowardice would only upset Ellie more, and that wasn't good for her or the baby. *Dear Lord, my sister was going to be a mother.* A smile spread across my lips at the thought of holding her little bundle of joy.

I gave El plenty of time to get settled on her plump pillows and carried the tray into her room. I wanted to have a conversation with her about how far along she was and ask some other questions I had for her, but it could wait.

"Gimme, gimme," she said as I approached the bed, making me chuckle.

"Is there anything else I can get you before I head out to run an errand?"

"Nope," she said between soft blows on her spoonful of hot soup. "This is perfect."

I kissed Ellie on the top of her head. "I won't be long, and I'm just a phone call away if you need anything."

"Thank you," she said sincerely. I saw tears forming in her big doe eyes and felt tears of my own threatening.

"It's going to be okay, Ellie. I promise."

I dropped one last kiss on her forehead and left her house to begin fulfilling my promise to her. The roar of Mistress's engine matched the rumble in my chest. One way or another, I'd make sure Ellie was treated with the respect she deserved.

CHAPTER
Six

Ben

I STOOD BENEATH THE SHOWER SPRAY AND LET THE HOT WATER BEAT down on my neck, back, and shoulders. Dinner at my mother and father's house was always brutal, but tonight had been especially difficult without my older brother, Bevan, there to help deflect their disappointment over our life choices. I had to put up with my mother's passive-aggressive bullshit while being blatantly ignored by my father. Why was I still seeking a relationship with them after all these years? Why did I want their approval so damn much?

My parents weren't disappointed that I was gay after they'd realized that my sexuality wasn't a choice. They loved having a token gay son to parade in front of potential clients to show how diverse they were. It amazed me that my self-absorbed father hadn't gone into a life of politics. My parents, however, were pissed that I had chosen a career outside of the family's corporate law firm. That was the choice they just couldn't abide. I'd rather someone stab me in the eye with a hot poker than read legal briefs day after day—or worse yet—help a slimy billionaire escape tax evasion charges.

I knew I wanted to do something to utilize my overactive imagination and creativity, but I wasn't sure what field I wanted to work in until Jeremy Jacobs's dad came to our middle school for career day. He got paid to come up with jingles, commercials, and print advertisements, and I was in awe of him. I had asked Mr. Jacobs a million and one questions after he was done talking to the class. He patiently answered every question and even stayed a little after class to give me some ideas on what courses I should take in college to give me an edge after I graduated. He stressed that digital art would have a major impact on the industry, and he'd been absolutely correct.

I had found what I wanted to do with my life. That night, I'd gone home and made the big announcement to my parents over dinner. They hadn't been impressed at all and even laughed it off as a prank, but it wasn't a joke to me. From that moment on, I secretly created ad campaigns for products I saw on TV in a sketch book Bevan had bought me for my birthday. I watched commercials and studied print ads to determine what worked well and what could've been done differently. I took as many art classes as my high school schedule would allow along with graphic design.

My parents threatened to disown me if I didn't follow in my father's footsteps, so I called their bluff. They didn't speak to me for my entire first year of college, and it was the best thing to ever happen to me. I learned how to live my life in the real world without their influence. I learned to stand on my own two feet and became independent. It was the happiest year of my life. Then Bevan gave up practicing corporate law to become a private investigator. Suddenly, my career path wasn't so bad.

Daniel and Beverly St. Claire were both products of privileged homes without parental guidance or concern. I always found both sets of my grandparents to be cold and completely uncaring. My parents had both been raised by nannies and carried on that tradition with their own offspring. It still amazed me that my vain mother had even allowed herself to become pregnant. There were many times growing up that I wished someone else was my mother and would come get me and take me to my real home. Sadly, that day had never come, and I was stuck with the family I had, but I refused to let their attitudes get me down anymore. Instead, I continued living my life the way I wanted to, not the way they still wished I would. Though I'd always thought my reason for avoiding any type of relationship was due to my schoolwork at first and then my workload after I graduated from college.

I started feeling a little better, and the tension from dinner started to leave my body until I remembered I hadn't contacted Xavier yet. I kept putting it off because I hadn't yet come up with a subtle way to let him know I was into him and not his sister. I had picked up my phone several times throughout the day to text or call him, but each time I got interrupted by a call from a client or an ad exec needing me to approve ad copy. I decided to call him as soon as I finished my shower and set about washing my hair and body, suddenly eager to hear his voice in my ear.

I had just rinsed the shampoo from my hair when I heard my doorbell ring over and over, followed by a fist pounding loudly. I shut the water off immediately, threw a towel around my waist, and jogged to the front door, thankful I had carpet on the stairs or else I probably would have tumbled down them. I couldn't imagine who would be knocking so desperately and feared something was wrong with Mrs. Hernandez.

I flung open my door and found an enraged Xavier Cruz on my doorstep. He opened his mouth to say something, but instead, it hung open as his eyes raked me up and down. Sure, I should have called him before now, but the anger on his face didn't match my crime.

"I was going to call you when I got out of the shower, Xavier. I'm sorry I didn't call you sooner, but I got really busy at work and…"

"You son of a bitch!" Xavier's enraged voice cut off my explanation. He placed both his hands on my chest and shoved me backward into my home and then slammed the front door closed behind him. He was surprisingly strong. "You got my sister pregnant, and you think you're just going to abandon her?" He advanced on me, but I was so lost in his gorgeous whiskey-colored eyes that it took several moments before I could react. He had his arm cocked back ready to strike me before his words penetrated my skull. I dodged to the left just in time to miss his punch.

"Wait just a damn minute." I spun to the side to avoid another swing. I lowered my shoulder and drove it into Xavier's midsection, pinning him against my door with my taller, heavier body. His chest rose and fell against mine as he labored to catch the breath I'd knocked out of him. "I. Did. Not. Get. Ellie. Pregnant." I returned his fury tenfold. *What the fuck had made him think I'd knocked up his sister? Oh yeah, he thought I was straight.* "I've never had sex with a woman in my life."

"Are you trying to tell me you're a virgin after you practically confessed to being a manwhore the other night?" Xavier slammed his lower body against mine, trying to push me off him. "Oh," he said almost breathlessly. It was then that I realized I had lost my towel in the scuffle and my dick was reacting to his nearness. I watched his Adam's apple move up and down as he swallowed hard. Xavier's eyes opened wide, and his breath ghosted over my damp skin, causing my nipples to harden to painful points.

Screw subtle! I was going all in. "No, Xavier, I'm not telling you I'm a virgin. All my slutty behavior has involved men because I'm gay. Obviously." I emphasized my excitement by rubbing my erection against the front of his jeans. I should have been embarrassed by my bold behavior, but I wasn't in the least. I placed my hands on his hips and lowered my mouth until it hovered over his full, perfect lips. "I've wanted to taste *your* lips since the first time I saw them. I sat there watching your mouth move as you spoke to me at lunch that day. Everyone else saw how captivated I was by you, *except* you. I'm going to taste them now, Xavier."

I slid my gaze up from his trembling mouth to look into his eyes, gauging his reaction. I saw nothing that indicated I should back away. In fact, I saw just how badly Xavier wanted to taste my lips too. I raised my hands and placed them on both sides of his face, and cupping him gently, I lowered my mouth to his. My eyes drifted shut and a happy sigh escaped from me as the plush softness of his lips pressed against mine.

I traced his full bottom lip with my tongue until I reached his lip ring. I gently sucked the hoop between my lips, reveling in the sinful moans coming from his throat. Xavier wrapped his hands around my biceps, burning my skin. I tilted his head back and deepened the kiss by sliding my tongue between his parted lips. The taste of him spurred me on and my hands slid from his face to his neck and farther down until my palms rested against his pectoral muscles.

I broke our kiss suddenly, trying to calm myself down. I let my thumbs trace the outlines of the barbell nipple rings I had just discovered. "Are you pierced anywhere else?" I asked, joking and breathless.

"Yes," he replied, his voice barely above a whisper. His wicked smile made it impossible for me to know if he was teasing me or being serious. There was only one way to find out. I slid my hands down to his waist and grabbed the hem of his T-shirt slowly lifting it up while our eyes remained locked on each other. Xavier wanted this just as badly as I did, which he proved when he raised his arms above his head to help me remove his shirt. I missed the feel of his hands on my skin during their brief absence and was ecstatic when he grasped my biceps again.

I tossed his shirt to the floor and reached behind him to lock the front door. "You're all mine now," I whispered hungrily in his ear.

I kissed a path along his strong jawbone until I reached his chin. I captured his mouth in a hot, frenzied kiss while I teased his hard nipples and the piercings with my thumbs. Xavier dug his nails into my flesh, which only turned me on more. I couldn't remember a time I'd been so hard and in jeopardy of blasting off so quickly.

Xavier whimpered when I pulled my mouth from his and relocated it to his neck just below his ear. I smiled against his tender flesh before sucking it between my lips. The urge to mark him was insane and caused me to feel momentarily off-balance. These feelings were wholly new to me, and I shoved them aside rather than examine them. I had more important things to concentrate on, such as living out my year-long fantasy.

"Ben." Xavier groaned my name when I kissed a path down his neck and across his collarbone. "Your mouth feels even better than I imagined it would." I kissed down the center of his chest and over to suck his right nipple hard between my lips. "Fuck!"

It was my turn to moan and groan when he tangled his fingers in my hair and held my head against his chest. I alternated between licking and sucking his nipple before placing open-mouthed kisses across his chest to the other hardened disc, which I gave the same teasing treatment. Xavier's nails scraped against my scalp sending my lust into overdrive.

I kissed a path down his chest while I lowered myself to my knees. Once there, I traced the treble clef tattoo that surrounded his belly button with my tongue. His tight abdominal muscles spasmed beneath his skin as I swirled my tongue along the tattoo's lines over and over. Xavier's well-formed vee delineating his hip muscles peeked out of his low-rise jeans, catching my attention next.

"Please, Ben." Xavier's plea was followed by an attempt to guide my mouth where he wanted it most.

I wasn't ready to play along yet. I nibbled the trembling flesh over both hips until I was satisfied. By then, Xavier's hard-on was trying to fight its way out of his confining clothes, and I was more than happy to set it free. After all, I wanted to see where else the sexy man was pierced. I slowly unbuttoned his fly, drawing out my anticipation. Finally, his jeans were open in a wide vee, exposing his light-blue underwear beneath.

My mouth watered at the sight of his precum saturating the fabric and the blunt, round protrusion of a piercing pressing against the fabric just beneath the bulbous head of his cock. I couldn't resist pressing my nose against the cloth and breathing the smell of him deep into my nostrils. "Christ, you smell good, but I bet you taste even better." I hardly recognized the deep timbre of my own voice.

"Suck me, Ben." Xavier thrust his bulge tighter against my face, pushing the wet fabric on my lips and chin.

I peeled his underwear down until just the head of his cock and the piercing were exposed. "I've never seen one of these before and didn't know how hot I'd find it." I traced my tongue around the circumference of the ball and then flicked it with my tongue. Xavier's precum dribbled over the head, and I lapped the rest of it off his crown. "What made you decide to pierce your cock?"

"It drives men wild when it pegs their prostate again and again," Xavier said between clenched teeth. "The way men practically cry during their orgasms makes up for the temporary pain I felt." He thrust his hips, gliding the tip of his cock over my tongue. "It's been a very long time since I've had the pleasure of using it, though."

Meaning he was most likely versatile and had only bottomed recently, or he'd been celibate for a long time. I rarely bottomed for anyone, but the orgasm he was promising me made me want to grab my ankles and hold on for dear life. Right then, I just wanted to drive him wild, make him come, and taste him on my tongue. I was confident I could give him the best blow job of his life. I just hoped his piercing wouldn't get lodged in my throat.

I slid my hands inside his underwear to cup his firm ass while I continued to bathe the tip of his cock with my mouth. I hooked his jeans and underwear and slowly pulled them down his toned legs to midthigh. I loved the feel of his crisp leg hairs tickling my palms. I sucked every newly exposed inch of his cock into my mouth until his smooth balls pressed against my chin and his neatly trimmed pubic hair tickled the tip of my nose. *That's right, baby. No gag reflex.*

"Fuck," Xavier cried out while yanking on my hair. "Jesus, Ben, your mouth…feels…so damn…good." I ratcheted up my torment a little by massaging his balls. I pulled off his dick to suck a smooth orb into my mouth before switching to the other. "I want to fuck your mouth, Ben. Now."

Xavier's need for me drove me wild. I maintained eye contact with him as I slid his erection back into my mouth. I reached between my legs and took my throbbing cock in my hand and jerked myself off while Xavier fucked my mouth. The sounds he made, the way he said my name, and the tugging on my hair drove me to the brink too quickly, but I couldn't ease up on either of our cocks.

"Going to come," Xavier warned, but I already knew by the way he trembled harder and his balls pulled tighter to his body. One of his hands held my head closer while the other tried to push me off as if he were at war with himself. "Pull off if you…" He didn't get to finish his sentence before

46

he was shooting over my tongue and down my throat. I moaned at the first taste of his salty essence and fisted my dick faster and harder.

A fire lit his eyes from within as he watched me jack off while licking his dick clean. It only took a few more pulls before I shot my load all over the hardwood floor between my knees. The force of my orgasm left me reeling for several seconds, and I leaned my forehead against one of Xavier's thighs. He ran his fingers softly through my hair as I fought to catch my breath. The gesture was tender in contrast to the frenzied pace of the blow job I gave him.

"Okay, so you're gay," Xavier said, breaking the silence.

CHAPTER
Seven

Xavier

BEN CHUCKLED AGAINST MY THIGH, CAUSING ME TO LOOK DOWN AT him. It was then I realized I was still running my fingers through his soft black hair. The moment was too tender for the rawness I'd been feeling, so I removed my hands and let them fall to my sides.

"At least we got that settled," Ben replied, using his discarded towel to clean up the mess he'd made all over his floor. I tried not to think about how hot he looked when he was jacking off at my feet. He placed one final kiss on my leg before he rose slowly. I took a long moment to look over Ben's gorgeously formed body once my heart, lungs, and brain began functioning normally. "If you don't mind, I'm going to go upstairs and get dressed, and when I get back, you can tell me what the hell is going on."

"I should probably just go," I replied, feeling like ten kinds of fool. "It was a huge mistake coming here." Then I remembered my near nakedness and immediately started to dress so I had a reason to look away from his gorgeous eyes until I could pull myself together. I really screwed up, and I wasn't sure how to get out of what I'd just let happen.

"I don't think so, Xavier." His voice was so firm and controlled I couldn't help but stop midmotion and look at him. "You'll be here when I come back downstairs, and we're going to talk through what just happened. I'm trying not to be offended that you thought I was straight and that I would be careless enough to get Ellie pregnant, then cast her aside like yesterday's garbage."

"Ben…"

"Stop," he said in that demanding tone I was starting to find really sexy. "I will just track you down if you leave my house without talking to me. So let's just face this head-on right now." He turned and began walking up his steps without waiting for my agreement. "Stop staring at my ass, Xavier, or I'm going to start thinking that you don't believe what just happened was a mistake after all."

I smiled in spite of the confusion clouding up my mind. I didn't really regret the blow job, but I knew I would have been better off not knowing how Ben's lips had felt around my cock or the sounds he made when he came. I was better off not knowing that Ben had wanted me for a long time because nothing could ever happen between us. He wouldn't want me once he found out what I'd done or who I'd let myself become over the last year. I would've been better off not knowing how good he could make me feel because learning that Ben was gay and available changed nothing for me. I still needed to focus my time and energy on getting stronger and staying sober.

I finished dressing and walked into Ben's living room to wait for him. I wasn't sure what I expected his house to be like, but it wasn't the warm, inviting space around me. The decorations on the walls consisted of framed posters of legendary rockers from the '60s and '70s, classic ad posters from many eras, and an antique-looking world map that was nearly as long as his brown leather sofa. There were bronze pins stuck in several countries, and I wondered how many of those were places Ben had already visited and which were ones he still planned to explore.

I turned away from the map and let my eyes roam over the large steamer trunk that served as a coffee table. In a corner of the room, there was an antique globe on a bronze pedestal and beside it sat a record player on a table made of dark wood. My eyes locked on the stacks of vinyl records that were stored on a shelf below the record player.

Ben's home made me want to sit back, kick my feet up, and just breathe. In fact, I felt better breathing in his air than I had in any other place since I'd arrived home. I would be lying if I said it was the blow job and not the man himself who'd made me relax. There was something calming about being in Ben's presence; it was as if nothing and no one could hurt me. I'd found that comfort in only a handful of people during my short lifetime, and it concerned me that I'd found it with him so easily. He was practically a stranger to me.

Ben's calm demeanor contradicted his controlling words and the voice he'd used to keep me here while he changed. Maybe it wasn't a contradiction at all and his calmness and control went hand in hand. Damien had used many unpleasant tactics to control me and get what he wanted from me, and I'd spent more than two years under Damien's abusive thumb. So why didn't Ben's dominant attitude alarm me? Why was Ben able to calm me where Damien had only scared me? It didn't really matter because I had already decided I wouldn't allow myself to spend much time around Ben. He was just another addiction waiting to happen.

"Penny for your thoughts," Ben said softly from behind me. I'd been so lost in my head I hadn't heard him come down the steps. He must be able to move like a jungle cat stalking prey. "You look like you're carrying the weight of the world on your shoulders," he said when I turned to face him. "I'm a good listener, and anything you tell me will stay between us. I promise not to go running to Ellie."

I nervously rubbed the back of my neck while searching for a response. "I appreciate that, Ben, I really do. These are things I just need to work through on my own." He had no idea how tempted I was to curl up on his couch and tell him the sordid pieces of my past. The only thing that held me back was fear of seeing disgust in his eyes. No, I needed to fix myself this time. "You're right about one thing. We do need to talk about what just happened, and I do owe you a huge apology. I guess that's two things."

"I'm not keeping score," he said, a wicked gleam entering his eyes. "Do you want something to drink before you grovel?"

"No thanks," I replied around a grin. Ben gestured with his hand for me to have a seat on his couch, and I complied. "I'm sorry I jumped to conclusions and accused you of getting my sister pregnant," I told him when he sat beside me.

"And casting her aside. Don't forget about that part."

I nodded. "Yes, I apologize for that too."

"How about saying you're sorry for thinking I was straight?" The word *straight* was said with so much disgust that it almost made me laugh. The expression on Ben's face matched his tone, and I was afraid I really had offended him.

"I..."

"That's almost as bad as you accusing me of casting Ellie aside, Xavier."

"Ben..." I knew my voice almost sounded exasperated, but I was cut off before I could say more.

"I'm very gay. I think I just showed you how gay I am, but if you need another demonstration..."

I held up my hand to stop him when he leaned toward me like he was going to kiss me. "That can't happen again."

"It can't?" Ben's brow furrowed in confusion.

"No."

"Can I ask why? You seemed to really enjoy yourself, and I know I enjoyed it."

"It was fine, Ben." I waved off his line of questioning, hoping to move on so I could get out of there and go home.

"*Fine?* It was *fine?*" Ben's voice rose in pitch, and his eyes bugged out comically.

"Nice," I responded.

"*Nice,*" Ben said, using air quotes, "isn't good either. Fuck!" He threw his hands up in the air out of frustration. "I thought I gave great head, but apparently I have delusions of grandeur. Jesus, I better start working on my skills. Are you sure this can't happen again? I can do better, Xavier." His gray eyes implored me to give in to him.

I would have been mortified by that point if I hadn't caught the mischievous twinkle in his gaze. I realized it had been too long since I'd laughed and joked with someone, and I missed it. I wanted to play along, but I feared playing with words would lead to playing with each other's cocks. I needed to keep my dick to myself, and I selfishly wanted Ben to do the same.

"I'm certain it can't happen again. It's not you…"

"Don't finish that sentence. Holy shit! You're killing me tonight, Xavier." Ben dropped his head into his hands and scrubbed his face briefly before looking back at me. "Were you seriously going to say 'it's not you, it's me' just now?"

"Yes. No. I… Maybe." I let out a frustrated growl because Ben had had me flustered and stuttering from the moment he'd come down the steps. I wanted to say what I needed to say and get the hell out of there before I made an even bigger fool of myself. "Look, Ben, your blow job skills don't need fine-tuning because they're fantastic. Your performance is not the problem. *I* am the problem, and I need to spend all my energy fixing *me* right now."

Ben took a deep breath and nodded slowly. "I respect that, Xavier, but let me just remind you that you aren't alone. You are surrounded by people who would do anything to help you, including me. You don't know me very well yet, but you can trust me."

I instinctively knew that was true. "Thank you for that, Ben. I do know I am a very lucky man with a wonderful support system, but I've leaned on them my whole life, and it's time I stood up on my own."

"Okay."

We stared at each other for a few minutes longer before I broke eye contact. I had to look away because Ben's quicksilver eyes were pulling me in, and if they did, I wouldn't want to let go. I could have easily allowed myself to get lost in him, but what I'd told him was true. I needed to fight this battle on my own. "I'm sorry for the way I barged into your house and accused you of terrible things, though."

"Like being straight?" Ben's wry grin told me he had forgiven me.

A genuine smile spread across my face for the first time in ages. "Yes, that too."

"You're forgiven, Xavier." Ben answered with a smile of his own. "You were just looking out for your sister, and that's something to be admired." I looked away from him again because I didn't believe there was much inside me worthy of admiration. "I didn't even know she was seeing anyone. I'm shocked she didn't tell me because I thought she told me everything. Why wouldn't she tell me she was dating someone?"

The confusion in his voice pulled my eyes back to him. "She didn't say his name. She just kept repeating that she thought he loved her and that she was different from the rest of them. Ellie's really beating herself up over this, and she's not feeling good at all. I'm really worried about her, Ben. Will you please let her be the one to tell you?"

"Hey," he said softly, placing his warm, strong hand on my shoulder. "I'll wait for her to tell me about the pregnancy no matter how bad I want to demand who this son of a bitch is so I can beat his ass. Ellie has us, and we won't let her down, Xavier."

"Thank you." I rose to my feet. "For everything."

"Do you mean the *fine* and *nice* blow job?" he asked, standing up beside me.

"Quit fishing for compliments, Ben. It reeks of desperation." I wasn't sure how to say goodbye to him after what we'd just shared. A fist bump and an attaboy? An awkward pat on the back? Ben followed me to the front door and opened it for me like a gentleman. "Well, it's been real." I nearly cringed at my lame attempt at a goodbye.

"Xavier." There was that calm but captivating voice again, and it had me stopping in my tracks. Ben pulled me into him and wrapped his arms around me. The next thing I knew I was resting my forehead against his shoulder and allowing him to hug me tight and give me comfort. "You're a lot stronger than you realize, and I know you'll overcome the demons you're fighting. I'm here if you want to talk, yell, or practice *your* blow job skills on me. I'm altruistic like that."

I pulled back from his embrace feeling a thousand times better than before I'd arrived on his front porch. "You'll be the first guy I call if I decide I need to practice." I shot him a playful wink and walked away from his house. I pretended he was moaning over my parting words and not my beautiful car that was parked in his driveway. I drove home knowing I'd be thinking of that blow job and the comfort I'd found in Ben's presence no matter how much I wished I could forget both.

CHAPTER
Eight

Ben

"**A**RE YOU JUST GOING TO PRETEND YOU DON'T KNOW WHAT'S GOING on with me?"

Ellie had snuck in behind me as I entered my office and asked the question just as I took a sip of hot coffee. The liquid went down the wrong way causing me to cough and sputter for a few minutes before I could speak. I shut the door so my personal assistant, Ian, wouldn't overhear our conversation. "Damn, you scared the hell out of me, El." I finally turned to face her.

She just stood there with her arms crossed over her chest, tapping her foot. My tiny friend looked tired but a little better. Maybe telling someone about the pregnancy had relieved some of her tension. "Xavier told me he went running over to your house and accused you of getting me pregnant."

Her lip twitched slightly indicating she wasn't as annoyed as she was pretending to be.

"He just volunteered that information?" I knew he hadn't. I raised a brow skeptically, which was met with an arrogant lift of her brow in return.

"Of course not," she said with a proud wave of her hand. "I know how to get the truth out of him after all these years. He came home dragging his tail between his legs, and I knew he'd done something he wasn't proud of." Her words pierced my heart because I knew which part he regretted, and it wasn't just the accusations he'd made. "He admitted to storming over to your house, but he didn't tell me what happened after he got there. Obviously, you set him straight about not being straight and told him you're not my baby's daddy. Then what?"

"Xavier and I are both adults, Ellie." I kept my tone calm and neutral, not wanting her to know just how bad her earlier comment had hurt.

"That's debatable, Ben," she threw back. "He was too mellow for nothing to have happened, so don't even go there with me. I thought we agreed you'd take things slow with him. What happened to subtle?" She narrowed her eyes and watched me closely as she waited for my reply.

It flew right out the door he shoved open. I walked to her and placed my hands gently on her shoulders. "El, I'm not discussing what may or may not have happened between Xavier and me with you. It wouldn't be right." She blew out a frustrated breath, then pinched her lips together. "He's much stronger than you know, stronger than any of you give him credit for, and he'll prove it."

"Xavier's strength has never been a concern. I just feel like he was into something very unhealthy for him, and he needs time to heal and pull himself back together." I heard the plea for my understanding in her voice. Her eyes teared up with concern over her brother.

"Which is exactly what he told me last night, El." I gave her a quick hug and sat down at my desk. I pointed to the visitor's chair, letting her know this conversation wasn't over—not by a long shot. "I appreciate you deflecting the attention onto Xavier and me, but that's not going to fly. I believe there is something you need to tell me. Let's start with the name of the man I'm about to fuck up."

"You could've warned me Hurricane Ellie was on her way," I said to Xavier as soon as he answered. I was calling from the back seat of a cab as I headed to the airport for an unexpected trip to Tampa.

"Shit! How bad was it? She laid into me for a solid hour last night about my activities with you and then again first thing this morning. I thought I had her calmed down before she left, but I guess not. I'm sorry, Ben." I heard the apology in his voice, and I didn't want him to stress over it. I meant to tease, but it appeared I'd had the opposite effect.

"I didn't call you for an apology." I aimed for comforting but wasn't sure I'd hit my mark.

"Then why did you call?" Xavier went from concerned to confused pretty quickly, which was only fair because he had the same ever-changing effect on my moods. I tried not to let the fact that he didn't want to talk bother me. I had to believe the crazy pull I felt toward him meant something beyond just a physical or chemical reaction.

"I got *his* name out of Ellie." There was no attempt to keep the smugness out of my tone.

"How did you manage that?"

I liked the awe I heard in his voice, but it made it hard for me to focus on our conversation. "It took a lot of back and forth with her, but I eventually wore her down. My brother, Bevan, is a private investigator, and I asked him to look into the guy. I figured you and I could check him out when I get back from Tampa."

"You're leaving?"

Did I detect disappointment in his voice? Dare I hope? "It wasn't a planned trip," I explained. "I'm filling in for an ad exec who got sick. I should be back tomorrow night, and I'm confident Bevan will have the information we need. Are you interested?"

"Like a stakeout?" I definitely heard humor in Xavier's voice. "Could be interesting, but you're going to need to drive because Mistress doesn't blend in."

My overactive imagination kicked in, and I envisioned Xavier and myself sitting in the front seat of my car, but we were doing some serious making out and heavy petting instead of staking out the jerk who'd gotten Ellie pregnant. I could almost hear the sound of Xavier breathing heavily in my ear as I nibbled his neck. I could almost feel his breath on my skin.

"Hey, buddy, we're here," the cabby said loudly, pulling me out of my fantasy just when it had started getting good.

"Sorry," I said sheepishly to the driver as I swiped my card to pay my fare. I grabbed my garment and carry-on bags and slid out of the cab. "I'll drive." I turned my attention back to Xavier as I entered the airport. "We can grab dinner first," I offered.

"It won't be a date, Ben."

Slow and Steady. Be what he needs and nothing more. "Of course not," I agreed. "I *was* listening when we were talking last night. No dinner. We'll check this douche out for Ellie's sake and no other reason."

"Okay," he said hesitantly after a short pause. "Are you planning on confronting him or just finding out more about him?"

"I hadn't planned to confront him," I said honestly. "Ellie said she wants nothing to do with him, and that is good enough for me. I just need to see what kind of guy he is with my own eyes."

"Call me when you're ready to set something up."

"I will. Take care, Xavier." I was reluctant to say goodbye.

"Thanks, Ben. I hope you have a safe trip."

We said our goodbyes after that, but his soft voice and image still lingered in my mind. There was a part of me that demanded I forget about this thing with Xavier and walk away before one of us got hurt. I suspected I'd be the one who got hurt, and that was something I wanted to avoid at all costs. I led a very happy and emotionally tangle-free life. As much as that all made sense, I didn't want to listen because something bigger than Xavier and me was at play here.

All I knew was that I suddenly wanted more than a tangle-free life. I blamed it on spending time with Gray and Chase, who were totally devoted to one another. They had opened my eyes and taught me that not all relationships were toxic cesspools. I wanted to get messy and experience the gamut of emotions a healthy relationship could bring, but was Xavier the right fit for me? There was only one way to know for sure, but I warned myself to proceed with caution. I whistled as I boarded the plane with an extra bounce in my step. I, Bennett Matthew St. Claire, had decided to live outside the box and embrace the mess.

CHAPTER
Nine

Xavier

I WAS STILL SMILING WHEN I SLID MY PHONE INTO MY FRONT JEANS pocket. I checked my watch and noted that Gram would be arriving any minute, as she was hardly ever late. Gram was one of those people who thought being on time was arriving fifteen minutes early. She'd set a great example for us on so many levels, which was the main reason I had invited her to breakfast at my favorite childhood haunt. I needed to be a man, look her in the eyes, and apologize for letting her down.

I sat back in the diner booth and put off those thoughts until she arrived. Instead, I thought about how I hadn't had even one bad dream last night. In fact, I'd woken up in the early morning hours with the echo of a new melody in my head. It was only a few notes that had penetrated my sleep, but it was a step in the right direction. I wasn't sure what had caused the melodies to return because nothing had changed since they'd left me. Well, Ben's amazing blow job happened, but that was an unlikely connection. I suspected stress was behind my inability to create music, so perhaps being back with my friends and family was enough for me to relax and let the creative juices flow.

"Sorry I'm late," Gram said in a rushed voice as she approached the booth. I looked at my watch and noted she'd arrived only twelve minutes early instead of the usual fifteen. "That Lennie is a hard man to walk away from in the morning." Gram shot me a wink, and I tried not to cringe. I could have lived the rest of my life without knowing what Gram and Lennie had gotten up to before she'd come to have breakfast with me.

"Thanks for meeting me, Gram."

"Xavier, you sound so damn serious this morning, and I've not had enough coffee for that yet." She held up her hand, and a waitress magically appeared. "I'll have coffee and my grandson sounds like he needs prune juice already at only twenty-six years old."

"I'll have coffee," I told the young waitress. I couldn't keep the grin off my face as she walked away. "You're something else, Gram."

She reached across the table and grasped both my hands. "There's that beautiful smile I've been missing. I expect to see it more often, you hear me?"

"Yes, Gram."

"Good." She looked around the diner for several minutes before turning her focus back on me. "Damn, this place hasn't changed a bit in twenty years. It's probably been just as long since it was last cleaned."

"I heard that, Agnes," came a booming, masculine voice from the kitchen. "You better watch it."

"Or what? You'll stop using your *special sauce* in the pancake batter? What kind of grown-ass man names his diner Spanky's?" Gram fired back.

Moments later, a grizzled-looking man came out of the back and approached our table carrying a tray with two cups and a carafe of coffee. He would have looked scary if not for the crooked grin splitting the lower half of his face. Gram stood up to greet him, and he pulled her into a bear hug after he set the tray on our table.

"It's so good to see you, you old broad. How the hell are you doing?"

"I'm doing great, Reggie. I'm still writing my books and living at the old folk's home where Chase and Xavier dumped me."

Reggie looked at me and then back at Gram. "Kids these days." Reggie shook his head in exaggerated disappointment.

Gram lived in a posh retirement community by choice. Although, she liked to joke that Chase and I had tricked her into getting in the car by telling her we were going for ice cream and then dropped her off at the curb of the old folk's home and sped off. There was a reason Gram was a successful writer; there was no end to her imagination.

"It's good to see you home, Xavier." Reggie patted me on the back hard enough to dislocate something. It felt really good to be home, which I told him. "Do you both want your usual orders?" Gram and I said we did, and he returned to the kitchen to begin preparing our food.

"I'm happy to have breakfast with you anytime, Xavier, but I sense you have something you want to get off your chest. All joking aside, I'm all ears, my darling boy."

I took a calming breath before I began. "Gram, I'm sorry I've let you down." I could tell she was going to interrupt and argue with me, but I really needed to say what was on my mind without interruption. I held up my hand to ward her off and continued. "You put all that time, money, and energy into my musical education, and I wasted your gift." I saw fire light up her pale blue eyes, and I knew I was quickly running out of time. "I had an amazing opportunity because of you, and I carelessly tossed it aside to join a rock band. I'm not sure I can even call it that since we didn't perform a single original song."

"Xavier." Her voice held a hint of admonishment.

"Please let me finish, Gram. These things have been on my mind for a long time now, and I need to say them to you."

"Okay, honey." Gram's compassionate gaze locked on me as she reached across the table and squeezed my hand. "You talk, and I'll listen." She gave me a slight nod to encourage me to continue.

"I'm sorry I didn't follow through with Julliard, Gram, because I might not have screwed up so badly if I had. I did things this past year that I'm not proud of and…" I had to pause to swallow around a lump in my throat. "I hate the person I let myself become. I'm working really hard to get back to me, but it's going to take some time. My first step is apologizing to the people I've hurt and disappointed. I owe you everything, including my life. I'm so sorry I let you down." I sat back and took a sip of my coffee when I was finished. The hot drink warmed the chill that had seeped into my bones at the thought of disappointing Gram. I stared at my coffee cup, afraid of what I might see when I looked into her eyes.

"Xavier, may I speak now?" I slowly raised my head, looked directly at her, and nodded. "I do not want to hear such stupid talk from you ever again. You do not owe me anything, do you hear me?" She didn't pause for me to answer, just marched on full steam ahead. "You were not some charity case I took in off the street. You were a boy who desperately needed unconditional love and a safe place to live. I have admired you since you were five years old."

"Me?"

"Yes, you. You were strong enough to be yourself when the people you loved and trusted tried to beat it out of you. It took a lot of courage for you to ask for that princess party, Xavier. You were a warrior then, and you're a warrior now. I know it, and so does everyone else. I can't wait for the day when *you* finally realize that. You'll sort through whatever you're going through and come out on the other side stronger than ever, baby doll."

"Thanks, Gram."

"Still not finished," she singsonged. "I encouraged you to forge your own path and march to the beat of your own drum from day one, didn't I?" I nodded my agreement. "Why then would you expect me to be upset when you chose your own path, one that was different from what *your teachers* chose for you?"

"You paid so much money to send me to that private school, and I didn't use any of the skills they taught me while I was in the band."

"Xavier," Gram's voice was full of exasperation when she lightly smacked the table in front of her. "I've seen your performances, and you most certainly did use the knowledge you received from attending Saint Cecelia's. I saw you play the guitar and piano beautifully, not to mention your amazing stage presence. Honey, I was just as proud of your rock shows as I would have been of any orchestra or symphony performance. To be perfectly honest, I would have much rather watched your band over an orchestra."

"Really?"

"Have I ever lied to you, Xavier?" She looked at me in disbelief.

"No, Gram, you haven't."

"And I'm not going to start now." She reached over and patted my cheek. "All I've ever wanted was for you to be happy then, now, and in the future." The waitress interrupted by bringing our food to the table. "Speaking of happy, I heard you left the bachelor party with Ben."

"Gram." My voice held a warning. I did not want to go there with her, but when the hell had that ever stopped her? Just hearing Ben's name had me reliving the events of the previous night. I dropped my eyes to my plate while I buttered and poured syrup on my pancakes. I hoped to avoid eye contact with her until I had my reactions to the memories under control. The last thing I needed was her meddling in my love life.

"Come on, Xavier, I'm not blind. Ben St. Claire has cocksucking lips the likes of which I've never seen before. He has those chiseled cheekbones, that square jaw, and that strong throat you just know can work a man deep."

I had started to eat in an attempt to dissuade her from talking, but that blew up in my face as a hunk of pancake got lodged in my throat when she blurted out the bit about Ben's cocksucking equipment. I, of course, had firsthand knowledge of his skills and couldn't agree with her more—not that I was going to say so out loud. I finally worked the pancake down my throat while she went on about Ben's attributes. I listened to her wax poetic about his ass, his hands, and his long legs. Jesus, I had noticed all those things too, but I couldn't allow myself to focus on them until I was whole again, which is what I told her.

"Nothing makes you feel grateful to be alive like a mind-blowing orgasm, but I'm betting you know that given the redness of your face. I'm not judging you, Xavier. Au contraire, I'm really proud of you for living a little."

"Gram, nothing will come of it." I wasn't sure who I was trying to convince—myself or her. I had this ugly internal battle going on where Ben was concerned. I wanted him to want me, but I was afraid to hope. What happened if I took a chance and he turned away from me when he found out about the drug abuse? I didn't think I could handle that kind of rejection.

"I've had a built-in bullshit meter my entire life, but it seems what I really need is a maudlin meter." Gram threw up her hands. "Listen to a wise old woman, kiddo. We only have one life to live, so you might as well experience it to the fullest. If Ben is who you want, then Ben is who you go after."

"Gram, I don't want him." *Liar!*

"Wrong, Xavier. I see the truth in your eyes. You don't *want* to want Ben, and you don't think you deserve him." She narrowed her eyes and pointed a finger at me. "Fix whatever needs fixing, but don't let a great thing slip through your fingers because you're afraid. You need to channel that five-year-old boy who bravely asked for a princess party for his sixth birthday no matter how many times he'd been told it wasn't right for him to feel that way. That little boy wasn't afraid then, and the wonderful man he's become shouldn't be scared now."

"Yes, Gram."

Next up on my apology tour was Millie Janikowski, my piano, violin, and guitar instructor at Saint Cecilia's School of Performing Arts. I'd had no idea what to expect that first day of school at Saint C's. I had mostly outgrown my desire to wear girlish things by high school, so wearing a school uniform didn't bother me so much. There was a huge advantage to wearing uniforms versus street clothes because everyone was equal, at least in dress.

My "fish out of water" feeling hadn't come from the way I dressed or how I felt on the inside. I was out and proud, and I didn't care what anyone thought of my sexuality. I had already faced the worst that could happen and survived. My insecurities came from my perception that I had inferior skills compared to the other kids. I figured most of them came from much wealthier backgrounds and had had the absolute best instructors money could buy.

I loved my original teacher, Mrs. Merrimen, but I thought the other kids had probably had more stringent and structured training. My recitals had consisted of Gram, Chase, and Ellie, where the other kids had most likely played for larger crowds. Mrs. Merrimen believed I was gifted and had what it took to get accepted into Saint C's. Gram agreed with her and took the necessary steps to get an audition for me. I'll never forget the look of happiness on Gram's face when my acceptance letter arrived. She'd taken us all out for a celebratory dinner at a swanky restaurant the following weekend, and I didn't understand how she could not be disappointed that I'd thrown all that away. Gram had never lied to me before, and I didn't think she was lying then, but hearing and believing were two different things.

All my nerves vanished the moment I walked into Mrs. Janikowski's classroom. She, like me, marched to her own beat. She wore wildly colored outfits with hair colors to match. It was shocking to see such a vibrant instructor working at the prestigious institution, but I had liked her teaching style immediately. My admiration had quickly turned into awe when she'd taken us to the piano room and played the first piece of music we'd be learning to play. It was also made very clear why the eccentric woman had been chosen to instruct us. She was magnificent as she'd lost herself in the music. I wanted to be just like her.

I knocked lightly on the doorframe before entering her classroom. Not much had changed in the years since I had graduated and moved on. The same posters were on the walls, the room arrangement was identical to my time there, and a familiar vivacious woman sat behind the large desk at the front of the room. Mrs. J's head popped up, and a bright smile lit up her face.

"Oh my goodness! Xavier Cruz, get over here and give me a hug," she exclaimed and rose to her feet. "It's been way too long since you've stopped in to see me." I walked to her desk and hugged her like she instructed. She patted me on the back several times and pulled back. "Where have you been? Surely that rock band of yours takes a break now and then."

"I'm no longer with the band, Mrs. J. I've come home for good." It was obvious by the expression on her face that she knew something more was at play, but she didn't ask. I appreciated that she didn't probe further because I wasn't ready to share the reasons why I'd left the band yet. I walked over and took a seat at one of the student desks in the front row while she sat back down in her chair. "I'm really sorry I let you down by not going to Julliard, Mrs. J. I know you probably think I've squandered my talent these last years, and I…"

"I don't think that, Xavier," she interrupted. "There were some instructors that were very upset you didn't follow that path, but I was not one of them. Look at me, Xavier." She waved her hands up and down her torso. "Do I look like a person who gives a damn what others think? You did what you needed to do at the time, which was explore your options, and there's nothing wrong with that. Do you know how many people float around life without taking risks? Hmm? Too damn many," she replied, answering her own question. "I was proud of you for spreading your wings and flying instead of going down the path that someone else had chosen for you."

"You were?" First Gram and now Mrs. J; it was almost too good to be true.

"I was," she said with a nod. "Can I ask why you're remorseful about that choice now?" I let out a deep sigh and was about to answer when she stopped me. "You don't need to answer that, Xavier."

"It's okay," I assured her. "I just don't like the person I became, and I've been wondering if I would've done better if I had gone to Julliard instead of to LA to join a rock band. I guess we'll never know."

"Your life isn't over, Xavier," she reminded me gently. "So you didn't go to Julliard, but was that ever really *your* dream?"

"Not really," I answered honestly. "It was an honor to be accepted, but I just couldn't see myself playing in symphonies for the rest of my life, but I didn't see myself performing cover songs from '80s rock bands and pop princesses either."

"I saw your show several times over the years when you were on the East Coast and once in Canada." Mrs. J's confession took me completely by surprise. "You do a better Tina Turner than Tina herself. Wow, you have some legs on you, kid." She winked at me, and we shared a laugh.

"You've seen me perform? Why didn't you try to visit me backstage or wait around after the performance and approach me in the parking lot?" Hurt and disappointment squeezed my heart. She'd been so close but made no attempt to see me.

"I did try to see you backstage on two different occasions, but your manager wouldn't let me back there and refused to even give you a message from me." She must have seen what I was feeling on my face because she leaned her elbows on her desk and rested her chin on her hands. "He's your problem, isn't he?"

I couldn't speak around the lump in my throat, so I nodded. I was so ashamed that I'd allowed Damien to control so much of my life to the point that he kept me from seeing the people I loved the most.

"Take it back," she said passionately. "You don't let a bastard like him ruin your life and dreams. Take back your life!"

"I'm trying, Mrs. J, but I'm afraid it's too late." I swallowed hard to keep the tears at bay. "I've lost my music," I whispered painfully, "and I don't know how to get it back."

"What do you mean?"

I explained how I no longer heard melodies in my head. And I missed it so damn much. My life used to have its very own soundtrack with every event creating a melody in my mind that I would turn into a song.

"It's because of the stress, Xavier. You'll get your music back as soon as you are at peace with yourself, which is what I suspect has prompted your visit to me today." I nodded in agreement. "Follow me, sweetheart," Mrs. J said and rose from her desk.

She led me down the hall to her music room and flipped on the light. I always loved how the lights gleamed on the shiny black surfaces of the grand pianos. Peace and harmony washed over me as I entered the room.

"Just play something, Xavier. Anything."

So I did.

CHAPTER
Ten

Ben

THE TRIP TO TAMPA WAS SCREWED FROM THE WORD GO. I ARRIVED on time with the materials provided for the presentation, but *nothing* I presented went well. The materials weren't in order, and the PowerPoint was sloppy to say the least. I would be having a very firm conversation with Drew when I returned home. I had mistakenly trusted him to put this together and was going to allow him to present it to the largest indoor aquarium in the United States without supervision. I wouldn't be making that mistake again. It was my job as creative director to make sure these errors never happened. I was angrier over *my* lackluster job performance than I was over Drew's.

Later that night, I sat in the hotel restaurant and ate dinner by myself. I was irritated by how my day had gone and because I hadn't heard from

Bevan yet. How freaking hard was it to find this Drake Anderson douche anyway? I'd given Bevan his name, where he worked, and the place where he and Ellie had met because I figured it was one of his typical haunts. Did I need to do his job for him too? Damn, I was in a foul mood.

I looked up from my phone again to find a raven-haired man with a pair of fuck-me blue eyes scoping me out. Things were suddenly starting to look up. If I couldn't get any information out of my brother, then I could at least get laid. The sexy stranger kept staring at my lips, and I knew what he was thinking. I'd been told plenty of times that men fantasized about how my lips would feel wrapped around their cocks. A memory of Xavier popped up in my mind as soon as the thought crossed it. I didn't owe Xavier my fidelity because he'd made it clear he didn't want to pursue anything with me. But try as I might, I could not get the memory of Xavier out of my head as he leaned against my door with his pants around his thighs and his beautiful dick buried in my throat. The memory was so tangible I could almost feel Xavier's fingers in my hair and taste him on my tongue.

I had a choice to make. I could screw a nameless man who I'd forget a few hours later, or I could take care of business myself and hope I wasn't alone in the bone-deep attraction I felt for Xavier. It seemed there really wasn't a decision to be made after all. I broke eye contact with the man and signaled for my check. I picked up my phone and called my brother so the guy wouldn't get the impression that I was asking for my bill so I could leave with him.

"Have you ever been in love?" I asked Van when he answered the phone.

"I'm trailing a cheating wife, which is why I haven't called you tonight with the information. Can I call you back?"

"Wait, is it our mother?"

Van laughed dryly on the other end. "As if our father gives a damn who she's sleeping with as long as it's not him."

"True, and it's not like he hasn't had the same mistress for the past five years or longer. Hell, we could have other siblings," I amended sarcastically. "Seriously, Van, have you ever been in love, or do you think our parents have killed any possibility of us having normal, healthy relationships?" I chewed on my lip while I waited for his answer. I wanted to believe I could have what Chase and Gray had someday, but our primary example of what relationships looked like was seriously screwed up.

"I've never been in love, and I don't know if *I'm* capable of love, but I'm not sure the same can be said about *you*, Ben. Daniel and Beverly had less of an impact on you because you refused to conform to their rules and demands. It's not just them either." Bevan blew out a frustrated breath. "Let's not forget what I do for a living, bro. I've yet to investigate a suspected case of cheating that turns up as an honest misunderstanding between spouses, and I doubt I could ever truly trust someone after witnessing the travesty of a marriage between our pathetic parents and all these cheating asshats." I could always count on my brother to be honest even if I didn't always like his answers. "Have you met someone special, Ben?"

How the hell was I supposed to answer his question? Yes, I'd met someone who piqued my interest, and I believed he was special, but the fact remained that nothing might ever come of it. I wasn't a defeatist, so I wasn't giving up, but I'd be an idiot if I didn't at least acknowledge that Xavier's scars might run too deep for him to ever trust again. I wanted to be the one he leaned on and trusted with all his secrets, but wanting and wishing wouldn't make it so.

"It's complicated, Bevan. I want him to be special to me, but I'm not sure he feels the same way." My answer was honest, even though it hurt to admit it out loud. It was good to talk to my brother about how I was feeling because everyone else I could turn to also knew Xavier as a friend or brother. So I told him all about the man who'd captivated me.

"It sounds like you just need to give him some time and space," Van answered when I was done talking. "Ben?"

"Yeah?"

"Just be careful, okay? It sounds like this guy was into something pretty bad in LA, and I don't want you getting sucked into something that could cause you to end up hurt." His big-brother concern made me smile. "Do you want me to do some looking around for you to put both our minds at ease?"

"Jesus, not everyone is a freaking cheater or criminal." I immediately regretted the defensive way I spoke to my brother when he was only look-ing out for me. I expelled a frustrated breath and lightened my tone when I said, "He's a good guy, Van."

"I'm not saying he isn't, Ben. There are a lot of good people who've made a bad decision or two, and it's caused them a lot of hurt. You're the only family I have, and I'm just asking you to be cautious. I'll respect your wishes if you respect mine and be careful."

It was the closest thing to a heart-to-heart conversation that Van and I had ever had. "I appreciate your brotherly concern and your advice. I prom-ise to be careful and take things slow."

Van and I talked about a few other things while I paid for dinner and made my way back to my hotel room. Alone. He ended the call when he reached his destination and needed to photograph the money shot. He promised to email the information on Drake Anderson to me later that night. I tossed my cell phone on my bed and took a long, hot shower while I mulled over Van's advice. I knew he was right to be cautious about Xavier. I had no clue what shit he'd gotten into, but there was no way I could walk away without trying. I wanted Xavier to be the one to tell me what had hap-pened; it would mean so much more than reading it in a report.

I checked my phone as soon as I had slipped on lounge pants and a T-shirt. I had missed two calls from Xavier while I was in the shower, but he hadn't left a message either time. My heart started to race because I knew he wouldn't have called me to chat. He'd made that clear during our con-versation earlier that morning. I called him back and held my breath while I waited for him to answer.

"Hey, Ben," he said in a whisper. "I'm sorry if I bothered you, but Ellie asked me to call you."

"What's wrong?"

"Nothing now, but we had a little scare this evening. Ellie had some cramping and bleeding, so I brought her to the ER. The doctor said she's fine and a little spotting and mild cramping is normal." He sounded relieved but tired. "We got to hear the baby's heartbeat, and it was the most amazing sound I've ever heard." I heard a hint of fear beneath the awe in his voice.

I wished I had been there to provide him comfort or at least a shoulder to lean on, but we weren't there *yet.*

I smiled because it was the first unguarded thing he'd said to me. "I'm so glad you called and let me know what's going on." A pearl of hope began to form, but his next words obliterated it.

"Ellie decided to take the remainder of the week off to rest, and she didn't want you to worry when you came back to the office and found her absent."

His emphasis that Ellie was the one who had wanted him to call stung just a little bit until I realized Ellie could have easily called me in the morning to let me know what was going on. Was Ellie playing matchmaker by trying to push Xavier and me into communicating, or was Xavier using her as an excuse to call me? I hoped for the latter.

"Did you hear back from your brother yet?"

I smiled to myself because I had my answer. "He was trailing a cheating spouse and said he'd email me the information tonight. I should be home tomorrow afternoon if you want to track this fucker down tomorrow night."

"Should be home?" Xavier asked. I told him about my screwed-up day, and it felt so good to have someone to talk to about it. "You must be really angry then," he stated once I finished recounting the meeting from hell. I tried to place the tone of his voice; it was somewhere between curious and timid.

"I was more disappointed than angry," I answered honestly. "I hate being embarrassed in front of clients because of poor planning and execution."

"What are you going to do about it?" Xavier asked softly, almost hesitantly.

I was certain there was more to Xavier's inquiry than what type of reprimand I had in mind for Drew. This was a test, not a question, and I was desperate to pass. "Well, I'm going to be supervising his ad campaigns a lot closer, and he won't be permitted to pitch to clients on his own until he's earned my trust again."

"So, no yelling or cussing him out?"

"That's not my style, Xavier."

"It's not your style in your professional life, but what about in your personal life?" Someone really had done a number on the beautiful man, and fuck if I didn't want to make it all better—by any means necessary.

"It's not my style in any aspect of my life, Xavier." I silently prayed he could hear the sincerity in my voice. Somehow earning his trust had become the most important thing in my life.

"I'm not available tomorrow night, but I am the night after if you really want me to go with you. Just let me know what time to be ready."

It was a small victory but one I would happily claim. We didn't chat for much longer, and our goodbye seemed a little awkward, but I didn't care. I was certain I had made progress, and if I had looked in the mirror, I knew I would have seen the goofiest grin on my face. That smile remained as I watched *SportsCenter*, read through my emails, and even when I fell asleep. It probably stayed on my face through my dreams.

CHAPTER
Eleven

Xavier

I DIDN'T HAVE ANOTHER NIGHTMARE, BUT THE NEW MELODY DIDN'T pay me a visit in my sleep either, so I woke with mixed feelings. I was grateful for a peaceful night of sleep without Damien haunting me, but I was disappointed about the lack of music. I was certain something should've broken free inside me after all the hours I'd played the piano at Saint C's the day before, but there was nothing.

I shoved the disappointment aside and focused on the positives I had going for me. It seemed that no one was disappointed with my choice to go to LA, except me, which meant I could move on with my life and be happy if I could just find a way to pardon myself. So that was what I decided to do as I jogged through the neighborhood in the cool morning air. I formulated a plan to start forgiving myself little by little, day by day. I would fight for the life I wanted, even if that meant battling myself.

Ellie looked like a whole new person when I got back to her house an hour later. The ER doc had prescribed an antinausea medicine, and it seemed to be working. She sat at the kitchen table eating oatmeal while the sun shone through the window and bathed her with its brilliant beams. She smiled at me as I entered the kitchen and poured myself a cup of coffee.

"You look so much better," I told her while leaning against the counter. "Are the pills working?"

"They seem to be so far." She got a faraway look in her eyes and smiled dreamily. "I'm going to be a mother," she whispered as if it was just sinking in. "I knew I was pregnant, of course, but it didn't seem real until I heard his or her heartbeat last night. I didn't plan on ever having kids and I didn't think I wanted to be a mom until I thought I was having a miscarriage." She focused her eyes back on mine and gave me a wobbly smile. "Thank you for being my rock last night, Xavier. I was scared out of my mind, but you gave me the strength I needed to stay calm."

"You've always been my rock, Ellie, and I'm glad I was able to return the favor." I walked to the table and dropped a kiss on the top of her crazy morning curls. "You're going to be an amazing mother. You were born to nurture and love, and my little niece or nephew will be the luckiest baby to have you for a mom. You're not our parents, and you won't ever be."

"Thank you, Xavier. Perhaps someday I'll get to say the same words to you."

"Who knows? Maybe." My words lacked conviction, though. It was hard for me to visualize a future with children in it. I had spent so much time on the road the last eight years that I hadn't given the possibility of starting a family much consideration. *Was fatherhood in my cards?* Only time would tell. "Do you need me to bring you anything while I'm out? I'll be gone most of the day, but I'll always have my phone nearby."

"I'll be fine, little brother. You go do what you need to do, and don't worry about me. I'm just going to lie around, watch some trashy daytime talk shows, and read a book. Oh, have you seen Gram's new vampire cover?

The model looks a whole lot like Gray." Ellie giggled softly. "I'm sure Gray does plenty of sucking, but I bet it doesn't involve blood."

I burst into laughter over her words and waggling eyebrows. "Jesus, El, you've been hanging around Gram too much."

"Your laughter is music to my ears, Xavier. You know, I'm not the only one who looks a hell of a lot better today. That must have been some phone call you had with Ben last night." Ellie gave me a lecherous wink.

"It lasted ten minutes tops," I said dismissively. "My mood today has nothing to do with Ben and everything to do with taking back my life and moving forward." I looked at the microwave clock and gratefully saw it was time to get my ass in gear. "Oh, look at the time," I said to Ellie, who shook her head at my avoidance. Besides, I had somewhere important to be.

"Hello, Lindsey," I said, shaking the small woman's hand after Miss Annette introduced us in her office. "It's nice to meet you. I asked Miss Annette if we could talk privately before you introduce me to Max. I just want to make sure you're comfortable, and I want you to sit in while I talk to your son."

"Thank you, Xavier." Her relief was palpable. "It isn't that I don't trust Miss Annette's judgment, but Max is all I have in this world, and I can't screw this up. I need him to be happy and healthy."

"I completely understand, and although we just met five minutes ago, I want to tell you Max is so lucky to have you for a mom. What kind of questions do you have for me?"

"I think I'm going to step out and give you guys some time to talk alone. Let me know when you want me to bring Max in." Miss Annette patted me on the shoulder as she left the room.

"I have more concerns than I do questions," Lindsey told me when we were alone. "I'm concerned about Max getting hurt at school if he chooses to wear feminine-looking clothes in the fall. I worry about finding the right balance between allowing Max to discover himself and protecting him. Does that make sense?"

"It makes perfect sense. It would be strange if you weren't worried about his safety and well-being. I'm not an expert on children, but I can tell you how *I* felt when I was his age and wanted to wear my sister's clothes." Lindsey nodded, so I told her how I had liked the textures and feel of girl's clothes against my skin. I explained that I was fascinated by sparkly accessories and nail polish. "It was never about my gender for me, but it could be for Max. There is a lot of good literature out there to help parents with children who identify with a different gender than what they were assigned at birth, and it would be a good place to start."

I knew Lindsey had to be feeling overwhelmed, because I certainly was, and Max wasn't my son, but I knew with the right information and the love I could clearly see on her face that everything would work out fine. I would gladly be a willing listener for Lindsey if she wanted someone to talk to. My biggest fear when I was Max's age had been facing my father's wrath, but Max wouldn't know that fear. Not with a mom like Lindsey.

"That's a good idea, Xavier. Thank you." She blew out a breath. "When did you know you were a gay boy who just liked to wear girl's clothes occasionally? When will I know how Max identifies?" Lindsey's worry was evident in the frown lines on her forehead and the downturned tilt of her mouth.

"Max will let you know when he figures it out," I replied honestly. "I always knew I was different from most boys, and I think it's something you inherently know. It clicked into place on the first day of first grade when I laid eyes on Mr. Williams. I crushed on him so hard the entire year," I said with a laugh.

"You must have gotten picked on in school, though, right? How did you handle it?" The worry in her voice carried through to her eyes as she looked at me. It was obvious that Max getting bullied was one of her biggest concerns. She didn't have to worry about abuse at Miss Annette's preschool, but Lindsey logically was less confident about how Max would be treated once he started kindergarten. Not everyone was as kind and accepting as Miss Annette, who had a zero-tolerance policy for bullying. If only there were more people like Miss Annette in the world.

"Gram signed me up for piano lessons and art classes, so I had a healthy outlet for my anger and frustration over not fitting in. It was the best thing to ever happen to me. I love music, and I can't imagine not having it in my life."

"Thank you for your honesty, Xavier. Are you ready to meet Max?" She seemed lighter after our conversation, and that made me feel really good.

"Definitely."

Lindsey opened the door and motioned for Miss Annette to bring Max in. Lindsey stepped aside and lively little Max skipped into the classroom, stopping when he saw me sitting there. "Max, this is Xavier, and I asked him to come and meet you today. Can you say hi?" Miss Annette asked as she kneeled next to him, bringing herself down to his level to ease any discomfort he might have been feeling over having a stranger in the room with him.

Max looked at his mom, Miss Annette, and then finally locked his innocent eyes on me. "Hi, Xavier," he said softly.

"Hi, Max." I stuck my hand out, and he hesitantly shook it. "I like your shirt." I pointed to the light pink tee with a unicorn and rainbow on the front.

"You do?" He pulled his shirt away from his body and looked down at it. "Tyler said only girls and fairies wear shirts like this."

"I don't know who this Tyler person is, but I've known plenty of people like him my whole life, Max. You can't let Tyler ruin your day or take away your joy when you wear a shirt you love, okay?"

"Okay, Xavier." Max nodded his blond head with conviction and gave me a genuine smile.

I talked to Max for another thirty minutes, letting him guide our conversation. He was an amazing kid, and I enjoyed the time I spent with him and his mom. I exchanged phone numbers with Lindsey before I left and made her promise to call me if she or Max had any more questions or just wanted to talk. I'd do anything I could to help them. I was confident when I left Miss Annette's preschool that Max would be okay because he had a mom who would love and support him no matter where life took him.

I shook all over with an adrenaline rush after my ninety-minute kickboxing session, which was basically me getting my ass kicked. Taking control of my life was exactly what I needed, but the side effects of the spiked adrenaline and testosterone prodded me to do something really stupid.

I tried to convince myself I was just driving by Ben's house to make sure he'd made it home safely and that I wasn't going to pull into his drive and knock on his door. Fuck, who was I trying to kid? I needed an outlet for my adrenaline, and I trusted Ben, nothing more, nothing less.

I shut off my car and jogged up to his front door reminiscing about a few nights before, but this time the emotions singeing my nerve endings had nothing to do with anger and everything to do with lust. I rang Ben's doorbell and didn't have to wait long for him to answer. Like the first time, I shoved him inside his house and slammed the door behind me. Ben's eyes widened, and his nostrils flared when he easily read the heat and longing in my eyes.

"I need…" I couldn't finish my sentence. I didn't want to cross that line.

"What, Xavier?" He stepped so close to me I could feel the heat coming off his body. "I need to hear the words so there's no confusion about what you *need* from me. Tell me, and I'll give you whatever it is."

Ben placed his hands lightly on either side of my neck, a move that would normally have me jerking away from his touch. This was Ben, though, not a demon from my past, and he didn't want to hurt me. I saw it in his eyes.

"I need to fuck you, Ben." There, I'd said it, and I waited to see if he would give me what I desired like he said he would, but Ben said nothing. Instead, he took me by the hand and led me up the stairs to his bedroom. My body shook so hard with hunger that it scared me a little.

"Take what you need from me, Xavier." I pounced, kissing him as hard as I could while we tore our clothes off and tossed them into a heap. "Condoms and lube are in the drawer," Ben said between nibbles on my neck. He wrapped his big hand around my cock and stroked up and down, which only drove my need to stratospheric heights. "Are you going to make me cry from the pleasure you give me?" Ben asked me while he circled my piercing with the tip of his finger, and I heard the excitement in his voice.

"Like you've never felt before, Ben. Get on your hands and knees." I fisted my hands tightly to keep them from shaking as I watched him climb onto his big bed and present his ass to me just like I'd asked him to. I grabbed the supplies out of the drawer and climbed up behind him, taking the time to appreciate Ben's beautiful body. "You have a very sexy ass, and I can't wait to be inside it."

"It's all yours, Xavier," Ben said breathlessly, but there was something else in his tone, something I didn't want to think about, at least not at that moment.

His words sent a thrilling shiver down my spine as I poured some lube onto my fingers and rubbed them together to coat them well. Ben cried out my name when I slid a single finger inside his tight entrance, but it wasn't a cry of discomfort. His tight heat sucked me in all the way to my knuckle. He began rocking back and forth, working his ass on my finger.

"More," he urged, but his actions spoke louder. I obliged him by adding a second finger, stroking softly and slowly inside him. I curled my fingers, grazing his prostate and causing his breath to hiss out between his lips. "I'm ready," he practically growled at me, his need evident in his actions and words.

"I'll decide when you're ready, Ben. You're as tight as any virgin, and you'll need to be soft and pliable for the fucking I'm about to give you." I watched as goose bumps popped up all over his golden skin at my whispered words. I fingered and teased him a few times before I pulled out completely, eliciting a moan from him. I placed my hand between his shoulder blades and gently pushed down until his forehead rested against the comforter. "Do not touch yourself, Ben, because you won't need to."

In this position, I saw his firm balls and straining erection dangling between his spread legs. If my need wasn't so great, I'd bathe every inch of him with my tongue. I rolled on the condom and spread more lube up and down the length of my erection before pressing the tip to his opening.

I placed one hand on his hip and left the other on my cock while I fed my hard length inside his quivering hole.

The urge to drive deep inside him was almost too severe to ignore, but I kept a tight grip on my control and slowly worked him open until I buried my cock to the hilt. Ben's scorching heat hugged my dick tight, making my eyes roll back in my head. Ben and I released matching guttural moans at the same time. Up until then, my piercing had just barely grazed his gland, but that soon changed. I pulled back until only the tip of my erection remained inside him.

"Xavier." My name was part plea and part curse. "Take what you need." I snapped my hips forward, aiming my cock at that glorious spot that would drive him to ecstasy after only a few strokes. "Fuck!" Ben roared, and I knew I had hit my target.

I pounded into him time and time again, gritting my teeth and tensing my muscles to stave off my orgasm. I had one hand fisted in his hair and the other squeezing his hip so hard I would likely leave a handprint.

"Oh my…God. So close, Xavier. Right fucking there." Ben roared as he came all over his comforter. I released his hair to grip his hips with both hands and drive harder and deeper, chasing my own orgasm.

"So tight," I told Ben as his ass continued to spasm, gripping me harder than anything I'd ever felt before. I threw my head back, closed my eyes, and clenched my teeth so I wouldn't call out his name as my climax ripped through me. His body turned boneless beneath me as I kept pumping in and out of him until the final tremors faded from my body.

I wanted to say it had just been the adrenaline that had contributed to the intensity of my orgasm, but what was the point of lying to myself? Still, doubt and regret creeped in as my body cooled and my heart calmed down. I wanted to pull out of him, clean up, and get the hell out of there, but I stayed put.

"You've already left me even though your dick is still semihard and lodged deep inside me."

CHAPTER
Twelve

Ben

XAVIER TENSED BEHIND ME, AND I INSTANTLY REGRETTED MY words. Maybe I shouldn't have said anything to him, but it pissed me off that he was emotionally distancing himself when he was still inside me. I hadn't asked him to come over and fuck me, although I wasn't complaining. He'd shown up at my house for himself, and I'd eagerly given him the outlet he craved. I knew why he'd come, and I also knew he hadn't changed his stance on our nonrelationship, but he could have at least waited until he pulled his dick from my ass before he started withdrawing emotionally too.

It was while I was chastising myself for not keeping my mouth shut that I noticed Xavier's body had begun to shake and tremble. I recognized the signs that he was coming down from an intense adrenaline high and disengaged from his body. His eyes were wide and haunted, his lips trembled, and he was clammy and cold with cooling sweat.

"Xavier, look at me." I placed both my hands firmly on his shoulders and gently shook him to bring his focus back to me. His whiskey-colored eyes latched onto mine, and the haunted look slowly shifted to one of embarrassment. "Don't go there right now. Let me help you if only for tonight." I gently kissed his lips before releasing his shoulder and taking his hand in mine.

Xavier remained silent as I led him into my bathroom, turned on the shower, and gently removed the condom from his sensitive cock before dropping it into the trash can. I guided him into the shower once the water warmed up, placing him directly under the spray. Xavier tried to avert his gaze, but I didn't allow it. There was nothing for him to be embarrassed about, and I wanted him to know that. I placed my hand beneath his chin, raising it until his eyes met mine. He opened his mouth, and I knew he was going to start telling me all the reasons why this had been a mistake. I pressed my finger to his lips to stop him because my ego couldn't take another blow just then.

"It wasn't a mistake, Xavier." He released a soft sigh against my finger, and I removed it from his lips.

"I'm broken, Ben. You wouldn't have let me inside your house, let alone your body, if you knew just how wrecked I am."

His body trembled beneath the hot spray, and up until that point, I had left a gap between us to give him the space I thought he needed. I pressed my body against his, tucked his head beneath my chin, and wrapped my arms tightly around him.

"You don't deserve to be treated like this." Xavier's hot breath puffed across my chest as he tried to pull himself together.

"Just hold on to me." My words were firm yet gentle. I wanted to soothe him, not bully him. Slowly, Xavier wrapped his arms around my waist. "I decide what I deserve and what I can and can't handle, okay?" Xavier nodded slightly, his forehead barely moving against my collarbone. "Furthermore, you are *not* broken, Xavier. A broken man does not fight this goddamned hard against his inner demons. He gives in and allows them to consume him. You are not that kind of man."

"You don't know what you're talking about, Ben. You've probably never had a bad day in your whole life. You're the kind of guy I want to be but can't figure out how to become." His once relaxed body stiffened in agitation, and he tried to take a step back, but my firm grip on his hips wouldn't allow him to go far. "Don't hold me against my will." Xavier's voice was nearly a snarl, one I assumed came from a place of abject fear. "Never again will I allow myself to be a victim."

It was then that I realized Xavier's scars went much further than I'd first suspected. Rage boiled beneath my skin at the thought of someone holding him down and taking something from him he didn't want to give. I loosened my grip and was surprised when he chose not to step out of my embrace. I worked hard to keep my breathing even so as not to give away the fury I felt on his behalf. I was afraid he would think my anger was aimed at him.

I gently pulled his head up so he couldn't hide his eyes from me. I needed him to not only hear me but to see the sincerity behind my words. "I didn't have the fairy-tale upbringing you've pictured, Xavier, and I will gladly share my story with you anytime you want to hear it, but deflecting isn't going to help you tonight." I dropped a quick kiss on his forehead. "I see beautiful where you see broken. I see strong where you see weak. I see a man who is loved by so many, and it's a shame you can't love yourself as much."

"You don't know me, Ben." Xavier looked away in frustration. "You see a face you think is attractive and a body you want to fuck. You adore my sister and Chase and can't imagine how I could be so screwed up when they're so perfect. I appreciate your attempt at a pep talk, but you can put away your pom-poms now." His words practically dripped with disdain.

"There is no such thing as a perfect person, Chase and Ellie included. Ellie is *not* perfect, and Chase has more issues than a guest on Dr. Phil, but I love them both with all my heart. We all make mistakes, Xavier.

Don't confuse my kindness and concern with a scheme to get you naked either. I find it offensive." My irritation was evident in my tone.

"Oh yeah?" Xavier's sarcasm kicked up several notches. "What about your dick?"

"What about it?"

"It's hard and primed to fuck."

"Oh. Ignore that." I glanced down, and sure enough, the rocket was ready to launch. "You're wet, naked, and standing in my arms. He can't help himself!" Xavier smiled crookedly at my explanation. "You're deviating from the original topic again." Xavier scowled at me, but I ignored him and said, "You *are not* broken or damaged. You're a man who apparently has made some mistakes and paid dearly for them. You're also a man who is trying to do everything in his power to atone for those missteps and make a better life for himself. That is a person to be admired, not admonished. I'd like to think I *deserve* to be friends with that kind of man."

"Ben." All the fight left him, and I once again held Xavier tight against my body. "Friendship is all I have to offer right now, despite how I behaved tonight. I was just really worked up after kickboxing class. It felt so damn good to feel like I was taking control of my life. The adrenaline rush was better than any high, but what goes up must come down, and the crash is painful." Xavier had confessed a whole lot with just a few sentences, either by accident or design.

"I'm just going to say one more thing, then you're going to let me take care of you tonight." I saw the protest forming on Xavier's lips and hushed him. "By taking care of you, I mean I'm going to help you clean up, let you borrow some clothes, and then I'm going to feed you before I send you home. That is what friends do for one another, right?" Xavier nodded reluctantly, so I continued, "Talk to someone, Xavier. It doesn't have to be a professional, and it certainly doesn't have to be me, but talk to someone about what you've gone through, or all this work you're doing will be for nothing. Will you at least consider it?"

Xavier looked up at me, and I saw so many emotions in his

expression—fear, regret, so much pain, and then determination. I was suddenly terrified he was going to talk to me and I wouldn't be strong enough to hear whatever he had to say.

Xavier took a deep breath and released it slowly. "My ex-boyfriend nearly killed me in a jealous rage a few months ago."

CHAPTER
Thirteen

Xavier

"**M**AYBE WE SHOULD DO THIS AFTER YOU'VE HAD A CHANCE TO get dressed and eat something." Ben was trying to hold it together for both our sakes, but if I stopped, I knew I wouldn't start again.

"No. You said I needed to talk to someone, and you were right. I choose you. Please let me do this before I lose my courage." Ben started to put some distance between us, but I pulled him back. He wrapped me up tight, and I tucked my head beneath his chin. His strong arms made me feel safe, and the steady rhythm of his beating heart brought me comfort. "Has Chase told you anything about my former band manager and ex-boyfriend, Damien?"

"No. Chase would never betray your trust."

"A little over two years ago, our original band manager retired, and we hired Damien to take his place. Everything went really well at first, and we couldn't have asked for a better manager. He was great with promoters, vendors, our fans, and all the band members. We really gelled, and the crew was more like a family than a band." I took a deep breath, thinking of how perfect things had been in the beginning. "That said a lot because we were already pretty tight. Things started to change within six months, but it was so gradual that no one really noticed until it was too late." I tightened my hold on Ben before continuing.

"We had all made a pact in the very beginning that none of us would have a personal relationship with any other member of the band, road crew, or management. Honestly, it was an easy thing for me to agree to until I met Damien. He said and did all the right things, Ben, and I thought I was falling in love with him, but it was all a mirage. He saw how lonely I was and exploited it." I took a shaky breath, and Ben began to rub my back soothingly while I searched for the right words.

"Take your time," he said, kissing the top of my head tenderly.

"Damien started taking over little things under the guise of caring for me and making life easier so I could focus on my career. He made me feel cherished and adored." I shook my head at my own stupidity. "I was completely blinded by the fact that he was slowly taking over control of every aspect of my life from the people I could hang out with to when and where I ate and what I wore. It makes me sound so freaking stupid when I hear myself telling this story out loud. Like, how could I have been so blind to not see what was happening? But I'm being completely honest when I say it was so gradual that it felt normal by the time I realized I looked to him for every single thing.

"My relationship with my bandmates deteriorated at the same time because I had broken our pact when I began dating our manager. It didn't help that Damien constantly whispered in my ear that I was the standout performer and that he could help me rise above my small-time fame and get me a record deal. I'd stupidly believed him, and my ego grew to epic proportions. The guys staged an intervention, and I blamed it on their jealousy over my greatness rather than the genuine concern it was. It completely alienated me from my band, and that was exactly what Damien had wanted." Ben continued to rub my back, giving me the strength I needed to continue.

"Then Damien started to show his true colors. Gone was the man who had claimed to love me, and in his place was a jealous, possessive man who wanted to own me by any means necessary." I stiffened with anger. "He became verbally abusive and somehow convinced me that he was the best I could hope to have and that most of the time I didn't even deserve him."

Ben pressed another kiss on top of my head but remained silent.

"The only bright spot was Deacon, who was part of the security staff. He saw what was happening and befriended me when Damien wasn't around, which was more and more frequently when he was convinced he had me under his thumb. I knew I had to get out, and Deacon promised to help me. I knew it was divine intervention when Chase called to say he and Gray were coming out to LA for business and asked if he could get tickets to a show. I knew once again Chase was going to rescue me, and he did."

"What made you go back?" Ben's voice held no recrimination, just curiosity. His hands slid into my hair and began massaging my scalp in circles with the perfect amount of pressure.

"The band kept calling me and putting pressure on me to return. I heard they were facing financial ruin if they couldn't meet their concert obligations, which was true. I hadn't thought about them for one single second while I'd planned my exit strategy with Deacon. I'd been selfish, and the guys didn't deserve how I'd treated them because none of it was their fault. They knew I had seen the light about Damien, and they got him to promise things would be different and that he would accept that our personal relationship was over. I stupidly fell for that one too. I should have insisted they fire Damien before I returned.

"I had just spent a few months with Mr. and Mr. Happily Ever After, who made constant kissy faces at each other, and fuck if I didn't want that for myself. I got depressed and despondent in LA when I realized I had been duped by the band and Damien. It took me all of ten friggin' minutes to realize Damien had pulled them over to his side while I was away."

"How?" Ben asked. "Why not just try to find a replacement for you?

There had to be hundreds of guys willing to audition for the open spot. So why would they warn you away from him and then help him reel you back in?"

"Drugs," I replied emotionlessly. "My bandmates, who had only dabbled in a little bit of pot, became addicted to Ecstasy while I was here trying to get my shit together." I took a shallow, trembling breath and felt Ben tense around me. "I started taking E to forget about my shitty life about a month after I got to LA. I took E to get high and then smoked pot to bring myself down."

"Xavier." Ben said my name tenderly, which encouraged me to continue.

"I hated myself off the drugs and hated myself even more while taking them. Damien waited for the right time to make his move, and I stupidly let him back in. He was much more violent the second time around, whereas before, he mostly yelled and threw things." The hatred I harbored for the man made me tremble.

"I started looking into online counseling and tips on how to get sober and stay that way. I read every article I could find because I knew there was no way I could escape Damien's eagle eye to attend meetings or work with a sponsor in person. I was lucky to find a sponsor online and I felt real hope for the first time in too long to count." Ben relaxed a little at my admission, his gentle massage starting again on my scalp and back.

"I faked being high around the band and Damien while I weaned myself off the drugs. I put all my focus on the natural boost I got from working out instead of the artificial buzz I got from the drugs. It was working until Damien searched my phone, tablet, and laptop and saw the emails I sent back and forth to my sponsor, Kevin.

"Damien was waiting for me in my dressing room when I got done performing one night. He blindsided me with a violent attack, and I ended up handcuffed to metal furniture that was bolted into the concrete floor. He told me how he was going to destroy Kevin's life by convincing his wife that he was having an affair with me because in his crazed mind that is what Kevin and I were doing." The memory of the chilling terror I'd felt made me shiver, but I needed to finish telling my story. I needed Ben to understand.

"Damien struck me in the face repeatedly while he yelled about how only he could have me. I knew I was going to die when he wrapped his hands around my neck and began to squeeze the life out of me. I felt my life slipping away, and I welcomed it, Ben."

"No. Please don't say that, Xavier," Ben whispered brokenly.

"I figured death was my only escape from him. Then members of the band kicked down the door when they heard Damien screaming about killing me. They saved my life, and I used the damage to my face and neck as collateral to escape that bastard once and for all."

"Did you go to the police?"

I shook my head. "I know it was wrong of me, but I was too ashamed, which is how abusers want their victims to feel, too embarrassed to talk. I just wanted to get away, but I documented my injuries and got statements from the witnesses. The other band members were willing to let him get away with a lot but not murder. There was no doubt in any of our minds that I would have been dead had they not kicked in the door."

Ben held me tighter but didn't say anything. It was then that I noticed we were both shivering because the hot water had run out sometime during my confession. I'd been too lost in my memories to feel the temperature change, and Ben either hadn't noticed or hadn't wanted to interrupt me. "Let's get dried off and dressed, and you can tell me the rest while I make you something to eat." Ben stepped out, handing me a towel before wrapping himself up in his own.

We dried off and dressed in silence, neither of us speaking until we were in his cozy kitchen. I watched as Ben calmly pulled ingredients out of his refrigerator and began to assemble a grilled ham and cheese sandwich.

"Soup?"

"Just a sandwich is fine," I replied. "Thank you for doing this, Ben." He paused and looked over his shoulder, offering a comforting smile. I was so relieved when I didn't see disdain and censure in his beautiful gray eyes. "Aren't you going to eat?"

"I already ate a few hours ago." Ben turned his focus back to cooking my sandwich and then asked, "Are you ready to tell me the rest of what happened?"

"Uh, Damien was finally subdued by the rest of the band and a few of our crew members drove me to my apartment and helped me pack up my stuff, then checked me into a hotel about forty-five minutes away. One of them followed in Mistress so I wouldn't be stranded without a vehicle when I was ready to move on. They even brought me enough food and bottled water for the little hotel fridge so I could stay inside for a few days. I realized the next morning why they thought I might want to hide.

"I didn't recognize myself in the mirror. My face was battered, bruised, and swollen, and my neck bore ten angry fingerprints from the man who tried to love me to death." A shiver racked my body as I remembered it all again so clearly. "I'll never forget the sight of blood-tinged water sliding over my body and washing down the drain in that hotel shower. I decided it was a symbol of washing away all the ugly and starting over clean. I convinced myself I would come out of the ordeal smarter and stronger.

"I stayed at the hotel for about a week, then I cleaned out my bank account and safe deposit box—those were the only parts of my life I hadn't let Damien control—and slowly began making my way back home while my body healed. I drove from the West Coast to the East Coast with both car windows down, letting the wind blow the negativity away. I still battle a lot of self-hatred, and I'm finding it hard to forgive myself, but I am trying."

Warm hands slid over mine where I had them clasped tightly together on top of the kitchen table. I was so caught up in the memories that I hadn't realized Ben had brought my sandwich to the table and settled in the chair across from me. I looked at his strong hands and remembered the feel of them on my body both in passion and tenderness. Then I looked into his expressive eyes that were damp with unshed tears, and for the first time in a very long time, something beautiful bloomed in my guarded heart. Hope.

Early the next morning, I heard the new melody in my dreams again. It wasn't the entire song, but it was several strands of music. I immediately sat up, turned on the lamp, and grabbed my notebook and pencil so I could document the chords as I'd heard them in my dream. Once I finished, I turned off the light and lay back down, but sleep eluded me.

I had been intimate with Ben on two occasions, and both times I had heard a part of the new melody I suspected would transform into a beautiful song. I wanted to chalk it up to coincidence, but I had never bought into that theory. I was a firm believer that everything happened for a reason, either good or bad. My brain cautioned me against moving too fast and letting my guard down too soon. My heart, however, was beating to the new melody I had only heard after finding comfort with Ben. It became the rhythm of us.

CHAPTER
Fourteen

Ben

"MRS. ST. CLAIRE IS HERE TO SEE YOU." IAN'S WORDS DROVE A railroad spike through my brain. I heard my assistant's unspoken thoughts because they were the same thoughts I had every time my mother came to my office for a visit. Neither of us were Beverly St. Claire's biggest fans. We'd commiserate over coffee as soon as she left.

Why the hell was she bothering me at my office? "Tell her I'm in a meeting, that I'm out of town, or better yet, you can tell her I'm dead."

"Um, sir..."

"I heard that, Bennett, and that's no way to treat your mother."

"Sorry, Ben," Ian said. If he were any kind of PA, he would have tackled her before she got through my door. His distressed voice made it impossible for me to be irritated with him, though.

"You can make it up to me later with a giant banana nut muffin." I hit the speakerphone button to disconnect the call, then turned away from my conference table where I had been reviewing Drew's revised mockups for the aquarium pitch right before my mother walked into my office. "Mother." I took in her outfit while I rose to my feet. It never ceased to amaze me that my mother dressed like the Queen of England every day regardless of if she was staying home or going out. The only thing missing from her ensemble was a hat.

"Bennett, I stopped by to ask a favor of you, but it's *obvious* you don't want me here." Beverly's performance of unappreciated mother was worthy of an Emmy, and I shuddered to think what they'd call a daytime soap opera based on my family.

"I'm very busy and have a lot of responsibilities." I refused to fall for her poor, poor pitiful me act. I especially wouldn't let her ruin my day because I had a stakeout to plan with Xavier for later that evening. I needed to see him to reassure myself he was doing okay after such an emotional night. "What can I do for you, Mother?"

"Well, I see where I rate." Beverly huffed and rolled her eyes so dramatically that I nearly clapped my hands. "I'd like for you to escort me to a charity function in a few weeks." I groaned loudly, but that didn't faze her. "Your father and I have donated a lot of money to support LGBT youth in *your* honor, and the least you can do is go with me. Your father is otherwise *engaged* that evening." That was Beverly's euphemism for when my father spent time with his mistress. "I supported you when you came out as gay, but not every child is so fortunate, Bennett. I'd think you would welcome my efforts."

Christ on a cracker! My mother's idea of supporting me was a joke but not a funny one. "When is the event, Mother?" I didn't feel like I owed her a damn thing, but she was still my mother, and I would show her respect whether she was deserving or not.

"It's three weeks from Saturday. You'll need to pick me up at six," she added gleefully.

I entered the date and time into my phone's calendar and looked back up to find her smiling smugly at me. It occurred to me that something else was at play, but I didn't have time to figure out what. "Is there anything else we need to discuss?"

"No, that will do for now. I'll let you get back to coloring." Beverly whirled and left my office, leaving behind the cloying smell of her over-priced perfume.

A few minutes later, Ian rapped timidly on my door before he opened it and peeked around the corner to gauge my mood after the ice queen's visit. I was rooted to the same spot I'd been in when she'd driven her ice pick through my heart. *Coloring? Is that really what she thought I did? Why did I continue to attempt a relationship with her?*

"Ben, do you want that muffin now? I can run downstairs and get it for you." Ian's voice was soft with understanding. I looked up at him and saw concern etched on his face. His cheeks were bright pink, which made his freckles stand out. "Why are you staring at me like that?"

"Why is your face all red and why are you talking to me like I'm a wounded animal?" I cocked my head slightly to the side and studied his posture. Ian always carried himself proudly, but right then he resembled a whipped dog. "What did Cruella say to you?"

"It was nothing you need to get upset about." Ian's words said one thing, but his body language said something entirely different. Ian was normally vibrant and bubbling with enthusiasm, but this Ian was downtrodden. This wasn't the first time my mom had said or done something to my assistant, and each time I'd let him blow it off. But not anymore.

"Come in here and shut the door." My tone made it absolutely clear I wasn't asking. I rounded my desk and sat in my comfortable chair, then gestured for him to take a seat. "I want you to tell me what happened."

"I'm afraid you're going to get furious." At who? Him or my mother? Ian wouldn't look at me, but why? "I should've told you as soon as I was hired, but I really needed this job after Josh and I broke up."

"Ian," I began, leaning my elbows on the desk, "I don't have time for games. I need you to tell me what my mother says to you every time she stops by my office. Look at me." I slapped my hand on my desk when he didn't immediately comply. Ian flinched and jerked his gaze up to my face. "What the hell is going on?"

"Your dad's mistress is my mother." He blinked rapidly while he waited for the news to sink in.

"Oh my fucking God." I threw my head back and laughed hysterically. "That's freaking hilarious." I slapped the desk a few more times over the ridiculousness of the situation. "My coldhearted mother—who hasn't been a faithful wife in probably two decades or longer—is holding a grudge against you because your mother is my father's mistress? Oh, I can't wait to tell my brother." My humor dissolved quickly when it occurred to me that maybe...

"No, I'm not your brother." Ian answered my unspoken question, which was nothing new. The awkwardness of the moment was broken when Ian giggle-snorted at the look on my face. "You don't have to look so relieved we're not related. Jackass!"

"Christmas is expensive enough when I have to buy you a gift as my personal assistant. I'd really have to step up my game if you were my half brother too."

"Sure, that's what you were worried about." Ian's normally confident façade slipped, exposing his vulnerability.

"Did you know before I hired you?" I asked.

"I knew Daniel had sons, but I didn't know one of them worked here. I simply responded to the job posting I saw online. I figured it out when you interviewed me because you look so much like *him*." Ian's obvious disdain for my father was palpable.

"I'm surprised you didn't run right then and there." I couldn't help but wonder what he had witnessed to make him dislike my father so much... well, besides the obvious. "Is my father good to your mother?" I wanted to take the question back as soon as it left my mouth.

"There's not a simple yes or no answer to that question, Ben." Ian's hesitant tone did nothing to appease my regret for opening that particular can of worms. "Daniel treats my mother very well, and I think he's truly in love with her. He'll never leave your mother, though, and I resent the fact that my mom pines for a man who doesn't love her enough to either give her the life she deserves or let her go. I don't dislike Daniel, but I distrust him. I feel like he's led my mother on for five years, and she believes him when he says they'll really be together someday. Do you honestly see that happening?"

"Not unless Beverly dies." Ian flinched at my blunt response. "Beverly was handpicked by my grandparents to marry my father based on her pedigree, and my father won't risk losing his social status, career, and access to the family trust to be with your mother, so you are absolutely correct to resent him being in your mother's life. I'm certain she deserves a hell of a lot better than him."

I sat back in my chair in stunned silence because I meant what I had just said about his mother deserving more. I had spent my entire childhood and teenage years being miserable as I watched my parents throw their affairs in one another's faces. I came to despise cheaters, including my parents, and their selfish ways to the point that I automatically disliked anyone associated with the act.

I thought back to how I'd made Chase's life miserable at every opportunity when I thought he had been screwing around with Gray's then-boyfriend, Devon. It took me a long time and some interference on Gray's behalf before I allowed myself to consider that Chase had also been a victim of Devon's betrayal. I accepted that there might've been more to the story and let myself get to know Chase—the real person, not the surprise birthday party crasher Devon had brought home to fuck when he thought Gray was out of town. God, the unconventional start to Chase and Gray's relationship still amazed me and made me smile. Now, I considered Chase to be one of my best friends and felt lucky to have him in my life.

"Oh." Ian's dejected tone snapped me out of my thoughts, and I immediately regretted my harsh answer to his question. "Well, I appreciate your honesty, even though it feels like you just punched me in the stomach." Ian closed his eyes for a few seconds before he reopened them and locked his laser-like blue eyes on me. "Will this impact our working relationship? I really enjoy working for you, and I think I do a good job." Ian sounded extremely nervous, and I wanted to put him at ease.

"This changes absolutely nothing, except that my mother will no longer be welcome here. That is one thing I can fix for you, and I will. You're not responsible for your mother's behavior nor am I responsible for my father's. You don't deserve to be treated disrespectfully by Beverly, and I wish you had told me sooner."

"Thank you." The gratitude in his voice made me feel like I'd accomplished something good, and it made my inner fixer very happy. "Seriously, do you want some coffee or something?"

"Not right now, but thank you." Ian smiled at me, got to his feet, and headed for the door. "Ian," I called out, stopping him before he could leave. "You're *excellent* at your job, not just good."

"I'll remind you of that in a few months when we have my annual review." Ian's sassy reply was emphasized by a dramatic exit from my office.

The rest of the morning passed quickly, and I was able to get a lot done. I decided to have lunch by myself so I could do some research on recovering from domestic abuse and drug addiction. I wasn't putting the cart before the horse, but I didn't want to do or say the wrong thing in my fragile new friendship with Xavier. Of course, I was interested in him beyond friendship, but I was willing to accept whatever he could give. Memories of Xavier's passion popped up in my mind. A broad smile spread across my face and my tender ass quivered. Yes, I would gladly do whatever Xavier needed to feel better.

I happened to catch my goofy smile in the reflection of a gift shop window as I walked past. I couldn't recall ever seeing such a dopey expression on my face before, and I laughed out loud at myself. A few pedestrians veered away from me as if they thought I was a lunatic, which only made me laugh harder. Then I noticed a display with a few items that would be perfect for the stakeout later that night, and I couldn't resist buying them for comic relief if nothing else.

CHAPTER
Fifteen

Xavier

THIS ISN'T A DATE. THIS ISN'T A DATE. I REPEATED THOSE WORDS TO myself over and over as I got ready for the stakeout. I still spent extra time choosing an outfit and trying to get my hair to lie right. I was probably two months past a haircut, and it was too shabby to style. I thought about bringing back the Rick Springfield look, then decided against it and made a mental note to book a haircut.

Ellie was curled up and asleep on the couch, and I was grateful because that meant I wouldn't have to lie to her about my evening plans. It wasn't like I could tell her the truth, and I didn't want her to get the wrong impression about me spending time with Ben. I had seen the hopeful gleam in her eyes when I'd come home from Ben's house the previous night. She didn't grill me about what we'd done because it was probably pretty obvious.

This was the most relaxed I'd been in over two years. It had felt great to unload my burdens to Ben without him looking at me in disgust or with loathing. Okay, the sex had been phenomenal, but I wouldn't let my mind go there knowing I would be locked in a car with him during the stakeout. It wouldn't take much for me to throw myself at him, and that wouldn't be fair to him.

Ben walked down his front steps as I parked my car in his driveway and got out. My eyes raked over his casual attire—jeans so old they were threadbare in places, a faded blue T-shirt, and a pair of Corona flip-flops.

"Evening," he said with a friendly smile. "You ready to stakeout this fucker?"

"As I'll ever be. What's in the bag?" I nodded to the reusable cloth grocery tote in his hand.

"Very important stakeout things, Xavier." Ben pushed the unlock button on his key fob, and we both climbed inside his shiny sedan. "So here's the plan," Ben said as he fired up the engine and backed out of his driveway. "Van gave me a description of Drake Anderson's car and his license plate number along with a list of several of his favorite haunts."

"Who's Van?"

"Sorry, it's the nickname I use for my brother, Bevan, unless I want to get under his skin, then I call him Bev." The smile in Ben's voice demonstrated how much he loved his brother. It made me nostalgic over the lost connection with my own siblings but all the more grateful for the bond I had with Chase and Ellie.

"The loser's name is Drake Anderson? It will be great to have his name and face to visualize at my next kickboxing class."

"Oh, when might that be?" Ben didn't bother to disguise his eagerness and wishful thinking that I might end up back at his house again after class, ready to screw my aggression out of my system.

I hated to break it to him, but I'd already started to research healthier ways to come down from the adrenaline high that didn't involve sex with him. One of the most common issues for people recovering from drug addiction was picking up another. Kevin referred to it as transference and warned me about it during our email conversations. I also read a lot about it in several articles during my online research. The most natural transference is to latch onto a person in place of the alcohol or drugs. I knew I wasn't going to avoid relationships forever, but I would evade them until I was strong enough to handle all the ups and downs that went with them. Besides, I still didn't trust my judgment after the last fiasco.

"Xavier." Ben's warm voice broke into my musings.

"Hmm? Oh, um, my next class is tomorrow night." I sat there wondering how I could tell him that there wouldn't be a repeat of last night without hurting his feelings or sounding like a dick.

"A massage or a soak in a hot tub or bath will help bring you down if you experience another spike like the one you had last night." Ben smiled wryly and added, "And masturbation works wonders for most things that ail us." Ben intuitively addressed my unspoken concern. A small voice in my brain reminded me that I'd been a little presumptuous to assume he wanted more than sex with me anyway. *Arrogant much?* "You might not have that spike after every class. Last night could have been an anomaly because you were taking steps to take back control of your life and your safety, so you were bound to feel excitement on a whole different level."

"How do you know so much about it?" My curiosity overrode my caution. I would have been lying if I said I wasn't interested in learning more about Ben.

"I was pretty chubby during my late childhood and early teen years," he replied. I looked over at him and let my eyes roam over his lean yet well-defined body. "It's true," he said as if he heard the doubt in my mind. "My home was a miserable, cold place for a kid, and Van was the only good thing I had in my life. He left for college when I was eight, and I became an emotional eater." Ben looked over at me and caught my stare. "Addictions come in many varieties, and one is not better or worse than the others because they are all mentally and physically destructive, Xavier. I was on a fast track to a host of health issues. Yeah, it might have taken longer to kill me, but the quality of those years would have been greatly diminished."

I turned to look back out the windshield and let his words reverberate through my skull. I'd never quite considered the points he was making, but then again, I hadn't really spoken to anyone, except Kevin, about addiction. No wonder Ben hadn't judged me for anything I had confessed last night. He'd been down a similar road and won.

"How'd you overcome your bad eating habits?"

"Daniel and Beverly tried just about everything to get me to lose the weight because I was an embarrassment to our family, which only made me eat more just to piss them off. They sent me away to summer fitness camps for a few years, but that didn't work. They tried counseling, but my parents didn't like being told they were part of my problem. Their solution was to find a counselor who told them what they wanted to hear—that I was a fat and lazy kid who didn't have a drop of ambition inside me when that was the furthest thing from the truth. Luckily for me, they never found that counselor." His voice was laced with dry humor, which confused me because there was nothing funny about the story he was telling.

"Their last resort was to hire a personal trainer to come to our house and whip me into shape and teach me a healthier way to eat. We already had a chef on staff, but they insisted this personal trainer be the one to prepare my meal plans." Ben laughed, and I looked over to see him grinning like a fool. "Good God, Xavier, I learned so much about myself that summer." His humor was contagious, and I found myself smiling with him, even though I was still confused about why we were smiling. "I took one look at Sven and knew my life had been irrevocably changed. My eyes took in all those tan, sculpted muscles and his beautiful face, and I realized I was gay as fuck."

Laughter burst from my chest like a shotgun blast, loud and widespread. "How old were you?" I asked when I regained my composure.

"Thirteen. It's a miracle I didn't go blind from jerking off so much." Ben's wide grin let me know he was enjoying this particular trip down memory lane. "To make a long story short, I was smitten, and I knew if I ever wanted to attract a guy like Sven, I'd need to lose weight and get into shape. He introduced me to all types of healthy foods, exercises, and activities, but the game changer occurred when he took me to my first swimming lesson. I took to the sport like a duck to water. We had a pool at our house, but it was more for looks than exercise. Sure, I splashed around and had fun in it, but that was nothing compared to the exhilaration of swimming competitively."

"I bet you were really good at it once you put your mind to it, weren't you?"

"I was," he agreed, nodding. "It took me close to two years to lose the weight and learn the techniques I needed to become a competitive swimmer, but there was no turning back once I reached that point." There was so much pride in Ben's voice. "Thanks to Sven and his unwavering support, I earned a swimming scholarship and a ticket out of my misery."

"Wow," was all I could think to say. Ben was so full of surprises, and it worried me how much I liked unwrapping him to find each one. I almost did a full-body shiver at the image of how I'd unwrapped and unraveled him last night. My dick stirred in the tight confines of my black jeans. There'd be no hiding my arousal in the tight denim, so I forced my mind to think about something nonsexual. "Are things with your parents better now?"

"Nope," he said casually, but his stiffening posture belied his calm, neutral response. "Okay, this is our first stop." Ben pulled into a parking lot of a dive bar I'd never been to. He competently backed his car into a secluded parking spot in a far corner where we could have eyes on both the front and side exits. "Will you hand me the bag?" It appeared the conversation regarding his parents was over. I wanted to learn more, but I didn't push him.

I reached behind his seat and lifted the tote he'd placed there when he'd gotten into the car. It was surprisingly heavy, and I admit I was curious about the things he deemed necessary for tonight. I handed the bag over to him and studied his smiling face as he sorted through the items.

"Every stakeout needs a disguise." Ben pulled a black ball cap with the words Task Force emblazoned on the front in large white print and handed it to me. He slid a matching hat on his head and went back to riffling through the bag. I slid the ridiculous hat onto my head and waited for the next piece of our costume, which turned out to be oversized aviator sunglasses. We slid the glasses on while looking at each other, and I was sure my goofy grin matched his. "I couldn't resist these when I saw them in a tourist souvenir shop."

I pulled the visor down and checked my appearance in the mirror. "I look like that bombing suspect from years ago. I'm just missing a hoodie," I told him, a hint of a whine in my voice.

"You look adorable," Ben countered, which I chose to ignore.

"What else is in the bag?"

"I brought us food," Ben answered then rushed to explain. "I know you said this wasn't a date, and I've accepted that, but I worked later than I anticipated, and I'm very hungry. It would have been really rude to eat in front of you without sharing."

"I could eat." My casual reply set him at ease, but I wasn't letting him off that easy. "There better not be anything in that bag that indicates you lured me here so you could seduce me. How'd you even know about this place?" Ben pulled out a file folder and handed it to me. I opened it immediately and read a shocking amount of information about Drake Anderson, including his home address, phone numbers, a photo of his driver's license, and a list of establishments he frequented. "Was this information obtained legally?" A chorus of raucous laughter broke out several rows in front of us in the parking lot, pulling my attention away from the file and the legality of the information it contained. "Please, for the love of God, tell me my sister wasn't hanging out in dive bars like this."

"Ellie told me she met Drake at the gym," Ben said. "I've never known Ellie to go to bars unless we all went out for a drink after work. We normally go to Bottoms Up where Chase used to work because the food is great, the beer is ice cold, and it has a great vibe."

"Yeah, I know the place," I answered. "I went a few times with Chase and Gray before I returned to LA last year." I looked back at the file in my hands and waved it slightly to get Ben's attention. "How does Bevan find out this information?"

"I don't know all his tricks, but I'm grateful for them. I need to learn all I can about this douche so I can help Ellie make sure he stays out of her and the baby's life permanently." Ben's devotion was another admirable trait, and it was becoming harder and harder to keep my guard up around him. Luckily, he started pulling food out of the bag and passing it out. "It's my specialty sandwich," he told me. "Thick slices of turkey breast, hickory smoked bacon, avocados, and herb infused mayo."

"Wow."

"Wait until you taste it," Ben said smugly. "I also brought Saratoga chips and bottles of peach tea and water because I wasn't sure what you liked to drink."

"Wow." I sounded like a parrot. "Thank you, Ben."

"Thank me after you devour your sandwich." Ben unwrapped his sandwich and took a hearty bite then moaned in pleasure. The sounds were similar to those he'd made when I'd had my dick inside him. I looked away from him and focused on my own sandwich. I took a bite and gave an appreciative moan of my own when the flavor combination burst over my tongue. "Right?" Ben asked around a mouthful of food. I couldn't answer, so I just nodded.

We made quick work of our food as the sun began to set. I looked over at Ben, and the content smile that lit up his face made me feel warm and gooey inside. I noticed a little smidge of mayo at the corner of his mouth, which almost resembled a little something I had left there a few days ago. Just that quickly, my mind derailed on a fast track straight to the gutter.

"You have a little something on your mouth." My voice sounded a whole lot huskier than a friend simply telling another friend about a little mayo on their face. Ben swiped the wrong side of his mouth, and I automatically leaned closer. "Here," I said, wiping the smudge away with my thumb. I licked the mayo off my finger without thinking, and Ben sucked in a shallow breath.

I sensed his hot eyes on me, even though they were hidden behind his dark sunglasses, and sexual tension started to build between us. I should have apologized for my little stunt since I was the one who'd jokingly accused him of parking back here so he could seduce me, yet I was the one acting inappropriately. I couldn't get my mouth to form the words needed to apologize.

"What was that on your tongue? Is that another piercing?" Ben whipped off his sunglasses and ball cap and tossed them on his dashboard, never taking his intense eyes off my mouth.

I had questioned my sanity when I'd stuck the piercing through my tongue before he picked me up. Was I deliberately trying to torment both of us? When had I become a shallow narcissist who needed constant attention? Worse yet, could I have possibly sent more conflicting signals to Ben? Try as I might, I couldn't tell him I was sorry when he looked at me with such heat in his eyes. I felt like I would combust at any moment.

"Yes." I finally found my voice but was only capable of the single-syllable response. My mouth was dry, and my throat felt scratchy. I should've reached for my drink, but I couldn't look away from him.

"Did you also get that piercing to drive a man out of his mind with pleasure?" I could tell from his half-lidded eyes that he was thinking about how it would feel to have that metal ball rolling up and down his hard shaft.

"Yes," I answered honestly and a bit hoarsely, then I cleared my throat before continuing. "Is that a pleasure you've experienced?" A war raged inside my brain while I waited for him to answer my question. I didn't want to think about another man pleasuring his dick with a pierced tongue. I wanted to be his first, but I had no right to think those things, though I couldn't stop myself from picturing doing that and more with Ben.

CHAPTER
Sixteen

Ben

Did Xavier have any clue just how fucking much his question had affected me? Did he know where my mind had gone the second I saw that silver ball poking through his tongue when he'd licked the mayo off his finger? I couldn't be sure because his expressive eyes were hidden behind his sunglasses. I reached over and pulled his disguise off, tossing it aside like I had my own. That was much better, and I had the answer to my question. He knew exactly where my mind had gone and how his question had affected me.

"No, I've yet to experience the feel of a little ball sliding up and down my cock, teasing that sensitive spot just beneath the crown while a lover sucks me off. I can only imagine how amazing it feels." I had to stifle the groan that threatened to escape with the thought. "Mmm, what about kissing? Does it feel amazing when a man kisses you with a pierced tongue?"

Xavier squirmed slightly in his seat, and I didn't need to look at his crotch to know he was just as affected as I was. I turned in my seat and faced him full on but resisted the urge to reach for him. I needed to let him be in control of what happened between us no matter how difficult it would be to wait. There was even a chance Xavier would never want more from me than what had already transpired. I knew that, and I would need to live with it, regardless of the physical attraction between us. I would never pressure him in to doing anything, especially after hearing about his abusive relationship with his former band manager. God, how I'd love to get my hands on that jerk.

"Yes." Xavier had taken so long to answer that I'd almost forgotten my question.

"I'll add that to my sexual bucket list." I was going for matter-of-fact, but my voice sounded too raspy to my own ears.

"Bucket list?" Xavier narrowed his eyes as if he didn't like the thought of me making a list of things I wanted to try with a man. "How long is the list?"

"Well, I just started it this week, so it's not very long. Oh, and you already helped me check off one item, so thank you." I shot him a playful wink.

Xavier turned in his seat so he was facing me. His eyes locked on my lips, and I knew he wanted to help me scratch off another item. Did he like being my first as much as I did? Was goading him into kissing me wrong when I could see how badly he wanted it?

"Ben." The raw need in his voice clawed at my guts and sent shivers up and down my spine. His pink tongue slipped out to moisten his lips, whetting my appetite for him. "I…"

"Xavier." I watched as his pupils dilated and nostrils flared. "You're in control here. If you want something, take it."

Xavier's eyes closed slowly, his body swayed slightly forward, and the tiniest of whimpers escaped his closed lips. His eyes opened, and I saw determination there. My heart started to pound out a staccato rhythm in anticipation as his body leaned closer and closer until his forehead was pressed to mine. Xavier's hands crept up ever so slowly until they cupped my face, and he ghosted his thumb over my mouth as he bit his own lip in anticipation.

We both kept our eyes open when his lips first brushed against mine. His lips were warm and soft, and it took every ounce of control for me not to press harder against him and deepen the kiss, eager to have his tongue in my mouth again. After several soft kisses, Xavier angled his head and licked a path across my lips.

"Open for me," Xavier whispered, and I happily obliged.

His tongue slid over mine so the smaller ball on the bottom of his tongue raked across the top of mine. I wrapped my lips around his tongue and sucked it deeper into my mouth. Xavier slid his hands into my hair where his blunt nails scored my scalp, eliciting a full-on body shiver.

I released his tongue with a sexy pop and let him kiss me however he wanted. He swirled his tongue around mine seductively slow, his piercing ramping up my lust tenfold. I kept my hands on the console between our bodies, not trusting them anywhere else.

"Touch me, Ben." Xavier didn't have to tell me twice.

I slid my hands up his torso, slowing to tug his nipples on my journey upward. I stopped when my hands reached his neck and lightly traced his pulse points with my thumbs. I angled my body closer to his, seeking out his heat. I wanted to feel his body pressed so tight against mine that not even air could fit between us. Never had a kiss affected me so damn much, and I never wanted it to end.

BAM. BAM. BAM.

Xavier and I jerked apart when someone pounded on the driver's side window. I clutched my chest in fear of a heart attack while my jackass brother laughed so hard he couldn't catch his breath. The finger-pointing and knee-slapping went on for a few minutes, which allowed my heart to return to a normal rhythm.

"Who the hell is that?" Xavier leaned around me to get a better look at the idiot.

"My asshole brother," I answered dryly. "What the fuck is he doing here?"

Bevan gathered himself and walked to the door behind mine, knocking on the window for me to unlock it and let him in. I shrugged at Xavier and clicked the unlock button. Xavier looked back and forth between Bevan and me, probably noticing how much we looked alike. We could pass for twins if not for the slight gray at Van's temples and the hint of crow's feet around his eyes.

"What are you doing, dickhead?" I asked as soon as he shut the door behind him.

"I knew you were going to be doing some sleuthing and wanted to make sure you didn't jump the guy and end up in jail for your pregnant friend." Xavier tensed beside me.

"Meet my pregnant friend's brother," I said sarcastically to Bevan. "Xavier, this is my older brother, Bevan, who's usually more tactful."

Bevan had the decency to look chagrined when he leaned forward and offered Xavier a hand. "I didn't mean any offense, Xavier."

"None taken." Xavier's tone wasn't convincing.

"It's a damn good thing I showed up because you two amateurs missed the fair-haired prince picking up his nightly piece of side action." Van nodded to a black SUV a few rows up and over to the right. Van snickered when the vehicle began to rock with the rhythm of a frantic fuck. "Lucky lady, huh?"

"Van," I warned. I couldn't be sure, but Xavier might have been watching this scene in horror, picturing his sister being treated in a similar fashion. The thought was enough to make my stomach pitch and roll, and I wasn't a blood relative.

"What? I'm not putting his sister down," Van said defensively. "I know nothing about her circumstances, but I've seen hundreds of douches just like Drake Anderson during my time as a private investigator. After he puts it to this woman, he'll stop and get his wife a little gift, then go home to her smelling like another woman. Disgusting. What's the point? I say we just keep playing the field, lil' bro, that way no one can make us feel as shitty as his wife will surely be feeling later tonight."

I glanced over at Xavier and found him watching me closely. I couldn't say how, but I knew my answer would make or break this fledgling little *thing*—for lack of a better word—we had building. I needed to answer honestly but be certain not to paint myself in a bad light.

"That's a pretty cold existence, though." I kept my eyes trained on Xavier while I continued. "I used to be pretty happy going from one dude to the next, but not anymore."

"Unh," Van grunted. "That's a pretty swift change of opinion, bro."

"Not really. I've spent the last year watching two wonderful men fall head-over-heels in love with each other. It's been the most enlightening experience in my life, Van. I mean, it's like they need each other to breathe. It's like nothing we've ever seen," I said, shaking my head. "I realized I want that for myself. Someday." Xavier said nothing, but he kept his eyes on mine, searching for any sign that I wasn't being sincere. I imagined he was mulling over every single word I'd spoken.

"Well, it sounds all romantic and nice, but I don't believe love lasts. I think too many times people confuse lust and hormones with love. People toss that *L* word around so casually these days that it carries no weight. But I hope your friends are the rare couple who make it work." Van leaned up and slapped me on the shoulder. "I hope you find that kind of relationship too, Ben, if that's what you really want." He sat back in his seat, then chuckled. "In the meantime, let's follow this loser and see if I was right."

We watched as Drake Anderson barely helped the lady out of the back seat of his SUV and didn't even wait for her to safely get into her car before he peeled out of the parking lot. *What a dick!* I pulled out behind him but didn't follow too closely. Van was the definition of a backseat driver as he instructed me on the proper way to tail a suspect.

"Stay two cars back."

"I am, Van."

"He's turning, Ben."

I snorted. "I see the turn signal."

"Don't pull into the same parking lot as him, dip shit," Van said. "You want to make it obvious? Go down to the sandwich shop next door, and we'll watch him discreetly from there."

I rolled my eyes but did as I was told. "Yes, Miss Daisy."

This was not how I wanted my night to go, but Xavier appeared to be having a great time as he laughed at the bantering and bickering between Van and me. We waited and watched as the cheating bastard went into the convenience store and returned a few minutes later with flowers and a bottle of wine.

"See? What the fuck did I tell you? I bet that wine tastes like panther piss." Van leaned forward until his head was between the front seats. "Let's finish this little stakeout, shall we? Let's follow this pathetic loser home."

I looked over at Xavier to see if he was okay with Van's plan, and he shrugged his shoulders in response. I took that as agreement and casually pulled out behind our guy because we all knew where he was going next and had the address. We parked down the street from his house, and I was grateful for the darkness that had fallen when I saw the light from the streetlamps bounce on the toys and bikes in the front yard, which indicated the sleazeball had already fathered children.

The front porch light came on when the asshole got out of his SUV and walked up the front walk to his door. His wife stepped onto the porch, and I saw the strain on her face even from a few doors down. She accepted the gifts and let herself be hugged by her husband, who didn't react when his wife went completely stiff in his arms. The wife remained on the porch for several moments after the cheating bastard went inside, smiling because he thought he got away with it again.

"She knows," Van said, breaking the strained silence, "just like they always do." He leaned back in the seat and let out a muffled groan that was full of frustration. "Take me back to my car, will ya?"

"Sure, Van."

I put the car into gear and drove us all back to the bar where our night had begun. The ride there was so quiet you could've heard a pin drop. I parked next to Bevan's car and was ready for him to get the hell out, but Xavier stopped him.

"Bevan, can I hire you to help me find a friend? I haven't been able to get in touch with him for a long time, and I'm worried."

Bevan looked as surprised as I felt, but it didn't stop him from pulling a business card from his pocket and handing it to Xavier. "Call me, and I'll see what I can do for you," he offered with a cool smile. "Ben, walk me to my car." It wasn't a question. I got out of the car and made sure to shut the door so Xavier wouldn't overhear our conversation. "What the hell are you doing?" Van whispered angrily. "Is that your idea of taking things slow?"

"Van, I've got this under control."

"It didn't look like it to me. It looked like you were about five seconds from car sex in public. I just want you to be careful."

"He's confided in me, and I'm perfectly fine with everything I learned. I promise I've got this. The absolute worst thing that could happen would be that he doesn't return my feelings. Yeah, it will hurt pretty freaking bad, but it won't kill me." I tried to convince Van…and possibly myself.

Van hugged me tightly. "Call me anytime. Day or night."

I agreed that I would and watched him get into his car and drive away. I smiled to myself as I walked back to Xavier because I had a new item to add to the bucket list: car sex.

CHAPTER
Seventeen

Xavier

I DIDN'T SEE OR TALK TO BEN FOR OVER A WEEK AFTER OUR STAKEOUT. Things felt strained and tense between us once he got back into the car and drove us back to his house so I could pick up my car. I was to blame for the edgy atmosphere because I was certain Bevan and Ben had had a discussion about me. I hadn't heard their words, but I could read their body language loud and clear. It had been obvious Bevan was expressing concern while Ben deflected it. I didn't want to come between the brothers, and their little conversation had helped me regain my perspective.

As much as I wanted Ben—and I wanted him bad—I couldn't let my attention get diverted from my recovery. I had made some huge strides in acceptance and forgiveness, but I wasn't foolish enough to believe I was anywhere close to being ready for a relationship. I spent the rest of the ride back to my car in almost complete silence, allowing myself to breathe in his scent and willing my brain to commit it to memory. I foolishly let my mind recall every second of our heated kiss.

Ben had tried to pull me out of my funk by asking if I was okay, and I had told him I was just tired. He accepted my answer, but I could tell he knew I was making excuses and pulling away from him emotionally. Again. He deserved so much better than I was willing and able to give. He deserved someone who was whole and able to give him more than quick, dirty fucks when the need became too strong. He deserved what Chase and Gray had found, and I wanted him to have it so badly.

Our goodbye in his driveway had been awkward to say the least with both of us saying the standard "See you around" or "Talk to you later" while knowing it wouldn't happen. I went home that night and dreamed more chords and lines from the rhythm of us. Like the time before, I recorded them in my notebook, but this time, my notes were accompanied by tears instead of a smile.

I had just been going through the motions of living during the days following the stakeout. I ate when I got hungry, slept when I felt tired, and worked out almost every free second in between. My body adjusted to the adrenaline rush from the kickboxing lessons, so I no longer experienced the crazed need to screw afterward, but I'd driven by Ben's house on more than one occasion. I found comfort in just seeing the lights on inside and knowing he'd open that door and welcome me in if I was brave enough to accept what he offered.

What exactly was Ben offering, though? Friendship? To be my fuck buddy? I believed Ben when he'd told Bevan that one-night stands just weren't doing it for him any longer, but that didn't mean he was looking for happily ever after with me. And what if he was looking for more with me? Could I handle it? I didn't know anything, except that I missed the sound of his voice, his laughter, and his delicious smell. I wouldn't let myself think about the way he tasted on my lips and tongue for fear of losing my mind.

So I lived a fairly miserable existence, enduring my self-imposed hiatus from Ben. I tried to put on a happy front for Ellie, who didn't buy it but had the decency to pretend she did. Then two amazing things happened that brought me hope and joy. I received an email from Ryan Productions in LA and learned that one of the original scores I'd written, produced, and submitted had been chosen for a new cable television series. It was a dream come true, and I couldn't wait to tell everyone. I picked up the phone to call Ben because he was the first person I wanted to tell. That should have been the eye-opener I needed, but it didn't immediately sink in. Chase called before I could dial Ben's digits, though.

"I need your help." Chase's frazzled voice snapped me to attention. "The wedding is in five days, and Gray insists on playing softball tonight. He says he's needed and can't let the guys down. Oh my God, Xavier, what if he gets hit in the face with a ball? Can you imagine the wedding pictures with my groom's face sporting a black eye or a facial fracture? I can't talk him out of playing, but I hope I can talk you into going with me to hold my hand and keep me calm."

It would seem like a small thing to anyone else, but to me it was huge. I was needed. Someone wanted to lean on me and let me shoulder their burdens for once, and there was no way I would let Chase down. I agreed to go with him, and he picked me up at six thirty for the game.

"I'm equal parts nervous and excited," he confessed while he maneuvered his vehicle down the road. "God, I don't want his beautiful face all messed up at any time but especially not on our wedding day."

"That covers the nervous part, but why are you excited?" I was confused how he could be excited over the possibility that Gray might get scuffed up.

"I get to see my man in his tight baseball pants." Chase's face flushed red, and he began to fan himself. "If it were left up to me, he'd wear either baseball pants or nothing."

"Glad to see you're still just as smitten with him now as you were when you first met." It gave me hope that maybe I could find that for myself one day, but I wasn't about to confess that to Chase, or he might start in about Ben.

"Ben also plays on Gray's team." Ah, there it was. I glanced over, and he waggled his eyebrows at me.

"Should I tell Gray you've been ogling Ben's ass?"

"He knows," Chase replied wryly. "I use it to get Gray all riled up so he has to remind me who I belong to." Chase's smile and laughter were infectious, and I found myself smiling like a loon. "You're in luck tonight because they're the home team, which means they'll be wearing their white pants instead of the black ones."

I didn't have a hard time picturing Ben's firm ass in tight baseball pants, which made my own pants a little snug in the crotch. Anticipation and excitement at seeing Ben bloomed inside me, but I tamped it down because I had no idea what kind of reception to expect out of him. I knew Ben wouldn't be cruel or mean to me because of the distance I'd put between us, but I was afraid his face wouldn't light up like it had the last time we were together.

All too soon, Chase turned into the outdoor sporting complex and drove past the soccer fields and sand volleyball pits until he arrived at the ball diamonds in the very back. I reminded myself I was there to support Chase and for no other reason, especially not to ogle Ben…

"Oh my God!" I heard myself exclaim loudly when I first laid eyes on all those tight asses in baseball pants, but more specifically when I saw the ass I craved most stuck up in the air while Ben bent over at the waist to stretch his glutes and hamstrings. I'd recognize that toned work of art anywhere and could easily recall how those taut cheeks had felt beneath my hands and how snugly it had—

"I know!" Chase's exuberant agreement interrupted my lusty thoughts, and I looked away before I got caught. "Mmm, there's my man. I'm going over there to give him his good-luck kiss. You can come with me or wait here. Your choice." Chase didn't wait around for an answer. He power walked his happy ass over to his fiancé for a kiss.

Gray wrapped his arms around my best friend and pulled him in. I couldn't help but watch the beautiful couple as they openly displayed their love for one another. *How would that feel?* I sensed eyes on me and turned to look in Ben's direction, and sure enough he had those silvery lasers locked on me.

My body perked up more and more with every step that brought him closer to me. His black softball jersey clung to his muscular torso and those ridiculously hot pants showed off his long legs and snuggly cupped the impressive bulge between his legs. What got to me the most was the joyful smile on his face. Ben was truly happy to see me, and once again, my spirit was lighter and happier in his presence.

"Hey, stranger," he said when he finally reached me. "How have you been?"

"I'm doing well." *I miss you*, I thought, but I left those words unspoken. The urge to wrap my arms around his neck and give him a good-luck kiss was overwhelming, so I slid my hands into my back pockets. "I actually have some exciting news I wanted to tell you about. I had just picked up the phone to dial your number when Chase called and asked me to come with him for moral support."

"He's still freaking out about Gray getting bruised up before the wedding, huh?" he asked. I nodded and Ben's happy laugh made me smile. "So what's your news? I want to hear it."

"Yo, Ben! Let's go," Jack Murphy, the sexy owner of Bottoms Up and sponsor of their team called out. "It's time to warm up."

"Ignore him. I always do. Please tell me the news." Ben eagerly looked down at me and smiled encouragingly.

"Now, Romeo!"

Ben started to turn around to confront Jack, but I reached out and grabbed onto his biceps. I feared for his safety if he took Jack on. "Go play your game, and I'll tell you afterward."

"Will you come to Bottoms Up with us after the game, or will that be a problem for you?"

His considerate nature was just one of many things that made the man so delectable. I caught myself staring at his lips and wanted to give him that good-luck kiss again. I tore my eyes away from his mouth and latched onto his gaze instead. He knew what I had been thinking because the same desire was reflected back at me.

"It won't be a problem for me," I replied honestly.

"Great," Ben said as he bounced on his toes. "See you after the game."

"See you," I replied to his retreating back. *Stop looking at his ass. Stop looking at his ass.*

"Would you look at that ass?" Gram asked.

Startled, I spun around and found Gram standing behind me, ogling my guy. *Did I really just think of Ben as my guy?* I decided to shove the thought aside to revisit later. "Really, Gram."

"As if you weren't just drooling over that tush," she said, clearly affronted by my tone.

"Guilty." I smiled and gave her a big hug. "It's getting kind of late, isn't it? Doesn't *the home* have a curfew for nutty broads like you?"

"Watch it, Xavier, or I'll bust your ass." Gram looked at me thoughtfully. "Maybe you're into that kind of kink so it wouldn't be much of a deterrent," she prattled on. "I could always threaten to move in with you. That ought to take the sass right out of you."

"You win, Gram." I threw up my hands in surrender.

"That's what I thought." She smugly linked her arm in mine, and we made our way to the bleachers. The soon-to-be husbands were nowhere in sight, and I wondered what they were up to. "Chase and Gray probably snuck off into the woods for a quickie." It was like the woman could read my mind.

"Did not, Gram." Chase's exasperated voice bounced off the metal stands as he joined us. "I just got Gray a Gatorade to drink during his game." Chase studied his grandmother closely. "I swear you get more and more inappropriate each year. When will we get to the grandma phase where you bake cookies for your grandsons?"

"Screw baking cookies," Gram said a little louder than Chase or I preferred. "I don't have time for that with all the *research* I need to do for my books." Chase and I knew *research* was code for watching gay porn.

"You ought to be an expert by now, shouldn't you, Gram?" Chase's lips twitched with barely restrained mirth. "Does Lennie know how much time you devote to *research*?"

I saw the smirk on Gram's face in reply to the question and knew we were about to get schooled. Again. "Why, yes, he does, my darling boy. In fact, he's *very* grateful for my newfound knowledge of the prostate gland.

I can make that beautiful man sing like an exotic bird." I dropped my head into my hands while Chase groaned in misery. "When are you two fools going to learn? Neither of you is a match for me."

"So true," I muttered into my hands.

"We bow down to you, Gram."

"Thank you. Now shut your yaps, and let's watch some ball. I'm contemplating a new series about closeted athletes. I think my first book will be about a baseball player who resembles our dear Ben. Mmm, that's a mighty fine ass." Ben's butt had starred in enough of my fantasies, so I guess it was easy to see why he was fodder for Gram's character.

As if he sensed my attention, Ben looked over at me from first base and shot me a wink. My stomach fluttered like a hundred butterflies had taken flight inside it, and my heartrate sped up at the thought of having him all to myself, even if only for a few minutes.

CHAPTER
Eighteen

Ben

I'D NEVER WANTED A GAME TO BE OVER AS QUICKLY AS I DID THAT NIGHT. I had always been a competitive player, but I turned into a savage beast on the field with the promise of alone time with Xavier bouncing around in my brain.

"You were on fire tonight, bro," Jack said after we lined up to exchange high fives. "Bring that with you to every game, yeah?"

"You almost hit for the cycle," Gray said as he jogged up next to me. "Little extra incentive tonight? Showing off for a certain someone perhaps?"

"I *was* motivated," I told Gray. He was the only person who hadn't urged me to proceed with great caution when dealing with Xavier. I'm not sure if he was clueless about the condition Xavier was in when he'd returned home or if he simply had more faith in Xavier's abilities to cope and deal with his issues.

"Good for both of you." Gray playfully punched me in the arm.

"Thanks for not denting your handsome face," Chase said to Gray as we approached our small fan club.

"Meh, I could've covered up a shiner with makeup for the big day." Xavier's casually tossed comment made everyone laugh but me. How many times had he covered up bruises his ex-manager had given him? I refused to refer to that guy as his ex-boyfriend because a boyfriend cares about you and doesn't beat you senseless.

"You kids all have fun," Gram told us when we reached the parking lot. "I've got enough material to get an outline done but not until after I spend some quality time with my beau."

Hugs and kisses were exchanged, then we split up into two cars. Gray had ridden over with me so it worked out great that he could ride to Bottoms Up with Chase and I would have Xavier all to myself.

"Tell me about your exciting news," I said as soon as we climbed into the car.

My heart had done summersaults and backflips when Xavier had told me he'd planned to call me. It was a giant leap in the right direction and did a lot to assuage my hurt over not hearing from him sooner. It was harder than hell not to call or text him, but I knew he needed space after the stakeout. He had erected a gigantic wall while I'd spoken to my brother. I tried getting him to open up to me that night, but he refused. Giving him the space he wanted was the only option.

"Several months ago, I submitted an original score I wrote and produced to a big-name production company in LA, and my music was chosen as the theme song for a new cable series." Xavier's excitement pulsated throughout his entire body so hard that I felt the shockwaves. "God, Ben, it's a huge dream come true for me. I picked up the phone to call you as soon as I received the email."

"Xavier, that's awesome." I pulled up to a red light and looked over at him. He was grinning from ear to ear, and resisting him was out of the question. I leaned forward and rubbed my nose against his, allowing him time to tell me no or push me away, but he did neither. I raised his chin with my hand and lowered my lips to his, kissing him in a whisper-soft brush of lips. The embrace was about celebration, not passion.

"Ben." My name was a whispered plea from Xavier's lips. He fisted his hands in my jersey and deepened the kiss by sliding his tongue into my mouth.

A low growl escaped my throat when Xavier took over, dominating the kiss. Again, I was willing to follow his lead, and I hoped it would take us back to my bed. I was just getting into the kiss when Xavier pulled back and looked up at me with hooded eyes. I saw his lips moving, but I was so lost in the sheen of moisture on his lips from our kiss that I didn't hear what he said.

My cell phone rang through my car's speakers, startling me back to reality. I saw that it was Chase calling, so I hit the button to answer him.

"The light is green, dickhead." Chase burst into laughter and disconnected. I looked in the rearview mirror when I heard an engine rev and saw that Chase and Gray were behind us at the light.

"*I'm* the dickhead?" I mumbled while Xavier grinned.

I drove to the bar with dread sitting in the pit of my stomach because I knew they were going to rib me over the kiss. I decided right then and there that I'd tell our friends that whatever was happening between us was our business, and they needed to butt out. The truth was, I had no clue what was going on between Xavier and me, so I wouldn't have been able to explain much anyway.

We followed Chase and Gray into the bar, and I envied the ease with which they held hands and the obvious comfort they found in one another. I wasn't lying when I'd told Van I wanted that for myself when the time was right. I glanced to my right and looked at the sexy man walking beside me. Was it the right time with the right man? There was only one way to find out.

The team scattered once we got inside the bar—some went to shoot pool, some sat down at tables, and others chose to go to the bar. My little foursome chose the latter, but we had to split up into two groups since we couldn't find four seats together.

I held up my hand and waved the bartender, Liam, over so I could order a beer. Xavier ordered a Coke, and it didn't take long for Liam to bring our drinks.

"Thanks, handsome." Liam winked after I handed him cash and told him to keep the change. I looked over at Xavier and found him watching Liam through narrowed eyes, and I shamefully hoped it was jealousy over Liam's flirting, but then Xavier spoke and killed my hope.

"Why does he look familiar? I can't place it, but he reminds me of someone."

I shrugged my shoulders because there had been something familiar about Liam to me too, but I hadn't been able to place it either. "So what happens next with your song?" I genuinely wanted to know.

"I'm going to call my old agent that I had when I first moved to LA and get some advice or possibly find a lawyer who can guide me through all the contract jargon to make sure I'm not getting screwed."

"I know a guy."

"An attorney?" Xavier asked, then followed with, "Who?"

"Van is a lawyer who specializes in contracts. I guarantee he could help you wade through the quagmire of legal jargon. Do you want me to call him?"

"I'm not sure that's such a good idea. I don't get the impression Bevan holds the Cruz siblings in very high regard." Ah, so that was the reason behind the atmospheric shift the night of the stakeout.

"Van is a good guy, Xavier, but he's really jaded because of our parents and the private investigation business he's established. He sees the worst this world has to offer, so he tends to be cynical and suspicious."

"I can appreciate that, but I don't want it aimed at me. I have enough stress trying to stay clean while rebuilding my life. That extra scrutiny just makes me itchy and jumpy, which causes him to leap to conclusions about why he makes me nervous." Xavier took a deep breath and blew it out. "I really wanted to hire him to locate my friend, but I haven't found the nerve to call him."

"The only thing that will change Van's mind is if he spends more time around you. If he gets to know you better, he will like you as much as everyone else does." I stroked a finger across his high cheekbone. "What's not to like, huh?"

"I'll give it some thought, but…" Xavier never finished his sentence because Chase rudely pushed between us.

"I just signed you up for karaoke." Chase's broad smile was in direct contrast to Xavier's look of horror.

"No, Chase." Xavier shook his head to emphasize his answer. "I'm not interested in performing in front of people anymore."

"Just one song. For me. Please? It will be randomly selected by the machine, so I promise I'm not trying to set you up."

"One song," Gray said as he joined our group. "You're up next by the way."

"Fuck me!" Xavier practically growled in response. "Come on, guys. Go up there and remove my name so I can sit here and talk to Ben in peace." Xavier's protests were too late because the karaoke DJ said his name through the microphone. A look of pure misery settled over Xavier's features when the bar began to clap and call out his name.

I leaned forward and kissed his lips lightly before I pressed my mouth to his ear. "You'll be amazing, and maybe it will help you face down some demons. Get up there and knock us dead. Own the song, the stage, and the night." I wanted to add that he could own me, but I thought it might be a little much.

Reluctantly, Xavier rose from his barstool and slowly made his way to the stage. The DJ handed him the microphone and pointed to the song that had been randomly chosen by the computer. I watched as Xavier's entire demeanor shifted from uncertain man to seasoned stage performer.

The crowd went wild when the intro to "Buttons" by the Pussycat Dolls began to play. Xavier's sexy-as-fuck hips began to sway and dip to the beat that was an eclectic mix of hip-hop and something else. His body became one with the rhythm and my dick pulsed in time with the music and his mesmerizing dance moves.

Then he began to sing, doing both the rapping and the singing in different voices. The crowd fell in love with his performance, and I was dangerously close to falling in love with the man. The air whooshed out of my lungs, and panic nearly consumed me as soon as the thought formed. I couldn't be falling for Xavier. I hardly knew him. Sure, he trusted me enough to bare his soul to me, and I was the first person he wanted to call when something positive happened to him, but that didn't mean he was developing feelings for me, did it?

Suddenly, I was the one feeling the need for some distance. All the reasons I didn't believe in love and happily ever after flooded my brain and overwhelmed me. I had thought about taking a chance and asking him to be my date to Chase and Gray's wedding, but I revised my plan on the fly. No, I wasn't willing to put my heart out there and watch it get stomped on. My tumultuous thoughts kept spinning around inside my skull like a destructive cyclone, threatening to ruin all the good that Xavier and I had started to build between us. I shook my head to rid myself of the negative thoughts, but a whisper of despair remained.

I forced myself to focus on Xavier and watched as he worked the crowd with both his body and talent. Our eyes met, and he smiled hesitantly at me as if he were privy to my inner turmoil. I hoped my answering smile eased his mind because none of my uncertainty was his doing. Xavier had been honest with me from the start, and I was the one who'd falsely hoped for more than he could or would give. And who the fuck could blame the guy? He'd been through hell and back and didn't need me putting pressure on him. I needed to walk away and give him time and space to make up his own mind.

"Well, what did you think?" Xavier asked when he arrived back at the bar. He started to take a drink from his glass of Coke, but Liam pulled it out of his hands.

"You left your drink unattended, so let me replace it for you, honey."

"Thanks, Liam. Just Coke on the rocks," Xavier reminded him before returning his attention on me. "What did you think?"

I think you looked beautiful. I think I could fall in love with you. I think I want to hold you in my arms all night while we sleep. Those thoughts all ran through my mind but were left unspoken. Instead, I said, "You were really awesome, Xavier." Maybe the sentiment in my words didn't show in my eyes because he looked confused. Damn it! I didn't want to say or do the wrong thing or cause him any grief or make him feel bad. I looked down at my watch like I was checking the lateness of the hour. "Listen, I need to head home. Do you want me to give you a lift, or did you want to grab a ride with Chase and Gray?" I didn't trust myself alone with him in my car, so I sent up a silent plea for mercy.

Xavier looked down the bar at his friends, who were in their own little world. He flicked his eyes back to me, and I saw the hurt and confusion I'd tried to avoid. "I'll hitch a ride with the lovebirds," he answered in a voice devoid of all emotion.

"Congratulations again on your song being chosen for the cable series. That's a huge accomplishment, and I'm truly honored you chose to share it with me." He looked as if he was waiting for me to say *but*, though there wouldn't be one. This was hopefully a *so long* and not a *goodbye*. "I'll be heading out of town for a few days, but I'll be back the day before the wedding. I'll see you then, okay?"

"Sure," Xavier answered flatly. "Goodbye, Ben."

"Not goodbye. It's so long for now," I said before I turned and left him at the bar. The painful, viselike grip on my heart sure felt like we were saying goodbye.

CHAPTER
Nineteen

Xavier

BEN WAS RIGHT. I KNEW I NEEDED TO HAVE A LAWYER LOOK OVER MY contract to make sure I was getting a good deal from Ryan Productions. I hadn't talked to my old agent for nearly two years because that had been the first relationship Damien had severed by planting seeds of doubt in my mind, and calling Estelle after all this time just didn't feel right to me.

That really left me with only one option because I needed to either submit an amended contract as a counteroffer for review or a signed contract stating I accepted their terms. I was in a hurry, and Ben had said I could count on his brother, and even though things were strained between us, I trusted him completely.

I wouldn't allow myself to consider the ramifications of Ben walking away from me at the bar. I hadn't heard from him since, but that wasn't anything new. Ben let me be in control of our friendship, and he followed my lead. *Could that really be called a friendship, though?* I asked myself. Friendship was a two-way street, not this "Simon Says" thing Ben and I had going on. It seemed like it had finally taken a toll on Ben, and he was tired of walking on eggshells around me.

I knew Ben had let me set the pace out of respect for the hell I'd gone through, and I appreciated it more than I could express, but I missed the calm command he sometimes exhibited. It wasn't anything like Damien's possessive control. Ben was able to yank me out of my head when I got lost in there, unable to move forward out of fear.

I retrieved my cell phone and sent Ben a quick text. *I'm looking forward to seeing you at the wedding. Save me a dance?* There, I'd made my move, and it felt really fucking good. I smiled to myself as I entered Bevan's downtown office. I looked around at the modern reception area in surprise because it wasn't at all what I expected.

"We get that look a lot," the receptionist said with a smile. "Were you expecting something more Bogart?"

I smiled sheepishly at being read so easily. "Busted."

"Are you Mr. Cruz?" she asked politely. No one had ever referred to me as Mr. Cruz. It reminded me of my father, and I didn't like it one bit.

"Xavier," I corrected. "I have an appointment at noon."

"Mr. St. Claire will be with you shortly. He's just wrapping up a phone call. Can I get you anything to drink? Coffee? Water?"

"I'm fine, but thank you."

I sat in a chair and perused the magazines on the coffee table. The chair was worn but comfortable as was the decor. It was a contrast to the Bevan I remembered from before, or maybe I had been using my defensiveness as a guard to keep from seeing the real Bevan, just as he probably did with me. I had just snatched up the latest copy of *Rolling Stone* and flipped it open when my phone buzzed in my pocket with an incoming text, and I pulled it out, fingers shaking. My heart kicked up a notch in hopes that it was a reply from Ben.

Warning: I have two left feet! PS I miss you too.

"Xavier." I jerked my head up and found Bevan watching me intently. "I suppose that goofy grin on your face means you're texting my brother."

"Uh, yeah," I said as I stood up.

"He has that effect on people," Bevan said with a smirk. "Come into my office." I followed behind him and took a seat in front of his desk while he shut the door to give us privacy. "Did you still want to hire me to find your friend?" Bevan didn't put an emphasis on the word *friend* with his voice, but his body language did as he sat behind his desk. He was Ben's brother and a very important part of his life, and I needed to put myself out there if I was ever going to earn his trust.

"I'm actually here for two reasons and, yes, one of them is to hire you to find Deacon." I reached into my messenger bag and pulled out the contract I'd received from the production company and a sheet of paper with every detail I knew about Deacon, which sadly wasn't much. "Here's what I know. It's not much, but I hope it's enough to find him." I slid the sheet of paper across his desk and waited for Bevan to pick it up. "Deacon helped me through a horrible time about fifteen months ago, and I haven't heard much from him since. I did get a random call from him at Christmas, but nothing since then."

"Why would he sever ties with you if he's such a concerned friend?" Bevan asked after he set the sheet down on his desk.

"I foolishly went back to the environment he helped save me from, and I think he, understandably, gave up on me."

Bevan leaned forward and set his elbows on his desk, pinning me to my seat with a very intense stare. "I don't find it the least bit understandable, Xavier. I would be a hell of a lot more vigilant if I thought my friend was in danger."

"Maybe he thought I wasn't worth the trouble. I'm sure a lot of people feel that way," I said with a shrug.

"Well, that isn't how I operate, and I guarantee Ben would agree with me." Bevan's brows lowered in frustration over my words. I decided to tell him what happened so he could see Deacon wasn't a bad guy.

I gave him the CliffsNotes version of my addiction and abuse rather than all the gory details. A few weeks ago, I would've wanted him to use this information against me to encourage Ben to turn away from me. Now, I hoped he could see past my mistakes and find a way to accept me, flaws and all. It scared me how much I wanted his acceptance, and I refused to analyze the reasons why at that particular moment.

"Well, you've certainly been through a lot," he said once I was finished. "I assume you've told Ben all this?" At my nod, he continued. "And he still wants to be a part of your life because that's what *friends* do. A true friend doesn't bail on you at the first sign of trouble, and they don't give up when you relapse into an unhealthy situation." Bevan blew out a frustrated breath. "I'll help you look for Deacon because it's important to you and you're important to my brother." Bevan saw the look of disbelief on my face and said, "You *are* important to him, Xavier. Don't hurt him." Bevan's no-nonsense tone made me shiver. "What's the other thing?" Bevan nodded to the contract that was forgotten in my hand.

"Ben said you specialized in contractual law." I handed the papers to him and waited while he read through it. "This is the opportunity I've waited for my entire adult life. I went to LA to make *that* happen," I said, gesturing to the contract. "The rock group was supposed to be a temporary gig until I was able to sell some of my original music. It took longer than I had hoped, and I took a twisty road of self-destruction, but here it finally is, and I don't want to screw it up."

"Congratulations! This is pretty awesome." Bevan punctuated the accolade with a hint of a smile, which I took as a major step in the right direction. "Tell me what your goals and concerns are, and I'll see how this contract measures up to both."

"Thank you." My relief was palpable.

Bevan and I spent the better part of two hours going over the document and making a few revisions where we felt necessary. He emailed the revised contract on my behalf and told me he would get back to me as soon as he heard back from the production company. He also promised to let me know what he discovered about Deacon. He walked me to the door but placed a hand on my shoulder to stop me from leaving.

"You've done a really good job of turning your life around in a really short amount of time. I see why Ben admires you so much."

Ben admires me?

"Yes, he does," Bevan said, answering my unspoken inquiry. "Don't look back, Xavier, only forward." I shook his hand and said my goodbyes, but Bevan's words stuck with me long after I left.

Was I important to Ben? Was I truly someone Ben admired?

The morning of Chase and Gray's wedding dawned with crystal-clear blue skies and hardly a cloud in sight. I hoped it was symbolic of their joyous union. My life was also starting to feel full of promise just like the clear, vibrant morning.

Bevan had called me yesterday afternoon to tell me the production company had accepted the amendments and would be sending a new contract for me to sign, and I decided to start looking for a place of my own as soon as I received my royalties. I had made quite a bit of money with the band and had been able to set a substantial nest egg aside, but I didn't want to dip into those funds unless it was an emergency. Thoughts of house hunting led to thoughts of Ben, and I wondered if he would mind going with me to look at houses when he was free.

Ben. My heart kicked up even more at the thought of seeing him again at the wedding. We'd exchanged a few flirty texts, but we had both tiptoed around the topic we really needed to discuss. Us. It was a conversation best had in person and not over the phone or via text. I pushed my thoughts of Ben aside so I could focus on the task at hand, which was putting on my rented tuxedo and preparing to meet the wedding party at the church. I refused to be late for Chase's big day.

I put Bess, my trusted Martin guitar, in my trunk and drove myself to the church. I saw Gray standing outside with his family, a captivating smile on his face. Could he be any more in love? I parked in the lot and said my hellos to the Wright clan, then went in search of the guy who was more brother to me than my own flesh and blood.

"Gray looks smoking hot in his tux," I told Chase as I entered the room he'd chosen to get ready in. "Wow, you look pretty amazing too." Chase spun around and modeled his gray tux for me. He radiated happiness from his toes to the top of his golden head. "You don't look like a nervous groom."

"That's because I'm *not* a nervous groom," Chase countered. "I'm so excited you're home and sharing this moment with me." Chase's eyes dimmed, and a frown marred his happy face. "I'm really sorry I've been so busy that I haven't made time to hang out and talk. Xavier…"

"No way, brother," I interrupted. "This is the happiest day of your life, and we aren't having any maudlin conversations." I was starting to sound a lot like Gram. "I'm doing really well, Chase, so please don't worry about me. We'll have plenty of time to get caught up when you get home from your two-week honeymoon in the Caribbean."

"You'll still be here when I get back?"

God, I had been such a selfish prick during my year-long hiatus, and I absolutely hated the stress I had put my family through. I reminded myself that there was nothing I could do to give them back the time we lost, but I could focus on making myself stronger and never repeating my mistakes. "I'm here to stay, Chase. I'm going to cat and house sit for you while you and Gray are off making happy memories. When you get back, we'll have a long overdue discussion."

Chase appeared mollified for the moment, but he was a natural born worrier. I took my thumb and smoothed out the frown still lingering on his brow. He had come a long way since he'd met and fallen in love with Gray, but his abandonment and insecurity issues still ran deep. I regretted wholeheartedly that I had contributed to his distress. He was the absolute best thing that had ever happened to me, and I would never let him down again. Chase pulled me into a tight hug, and I held on, so grateful to be alive and sharing this moment with him.

"There are my two beautiful boys." Gram stood just inside the room looking beautiful in her soft pink dress and matching hat. "Oh damn, here come the waterworks." She covered her mouth with her hand as happy tears slid down her face. She opened her mouth a few times to speak, but no words came out.

"Gram," Chase said her name softly and pulled her into a group hug between us. "We don't want red, puffy eyes for the wedding pictures," he said, trying to make her laugh.

Gram stepped back, opened up her purse, and pulled out a silk square of fabric in various shades of blue and green, reminiscent of the colors found in peacock feathers. "Gray had pocket squares made out of your mother's favorite silk scarf for the tuxedos," Gram said softly as she folded the material so it would fit inside the pocket on his chest. "He wanted to make sure she was included in your special day. I remembered this scarf of hers that I hadn't been able to part with and knew it would be the perfect thing." Gram swapped out the pocket square and smiled. "That guy, he's just so..."

"Thoughtful," Chase said when Gram couldn't finish. "I love him so much, and this means the world to me," he said, running his finger over the silky fabric.

Gram turned to me and replaced my square too. "You look so much happier since the last time we talked, Xavier." She stood on her tiptoes and kissed my cheek.

"I am happier, Gram."

"How's Ben?" The woman never stopped meddling, and I feared she would only get worse since Chase had found his dream man.

"He's been out of town on business these last few days, but he'll be here for the ceremony and reception." Bats—not butterflies—took flight in the pit of my stomach at the realization that I would not only be seeing Ben but dancing with him too. I recognized that my answer had done nothing to dissuade Gram, so I wasn't surprised by the words that came out of her mouth next.

"So, are you dating or just screwing?" At least she had the decency not to say *fuck* in a church.

"Gram," Chase admonished before I could answer. "Leave Xavier alone. You'll scare him back to LA before Ben can make an honest man out of him."

Gram looked at me with wide eyes as if she was actually considering if she was the reason why I had left for LA. That couldn't be further from the truth, and I needed to debunk it right then and there. "I did go to LA because of you but not for the reasons Chase jokingly implied. I was only able to leave because you taught me to be courageous and to follow my dreams. If not for you, I wouldn't be able to share my exciting news. I wasn't going to say anything yet because I wanted this day to be all about Chase." They looked at me with hopeful smiles. "One of my original soundtracks was chosen for a new cable show that comes out in the fall. Ben's brother helped me finalize the contract this week." I took Gram's hands in mine and directed my next words at her. "My dream wouldn't have come true without your unwavering love and support."

Gram gave a muffled little sob as she laid her head against my chest. "That is so exciting, Xavier. How long were you going to keep that amazing news to yourself?"

"I was going to wait until the newlyweds got back from their lovefest," I answered honestly. Gram lightly cuffed me upside my head. "Ouch."

"We're your family, and we want to know the minute something good happens to you so we can celebrate," Gram admonished. "You know how I love to throw parties. We'll have a big barbeque when the boys get back from their honeymoon."

There was a knock at the door, and Gray's brother, Preston, poked his head inside. "Pastor Simms asked me to find out if you're ready?"

"I've never been more ready for anything," Chase said.

"I'll let her know," Preston replied. "Xavier, you and I need to take our places at the front of the church."

I gave Chase and Gram one last hug, then followed Preston down the hall until we reached a side door that would allow us to walk in at the front of the church and take up our places on both sides of Pastor Simms at the altar. I looked around the church and appreciated the subtle decorations and small crowd that had gathered. Chase and Gray had opted for an intimate wedding by only inviting close friends and relatives.

The hair on the back of my neck stood up, and my skin suddenly felt too tight. I sensed an intense gaze aimed my way. I turned and found Ben's eyes locked on me. The smile that lit up his face warmed me from the inside out. Ben shot me a wink, and the bats in my stomach started to circle again. The connection between us suddenly seemed different, more intense, as if something had cosmically shifted whether we'd wanted it to or not.

Soft music began to play, pulling my focus to the back of the church where we waited for Gray and Chase to appear. The doors opened and everyone rose to their feet as the two men crossed the threshold, their hands entwined as tightly as their hearts, and began walking down the aisle toward the altar.

I knew I was still a work in progress and would be for the rest of my life since addictions didn't just disappear; they were managed and controlled. I also believed I had found a man who understood and related to my struggles in Ben. I was getting stronger every day, and with that strength came the belief that I did deserve happiness in my life. My eyes briefly met Ben's once more before the ceremony began. I couldn't be certain Ben was the man I'd spend the rest of my life with, but I knew he was the man I wanted to take a chance on.

CHAPTER
Twenty

Ben

I KNEW SOMETHING HAD CHANGED BETWEEN XAVIER AND ME THE MIN-ute our eyes connected in the church. To be honest, I knew something was different even when I was on the road. Xavier had initiated contact with me through text on more than one occasion, and I wasn't ashamed to admit how happy it made me feel, especially after the uncertain way we'd parted at Bottoms Up after the softball game.

My breath caught in my throat when he and Preston stepped through the door and got into position at the altar. The first thing I noticed—besides how freaking amazing he looked in a tux—was that he'd gotten his hair cut. Gone was the messy rocker look, but he'd left his hair long enough for me to yank the strands if he ever decided to use his pierced tongue on my cock.

I started to feel ashamed at the direction my thoughts were taking while in a church, but Xavier chose that exact moment to look into my eyes, and all my good intentions went up in a puff of smoke. The sunlight streaming through the stained glass windows landed on the altar, bathing it in a kaleidoscope of rainbow light suitable for the special occasion. Xavier's eyes looked like glowing embers in the sunlight. I couldn't look away from him, and it appeared he was equally enthralled with me. It was as if the rest of the world had disappeared and only the two of us remained. We stayed connected until the music began to play and the grooms made their way down the aisle.

I had attended plenty of weddings in my life but none I had enjoyed as much as Chase and Gray's. I had almost expected them to recite their own vows, but they both wanted the traditional words spoken and repeated to one another. I didn't consider myself an overly emotional man, but listening to them commit themselves to one another was a touching experience. The tenderness between them was like nothing I had witnessed before. At one point, Gray lovingly reached over and wiped a stray tear from Chase's face. Gray's voice broke during his vow recital, and Chase squeezed his hands to give him strength to continue. I was struck anew by how much I wanted that for my future.

Ellie sniffled beside me, and I reached over and held her hand. She smiled up at me with watery eyes before she leaned toward me. I lowered my head so she could whisper in my ear. "Don't think I missed the moment shared between you and my brother. He was so focused on you that he didn't see me smile and wave at him. Please don't hurt Xavier." Ellie punctuated her plea with a soft kiss to my cheek.

"I think you should start worrying about *me* getting hurt," I whispered back. Ellie raised a questioning brow, and I simply nodded in return. It was the candid truth and something I'd known from the very start—Xavier Cruz might never belong to me.

I waited for Xavier by his car once the ceremony was over and I had hugged and congratulated the grooms. I was feeling a little shaken by the pull I'd felt between us in the church, and I didn't want to wait until halfway through the reception to speak to him.

"Waiting for me?" Xavier's smile told me he wanted that to be the case.

"None other." My fingers itched to run through his shortened hair before I wrapped my hand around his nape and pulled him into a kiss. My crazy imagination kicked in, displaying the image in my mind. I could almost taste him on my tongue and breathe his masculine smell into my lungs. It only took a few seconds for my body to react to both my vision and his nearness. "This kind of feels like a scene from *Sixteen Candles*," I said with a smile.

"Do you have a pair of my briefs with you?" Xavier smiled mischievously as he played along.

"Do you make a habit of leaving your briefs around town?"

"At least I wear them." Xavier raked his eyes up and down my body, lingering on my crotch. "I noticed that on at least one occasion you went commando beneath your pants. I admit to wondering if that is a common occurrence with you." His hot eyes returned to my dick, and I stirred beneath his stare.

"I go commando often, but never to work or any other time I wear dress pants. They don't conceal much," I said, gesturing to the effect he had on me.

The temperature outside ratcheted up by about ten degrees due to the sexual tension between us. It was obvious as hell we both wanted to take the physical part of this thing we had going a step—or ten—further. The physical aspect was definitely not the reason we circled each other like wary animals. No, I was in uncharted territory, wanting more from a man than just sex. Xavier had barely escaped an abusive relationship, and I was completely out of line to even hope he would consider giving me more.

Xavier looked around the parking lot to see if anyone was paying attention. I did the same and realized most of the wedding party had already left for the reception and there were only a few stragglers left behind. Xavier stepped into me, taking me by complete surprise. The sun-warmed metal of his car was hot but the heat rolling off his body was scorching.

"Come home with me after the reception. I want to feel you inside me,

Ben." Xavier's warm breath blew across the sensitive flesh of my ear, and my knees nearly buckled. There was no way I could resist him.

"Wouldn't you rather come back to my house instead?" I turned my head so my lips were close to his. I slid just the tip of my tongue out and teased the corner of his luscious mouth. He'd removed his lip ring for the ceremony, and I missed it.

"I'm house and cat sitting for Mr. and Mr. Wright. There's a big, comfy guest bed with our names all over it. What do you say?"

"How long do we need to stay at the reception?" I asked. There was no attempt at hiding my enthusiasm.

"At least until their first dance as a married couple. It would really be in poor taste for me to skip out before I serenade them like I promised." Xavier rubbed his nose along mine, and I breathed him in, committing the moment to memory. This was so much more than just lust to me.

"That would definitely be in poor taste." I whispered the words against his lips before I closed the gap and pressed our mouths together. I needed a tiny taste of him if I had to wait hours before I could finally claim his body. I kept the kiss light with only a playful tease of tongue before I broke the kiss. "You taste delicious." I practically purred the words against his mouth.

A soft hum escaped Xavier's lips. His eyes opened slowly, and I read his naked desire—or desire to be naked—in their depths. It was the first time he had ever let his vulnerability show, and I silently vowed to never break his trust because it was so preciously given. I would be what he needed me to be whenever he needed it and hope I didn't get ripped to bloody shreds in the process. "Ride with me to the reception?"

I smiled broadly while shaking my head. "We'd never make it there in one piece. I'm calling a timeout while I get myself under control."

"Good call." Xavier stepped back slowly, and I missed the weight of his body pressed against mine immediately. He shot me a wink and walked around to the driver's side of his car. "See you on the dance floor," he said before he climbed into his car and fired up the engine.

I stepped away from the car and stood there watching him drive away like the lovesick fool I feared I was becoming. Then I remembered his parting words and walked to my car with dread. I really did have two left feet and could only hope Xavier was suave enough to make up for my clumsiness.

Dinner was consumed, toasts were given, and it was time for the grooms to take center stage on the dance floor. I watched as Xavier took off his tuxedo jacket and draped it over the back of his chair before he made his way to the stage. I was mesmerized by the confident way he picked up his guitar and approached the microphone.

"I asked Chase if he would let me choose the song to sing for his first dance with his husband, and he graciously agreed. I couldn't think of a better song than this for the two of you."

Xavier began to play the intro to "Bless the Broken Road" by Rascal Flatts on his acoustic guitar, and it was so beautiful that I nearly forgot to watch Chase and Gray together on the floor, but the *oohs* and *ahhs* finally pulled my attention away from Xavier. The love they felt for each other was evident as they danced closely while Xavier sang to them. Their foreheads were pressed together, their eyes were locked on one another, and they wore matching smiles. It was a beautiful moment, and I was lucky to be a part of it.

Once their dance ended, the DJ played an upbeat song to get everyone out onto the dance floor, including Gram and her boyfriend, Lennie. Xavier came down off the stage and crooked his finger at me. *Uh oh!* I thought he had wanted me to slow dance with him, not fast dance. I was clumsy at best during slow tunes, but I was Elaine from *Seinfeld* on the livelier songs. I was a jerking and twisting hot mess who couldn't keep rhythm, but that didn't stop me from going to him.

"I can't dance," I warned when we met on the floor.

"Only because you haven't had proper instruction." Xavier turned so his back was to my chest. I automatically wrapped my arms around his waist and pulled him close so we were perfectly aligned, his ass pressed snuggly against my package. "Relax and follow my lead."

Xavier began to move his body fluidly with the beat, becoming one with the music. I did just what Xavier said and allowed myself to relax, letting him guide me. There were some awkward moments at first where it looked like my hips were chasing him, but once I got the hang of the movement, Xavier spun out of my arms and faced me so we could dance while looking at each other. He was so gorgeous that I lost my rhythm at first but quickly caught on.

On and on we danced, one song after the next until we stopped to get a cold drink. We headed to the bar where Xavier ordered a Sprite. I debated about what to order because I wasn't sure how Xavier felt about kissing a man with alcohol on his breath and tongue. I planned on doing a hell of a lot of kissing, and I didn't want it to be a problem or a temptation he didn't need.

"You can order a drink if you want." Xavier had clearly misread the hesitation in my eyes. "It honestly won't bother me, Ben."

"I'll have what he's having," I told the bartender. Xavier looked skeptical, so I leaned in close to his ear so that only he would hear my words. "I have a feeling you'll be a much better buzz than I can get from alcohol." I could tell by his expression that he thought I was being corny, but I knew the words were the absolute truth. I downed my drink and set the empty cup on the bar. Xavier sipped his at a slower pace until I took it from him and set it on the bar when a slow song came on. "I've been looking forward to this since you texted me."

We hit the floor just as Ed Sheeran began to sing the first words of "Thinking Out Loud." Slow dancing with Xavier was like making love with our clothes on. I couldn't get close enough to him to suit me. My body literally twitched and tingled with the desire to feel his naked body against mine once more. My skin burned with awareness where his hands touched me. I lost track of time and everything around me. My sole focus was on the man in my arms and how he made me feel.

"You chose the perfect song for Chase and Gray's first dance and performed it beautifully." Xavier shivered when my lips touched his ear, telling me he was feeling the same insane chemistry between us. "Your speech was beautiful too." I didn't tell him that I wanted to be the one to bring that kind of happiness to his life. It scared me when the thought crossed my mind during his speech, and neither one of us was ready for that kind of declaration.

"Thank you, Ben." His eyes told me he was ready to go, so when the song was over, we tried to leave as discreetly as possible. We failed miserably.

No sex in my bed, was the text I received from Chase when I climbed into my car.

Eww, I sent in reply.

Practice safe sex, came from Gray, followed by, *Oh, and shut the bedroom door unless you don't mind a voyeuristic cat.*

Good to know, I replied, laughing as I hit Send.

CHAPTER
Twenty-One

Ben

MY THOUGHTS WERE ALL OVER THE PLACE AS I FOLLOWED XAVIER to the Wrights'. Did he want me to stay the night with him or leave after we were finished? Did this change the dynamic between us, or was I still willing to just follow his lead? I felt like a fish out of water, and it wasn't a comfortable feeling, though any discomfort was worth the sacrifice when Xavier was the prize.

I pulled up beside him in the driveway and cut the engine. I got out when he did and followed him up the landscaped pathway to the porch. I refrained from touching him like I wanted to as he unlocked the front door. Xavier tossed his keys on the table in the entryway, then turned to look at me.

"I've thought about nothing else besides how you'd feel inside me since the night of the softball game. I don't know what's going on here, Ben, and

I am making you zero promises, except that I want to be with you. I need to taste you, to feel you, and to learn every inch of you. That's the only promise I can make right this minute. Are you okay with that?" Xavier pressed his body to mine, which made it nearly impossible to think.

I forced my brain to absorb his words, mull them over, and really let them sink in. My body wanted him beyond anything I had ever known before, but there was a part of me that screamed at me to walk away before I got hurt. Could I casually stroll away from this man after being inside him, or would it completely wreck me? I guessed I would find out what my limits were because saying no to Xavier wasn't something I was willing to do.

"No promises." I recited his words back to him, then lowered my head to capture his lips in a slow, seductive kiss. This was my night to have him, and I wasn't about to rush it.

I walked him backward toward the staircase while I made love to his mouth. Xavier began to walk backward up the stairs as unwilling to break our kiss as I was. We were almost to the top when something crashed hard into the back of Xavier's legs. Xavier was midstep, so the momentum took us backward with his magnificent ass landing on the stair and my bodyweight pressing down on him.

I leaned back to make sure he wasn't hurt, but he pulled my head down to resume our kiss. Xavier tangled his hands in my hair and wrapped his legs around my waist, bringing our erections into contact with each other. His intense heat burned through our layers of clothes, and I couldn't wait to feel his skin against mine without any barriers.

I began to gently thrust my hips into the V-shape space between his legs, urging my body to go slow, to savor the moment, and not crush him beneath my considerable weight. I braced myself on my elbows above him, but Xavier's hands slid from my hair to my shoulders where he tried tugging me down. I was reluctant to pull away, but I wasn't willing to have sex with him on the steps.

"Bed." My voice sounded as desperate as I felt. I pushed up and held my hand out to help him up. "Lead the way," I told him when he was standing in front of me.

Xavier hit the light switch on the wall in the guestroom, then dimmed the lights. I wanted to tear his clothes off but instead chose to unwrap him slowly so I could relish the moment. I kissed the skin I uncovered and inhaled the smell of him. Xavier followed my lead for once and stripped me out of my clothes just as slowly. The gentle kisses he placed on my skin had me clenching my fists to prevent myself from going all caveman on him and throwing him to the bed.

Once we were completely nude, I laid him down on the bed and proceeded to reintroduce myself to his gorgeous body. I worshipped his soft skin with my mouth and tongue, lingering on his flat, dark nipples as I moved down his chest. He had removed his nipple piercings, and I missed them. I let my tongue trace the line that bisected his abdominal muscles and then his treble clef tattoo. Xavier jumped a little when I swirled my tongue inside his navel, making me chuckle. I nipped and sucked my way down to the trim patch of hair at the base of his erection. I remembered the feel of his hair tickling my nose while his dick pulsed and released in my throat.

I gave his pubic hair a little tug while I licked his erection from root to tip, making sure to linger on the piercing before I sucked the crown of his dick inside my mouth. I was thankful he hadn't taken away all my fun by removing all his piercings. Xavier writhed on the bed beneath me, chanting my name with reverence. He had a white-knuckled grip on the duvet cover beneath his body, and his head tossed from side to side on the pillow.

"Ben!" Xavier shouted my name when I took his full length deep inside my mouth. "Won't last." I pulled off slowly, then lowered to lick and lap at his tight sac before sucking his balls into my mouth one at a time. He leaned over, and I heard him open the bedside table drawer. "Here." Xavier's words were followed by a thump on the bed beside me.

I reached for the lube he'd tossed at me, opened the bottle, and drizzled some on my fingers. I sat back on my heels and spread his long, lean legs wider so I could see the puckered entrance to my own personal nirvana. Xavier squirmed when I traced lazy circles around his nerve-laden entrance with a lubed finger.

Low growls emanated from his throat as he raised his greedy hips, trying to impale himself on my finger. His growls of frustration turned into howls of pleasure when I slid one finger inside him all the way to my second knuckle on the first pass. Xavier's greedy hole sucked so tightly around my digit that I feared I'd lose control and come as soon as I slid my dick inside him.

"You're going to feel so good wrapped around my dick." I slid my finger in and out of him torturously slow. I soaked in every sound he made while my eyes greedily drank him in. One digit became two, circling and stretching while I teased his prostate on every inward thrust.

"Please, Ben. Just...I need more."

I worked Xavier until he was pliable and ready. I slid on the condom he'd pulled out with the lube and slicked up my dick before I pressed it to his trembling opening that was begging for penetration. I pushed gently until my dick passed through the tight ring, then stopped for a minute to let him adjust to my girth.

"Ben." Xavier's voice was laced with pleasure and need. His eyes were wide with wonder, and his mouth was parted so his breaths escaped in shallow gasps. "Don't stop."

I couldn't move for several seconds because I wanted to burn our joining into my brain. I didn't want to forget a single thing about this moment. Finally, I thrust my hips forward and buried my dick to the hilt in one smooth push. I braced myself on my elbows on either side of his head and lowered my mouth to his, making love to Xavier with both my body and my mouth. My heart threatened to beat out of my chest, but I kept my pace unhurried and controlled.

"So good," Xavier whimpered against my lips when we broke the kiss to suck in some much-needed air.

Need unfurled in my gut, clawing and shredding my insides raw, while my balls threatened to release their heavy load. I gritted my teeth and bunched my muscles to stave off my impending orgasm so I could make this good for Xavier. I didn't want him to think he was nothing more to me than just another ass to plow. Xavier had changed something inside me, and I knew I didn't want to go back to my old ways.

I leaned back and wrapped my hands around Xavier's thighs, pushed his knees closer to his chest, and placed his ankles on my shoulders. I may not have a piercing to drive him wild, but I had a few tricks up my sleeve I could use to unravel the man beneath me.

I placed my hands on both sides of his face, captured his mouth, and drove deep inside him on my first downward thrust. I circled my hips, pulled back, and thrust home again. Xavier fisted his hands in my hair and yanked. My mouth captured the sounds of his pleasure as I kept up the pattern of long deep thrusts followed by slow circles and an even slower retreat.

Xavier's cock was pressed tight against my stomach and rocked up and down the ridges and valleys of my abs with each push, leaving a trail of pre-cum in its wake. His snug, hot channel clamped down tighter around my cock, and his body trembled all over, indicating that his climax loomed near. I could've reached between our bodies and jerked his cock to orgasm, but I held back.

Xavier slid his hands down until they reached my shoulder blades, then he curled his fingers into my skin and clawed my back, urging me to fuck us both into the bed until we came. I ignored his attempts to spur me on until he sucked my tongue into his mouth, then nipped it with his sharp teeth.

If Xavier wanted a little rougher play, I would give it to him. I repositioned my knees then let myself have free rein with his pliable, willing body. My cockhead found his gland on every hard thrust home. Later, I'd think about why I referred to Xavier's body as home, but right then all I could think about was making his eyes roll back in his head from the sheer pleasure I gave him. I needed to make this moment count so he would remember it for the rest of his life, no matter what happened between us.

"B-B-Ben." Xavier stuttered my name as his eyes rolled back in his head, but I didn't stop to enjoy my victory. I fucked into him harder and deeper, knowing he'd be feeling me for days. "Oh hell!" His nails dug deeper into my skin, eliciting a snarling growl from me while my dick pistoned in and out of him. "Kiss me, please." Xavier's soft plea caught me off guard, but I gladly complied.

I pressed my lips against his, relishing the feel of the trembling, soft flesh beneath mine. The tenderness was my undoing. I reached between our bodies and began to stroke his dick, matching the pace of my thrusts, and it only took a few pulls before his hot release jetted out of his cock and shot all over my hand and his stomach.

The combination of the scent of his spent seed and his ass tightly squeezing my cock was more than I could take. I threw back my head and roared as my body ripped and splintered into a thousand pieces while the orgasm tore through my body, causing me to jerk and quake as I released deep inside Xavier. I lowered my head and locked my eyes with his while I rode out each wave of pleasure he gave me.

I opened myself up to him, letting Xavier see my vulnerability and how he impacted me. My chest felt raw with emotions I wouldn't express. It seemed like I saw the same emotions in Xavier's eyes, but I wouldn't allow myself to hope. Yet.

I lowered his ankles from my shoulders and pressed my body on top of his. I wanted—needed—to feel his lips on mine while I recovered from the overload of sensations. My body was so sensitive it almost burned, but hurting had never felt so good.

I pulled back and rubbed my hand through Xavier's shorter hair. "I forgot to tell you how much I like your haircut." I tugged on a few strands. "It's still long enough for me to pull when you work my cock over with your pierced tongue." I couldn't stop the smirk that followed my statement.

"I packed my tongue ring and brought it with me." Xavier traced my nose and lips with a finger, then his eyes met mine. "How much recovery time do you need?"

"Not much when you look at me like that," I answered honestly. "Shower with me?"

"Sounds like heaven." Xavier groaned and stretched his body beneath mine, reminding me that my semihard dick was still buried inside him.

I eased out of him and lowered myself down for one last kiss. I was cautiously optimistic that Xavier wouldn't kick me to the curb after our shower. He had asked about my recovery time, so surely that meant he planned to go at least one more round with me that night.

Meow.

Xavier and I jerked apart in surprise. Oliver sat on the bedside table, swishing his tail in apparent irritation. Fuck! We had forgotten to shut the door, and the Wrights' pervy cat had not only spied on us but had obviously found our performance lacking in some way.

"Out, Oliver," Xavier yelled, pointing to the door. Shockingly, the cat did as commanded. Xavier looked back at me with a sly grin. "Everybody is a damn critic these days."

"No doubt," I agreed. The bed shook as we laughed over the ridiculousness of the situation. "I gave you my best moves too."

"And I loved them," Xavier said. "I'm willing to be your test subject if you feel like you need more practice." His words reminded me of his first visit to my house when I'd offered to blow him as often as he liked to work on my own skills.

"Deal! Now seal it with a kiss."

Xavier laid himself over my body and kissed me with a passion that made my toes curl. We sealed the deal with several kisses that spilled over to our shower. Horny men, hot water, wet bodies, and the shower we were taking to clean up turned really, really dirty. We stayed there until the water went cold, then we dried off and climbed back into bed.

I wrapped my arms around Xavier and held him close. I had no clue what the next day would bring, and for once, I didn't care. Worrying about the future would deprive me of the beautiful moments I was sharing with Xavier. His breath fanned across my bare chest as he fell asleep in my arms.

It was everything I never knew I wanted until that moment.

CHAPTER
Twenty-Two

Xavier

THE MELODY RETURNED TO ME FULL FORCE WHILE I SLEPT SOUNDLY in Ben's arms. It started out as a dream like always, but it became so intense that it woke me and continued to play in my head until I got out of bed and went in search of my notebook. I sat in the living room with Oliver, who perched on the ottoman swishing his tail as if he was keeping time for me. I would've preferred to be in bed with Ben, but I had to record the music while it was so fresh in my mind.

It seemed like I wrote for hours, but in reality, it was only about thirty minutes. It had been so long since music had swept me away and kept me prisoner to its demand, and it felt unbelievably good. I was certain I was smiling like a complete goober as I made my way back upstairs to the room I was sharing with Ben.

I stood at the foot of the bed and stared at his sleeping form awash in the muted moonlight that snuck in past the minuscule spaces between the blinds. Ben was hugging my pillow as if he subconsciously knew I was gone and he missed me. The thought caused my heart to turn over in my chest, stutter to a stop, and finally beat again, albeit much faster than normal. I refused to think about why the sight of him missing me caused such internal conflict.

Enjoy the moment and quit looking for problems, I told myself. My brain instantly concocted a way that both Ben and I could enjoy the moment. I grabbed my tongue piercing off the dresser where I'd left it and put it in. I climbed back onto the bed and eased the covers down Ben's long body. He was lying on his side facing me and looked so peaceful that I almost felt guilty for waking him. Almost.

I gently pulled the pillow from between his arms and snuggled myself against him in its place. A happy sigh slid from him as he wrapped his strong arms around me. I tucked myself beneath his chin and began to tease and toy with the flesh on his neck, alternating nibbles, licks, and gentle sucking. Ben groaned softly, and I moved my mouth up to his strong jawline, following it until I reached his ear. Ben's arms wrapped around me even tighter when I began sucking his earlobe into my mouth.

"Xavier." His sleep-roughened voice saying my name caused my heart to summersault inside my chest. "Babe." That word and the reverent way he spoke it should've had me running for my life, but I couldn't muster the gumption to leave. Instead of running, it had me wanting to climb inside him and nestle up against his heart.

Ben's erection pressed against my stomach, demanding attention, but it would just have to wait. I wanted to take my time to learn every peak and valley of his stunning body. My good intentions were almost derailed when Ben slid his hand down the back of my boxers and began running his fingers up and down the crease of my ass.

Ben reached down with his free hand and pulled my thigh up so it lay over his hip, bringing our erections into direct contact. Our matching moans of ecstasy echoed around the moonlit room. Ben cupped my ass and pulled my hips toward him at the same time he thrust into me. It felt so good that I nearly forgot why I had started this seduction. I captured Ben's lips in a hot, lazy kiss that had my toes curling and my dick leaking. Ben suddenly pulled back from the kiss and captured my chin between his thumb and first finger.

"You put your piercing in." His eyes shone with delight at the discovery.

"I wanted to wake you up with a blow job, but I got a little sidetracked." I loved the way Ben's gray eyes turned lighter with lust, and they were nearly iridescent in the dimly lit room.

"Babe." There was that word again. "I might detonate at just the thought of you going down on me with those lips and using that tongue." Ben pressed his finger to my lips, and I sucked it into my mouth, rolling the metal ball around his fingertip just like I planned to do to his cock. I hollowed out my cheeks and sucked the digit hard. "Jesus, Xavier."

Lust rippled through his body, and it emboldened me to push him to his back so I could please him with my tongue like we both wanted. If there was one thing I knew at that moment, it was that I had to taste Ben on my tongue. I would not waste another second dwelling on my insecurities over my worthiness of his affection or my ability to handle emotional entanglements while recovering from drug addiction.

Ben worked my boxers down my ass and legs, and I kicked them off to the side. He fisted both our cocks in his large hand and jacked them slowly while our mouths met in a chaotic vortex of need. The feel of his cock gliding against mine was so sensual it had me on the brink of losing control and spilling into his hand. I released his lips and bit his pectoral muscle hard enough to pull a hiss out of him, but he released our cocks.

"I promise to make it up to you." I eluded his hands that kept trying to pull me back up and kissed the mark I'd made on his skin, then continued to learn every inch of muscle and sinew as I kissed my way down to his proud cock.

I made a deliberate show of sticking my tongue out as far as it would go so he could get a good look at what he'd been fantasizing about since the night of the stakeout. Just as slowly, I lined the metal ball up with the magic spot just beneath the head of his cock. I sucked Ben's crown inside my mouth and circled my tongue around so the ball massaged the spot just right.

"Fuck!" Ben's cry made me want to extract more lust-crazed sounds from him. I relaxed my throat muscles and slid his length all the way inside my mouth until my nose was pressed to his trimmed hair and my tongue teased the base of his cock. "Jesus, Xavier. Fuck… That's… Oh my God… So good."

I let his dick slide out of my mouth with a wet plop. "I'm just getting started." I lay flat on the bed between his sprawled legs. The super soft sheets teased my sensitive dick and I fought the urge to grind against them. "Reach behind you and grab the headboard and anchor yourself down so you don't float away." Ben grabbed two fistfuls of my hair instead. "That'll work too."

I worked his cock up and down, alternating from fast and hard to slow and sensual. Ben writhed beneath me, his every cry of pleasure ratcheting up my own desire. I found myself rubbing my erection against the bed beneath me at the same pace that I blew Ben. His strong body trembled, triggering a quake in my own. We were both on the cusp of orgasm, and the smallest touch would send us both over.

I palmed his firm balls and gave them a gentle tug. Ben raised his legs and placed his feet on my shoulders, thrusting his hips and fucking my mouth at the pace he wanted. His nails dug into my scalp as his excitement reached the precipice. One more pull of his balls and he tipped over the edge and filled my mouth with his earthy essence.

I came all over the sheets like a randy teenager the second his first shot splashed across my tongue. I bathed his softening dick until I was satisfied I had licked him clean. I looked up once I was finished and found his hot, intense eyes locked on me.

"Come here," he said huskily.

I climbed on top of him, and he held me against his chest. "Give me a second, and I'll return the favor," he whispered against my temple.

"Too late. I got too excited and made a mess all over the sheets." My ridiculous confession made me laugh in spite of the embarrassment.

"Damn, that's hot," Ben said, wrapping his arms tighter around me.

"It is?"

"Hell yeah, it's hot. You getting so worked up over exciting me that you came all over the bed is the hottest thing I've ever heard." Ben's hands lazily stroked my back up and down while he moved to get us into a more comfortable position. "Okay, I just found the wet spot with my leg, and it kind of takes the sexy out of it." Ben's laugh rumbled in his chest beneath my ear. It was a sound I wanted to get used to. "Do you happen to know where Chase keeps extra sheets?"

"Sure do. Gray sent me a text after the wedding and told me where I could find extra bed linens. You know, just in case."

"Smart ass."

Instead of getting up to change the sheets, I snuggled closer to Ben, letting the sound of his heartbeat and his warmth lull me back to sleep.

CHAPTER
Twenty-Three

Xavier

THE SMELL OF FRESH COFFEE AND SAUSAGE WOKE ME FROM A DEEP sleep, or it might have been the massive ball of orange fur that was standing on my back, massaging my bare shoulders with his paws. I gently rolled to my side, and Oliver sidled up and peered down at me. *Meow*. I scratched his ears, and Oliver closed his eyes, purring loudly.

"You're a handsome boy, Oliver." I laughed at myself for talking to the cat as I dug my fingers in just a little harder. Chase and Gray talked to Oliver like he was a person and often swore he knew what they were saying. I wasn't convinced, but I did know from the previous time I had house sat that he was a very smart animal. "You already know that, don't you, buddy?"

"Is it wrong that I'm completely jealous of the way you're stroking that cat's ears and his ego?" I jerked my head to look at the door and found Ben leaning against the frame wearing nothing but his briefs, watching me interact with the cat. "Breakfast is ready if you can pull yourself away from your furry friend."

"Oliver was waking me up for breakfast," I replied. "He's considerate like that and probably hoping I'll reward him with a piece of sausage."

"Turkey sausage," Ben corrected.

"Did you go out and buy groceries? How late is it?" I sat up and reached for my phone to check the time.

"It's only nine thirty, and the fridge is loaded with food, so I didn't have to go shopping. Gray left a note for you to help yourself." Ben straightened and stalked over to the bed. He looked like a powerful, sleek jungle cat on the trail of his favorite prey. I was his prey. Ben gently set Oliver aside and leaned over my body, capturing my mouth in a soft kiss. Ben pulled back just as I tried to take the embrace to the next level. He smirked as I chased after his mouth with mine. "I worked really hard on breakfast. Let's eat first, then you can kiss me as much as you want."

I reluctantly got out of bed, threw on a pair of shorts, and followed him downstairs to the eat-in kitchen. The table was already set with turkey sausage, crepes, fresh fruit, and coffee. My stomach rumbled at the delicious spread laid out before me.

"Yum! This looks amazing, Ben. I can't believe you went to all this trouble."

"It was no big deal. We both need to eat, so we might as well make it something nutritious and delicious." Ben gestured for me to have a seat at the table. "Let's dig in."

I sat and began to fill my plate. "This certainly looks delicious, but I'm not sold on the nutritious part."

"Ah, that's the trick," Ben said confidently. "There's always a way to make a healthier version of the foods you love. I replaced the pork sausage with turkey and exchanged the typical fattening crepe filling with honey-sweetened Greek yogurt, and now you have a meal that tastes great without all the extra fat, carbs, and guilt."

"Thank you." I found his gesture to be sweet and completely endearing.

"You're welcome." He pointed to my plate with his fork. "Dig in."

I wasted no more time and loaded up my plate with the mouthwatering food. We ate in silence for a few minutes before I worked up the courage to ask him a question that had been weighing on my mind since the night of the stakeout. "What exactly is the deal with your parents? You've talked about your unhappy childhood and dealing with obesity, then Bevan mentioned your parents are the reason both of you have avoided relationships and commitments."

Ben set his fork down, leaned back in his chair, and crossed his arms over his bare chest. I feared that I had stepped into territory I had no business visiting. I had the feeling Ben was the kind of guy who didn't mind shouldering everyone else's burdens but wouldn't ask the same in return. I was about to tell him to forget I had asked, but he began to talk.

"My parents, Daniel and Beverly, came from very wealthy families. Their marriage was practically arranged, and they've both been miserable since day one." I had the feeling Ben was glossing over a lot of it, but I was grateful he was opening up to me. "I don't know when their extramarital affairs actually began, but I can tell you that I learned about them when I was seven.

"I caught my mother kissing one of my father's associates at a dinner party at my house. Van and I were banned from coming downstairs when Dan and Bev had parties, but I wanted a book to read, so I snuck down to the library, which was connected to my father's home office. I heard some strange noises coming from the office, so I opened the door a crack and peeked inside. They had probably been doing a lot more than kissing, but I must've walked in toward the end so at least they were dressed." It was obvious from the bitter expression on Ben's face that this memory was particularly unpleasant and was still a cause for inner turmoil. I wanted to tell him to stop, but he continued talking.

"I had never seen my parents embrace, yet there was my mother wrapped in the arms of another man who was kissing her senseless. I was confused. I mean, what kid wouldn't be. And I ran and told my dad, who unfortunately was in the middle of talking to some guests." Ben looked at me with a wry look on his face. "I'm sure you can imagine how well that went over. Sort of like a lead balloon.

"Daniel was always quick on his feet, though. He gave me a condescending pat on the head and told the people in his group that I had read so many books that it was hard for me to tell reality from fantasy." Ben shook his head at the memory. "When I started to argue, he gripped the back of my neck and gave it a hard squeeze. I immediately shut up, of course, and went back to my room like he told me to." Ben sighed deeply as if he needed the break to summon the energy to tell the rest of the story.

"After the party, my parents fought so loud it woke me up. I heard them screaming at one another, then the sound of glass shattering. I was really scared, but I thought they might be hurt and need help. I creeped out into the hallway and looked through the bars of the wrought iron balustrade that wrapped around the entire second floor of our home." Ben stared into space as if he was reliving that moment.

"Ben, you don't have to tell me anything else." I reached across the table and covered his hand with mine. "I'm sorry I brought up these painful memories on such a beautiful morning. Please forgive me."

Ben shook his head, bringing himself out of his memories. "It's okay, Xavier." He flipped his hand over, linked our fingers, and continued the story. "Bev and Dan stood below me in the great room having the fight of the century. My father called my mother a whore for fucking around behind his back, and my mother countered, listing all the affairs my dad had had over the years. I had no idea what affairs were, but I could tell they were bad by the tone of their voices. My father asked my mother if I was even his son, and that was when shit got real. My mother charged at him with her fingers curled into claws. She scratched his face and hit him repeatedly." Ben ran his hands through his hair in agitation and his expression went vacant.

"Dan tried to deflect Bev's attack and repeatedly asked if I was his son. She told him yes each and every time, but he kept saying he didn't believe her, so she said she'd prove it with a DNA test. My father then yelled that it didn't matter what the test said because there was no way such an awkward, geeky kid could belong to him. My mother did nothing to defend me because she was still so angry her so-called honor was in doubt. The next thing I knew, Van wrapped me up in a tight hug, then wiped away my tears. He took me by the shoulders and told me not to pay attention to the two assholes downstairs. He told me they didn't deserve a kid like me and that I was better than both of them combined." Ben blinked his eyes and focused back on me once again. I was so happy he'd returned to me.

"Van is good people," I told him after I swallowed down the lump in my throat. "Jesus, I wish I had kept my mouth shut."

"Nonsense." Ben tugged on my hand until I leaned over the table and met him halfway for a brief kiss. "It's all in the past. Yes, my parents were—and still are—a negative influence in my life, but I've moved beyond it. I refuse to be jaded by their misery."

"What are your plans for the day?" I wasn't sure why I asked, except that I wasn't ready for our time together to come to an end.

"Um, just a bit of laundry. Do you have something in mind?"

The doorbell rang before I could answer his question. "Be right back," I tossed over my shoulder.

Bevan stood on the front porch looking drained and uncomfortable. "I tried calling your cell phone, but it went straight to voicemail. I stopped by your sister's house, and she told me I could find you here."

"I forgot to plug my phone in last night, and it must have died. I'm sorry you had to go to so much trouble. Come on in." I stepped aside so he could enter. Dread settled in the pit of my stomach at Van's stiff posture and serious expression. I sensed he had bad news for me, and I was instantly worried something horrible had happened to Deacon.

"I see Ben is also here, and I'm not sure if you want me to…"

"Hey, Van. What are you doing here?" Ben had snuck up behind me like he was known to do.

"I came to talk to Xavier, but I'm thinking now isn't a good time."

"Xavier?" Ben looked between us and then must have remembered the conversation from the stakeout when I had asked Bevan if he could help me locate my friend. I had never told Ben I had hired his brother to track

Deacon down and to help with my contract. Suddenly, it felt like I had gone behind his back, which was ridiculous.

"I hired Bevan to look for Deacon and to assist me with the contract like you recommended. He has already handled the latter, so I'm guessing he's here about the former." I looked at Bevan, and he nodded, indicating I was correct. "Whatever you have to say can be said in front of Ben. I have nothing to hide."

Ben placed a comforting hand on my shoulder because it was obvious Bevan was uncomfortable with the news he had to deliver and hesitant to do so in front of Ben. If something bad had happened to Deacon, I definitely wanted Ben to be there with me.

"Come in," I told Bevan again.

He entered the house reluctantly but sniffed the air appreciatively. "Do I smell coffee?"

"You do," I answered. "Come into the kitchen, and I'll pour you a cup. Are you hungry? Ben made a fantastic breakfast, and there's plenty." I was nervous, and I rambled when I got nervous. I looked behind me and saw the St. Claire brothers exchange a look and a half smile. It seemed they found my rambling amusing, but I didn't hold that against them. "How do you take your coffee?"

"Black like Ben's undies," Bevan answered. He raised a brow at Ben's nearly nude body but didn't say anything else.

I poured him a cup of coffee, and we all settled around the table. Bevan declined food, and I was too nervous to continue eating. I sat quietly waiting for Bevan to tell me what he had learned, and each second seemed like an eternity.

"Do you know anything about Deacon Bradley's life before he came to work as security for the band?"

"I honestly don't," I replied. "Deacon was very quiet and private. He didn't have a whole lot to say."

"What kinds of things did you talk about?" Bevan asked. "You said you were friends, and friends usually confide in one another. How close are we talking?"

I blew out a frustrated breath because I didn't understand his line of questioning. It seemed like Bevan was accusing me of something, and it made me very uncomfortable. "We chatted about music and sports when we spoke at all. I considered him my friend not because of the conversations we had but because of the way he shielded me from Damien when he was at his ugliest. I don't understand what information you're trying to get out of me, Bevan. I told you everything I knew about Deacon when I hired you to help me find him. Has something bad happened to him?"

"The Deacon Bradley you know doesn't exist."

I felt like Bevan was speaking in riddles. "I don't understand."

"Van, what's with all the subterfuge? Just tell Xavier what he needs to know," Ben demanded, sounding fed up and frustrated.

"Deacon Bradley is really Mark Bradley, a highly decorated sniper in the Marine Corps. His men gave him the nickname Deacon because his words were like gospel when going into battle. After he retired from the corps, he started working for a private security company, which is how he met you, Xavier." Bevan's deep sigh and expression told me I wasn't going to like what else he had to say. "He is currently wanted for questioning by the LAPD in a murder investigation."

"Murder? Holy shit!" I was stunned. *Deacon was suspected of killing someone?* I just couldn't wrap my head around it.

"Yes, murder. His bloody fingerprints were found all over the crime scene. He's vanished without a trace, and I'm not sure if he had help from the military because they don't want the reputation of their decorated war hero tarnished or if he's just gone off the grid."

This was too much for me to take in. I must have looked like a fish with my mouth gaping open then closing as I tried to formulate words. My brain was firing too many questions at once, threatening to short-circuit and blow a fuse. I could almost smell the smoke. Ben reached over, took my hand, and gave it a squeeze to remind me of his presence. I clung to it like a lifeline.

"I was unable to dig deeper to get more information about him be-cause I don't have the proper security clearance. Yes, I could've obtained the information, but I wouldn't be able to sleep at night for fear someone would slit my throat in my sleep." Bevan paused again, and I braced myself. "There's more."

"Of course there is." It wasn't fair that I used such a sarcastic tone with Bevan. He wasn't my enemy, and he'd only done what I had asked him to do. "Sorry, Bevan."

"Deacon is suspected of killing Erik Schafnitz, who you know as Damien Diamond."

"Oh my God." A bomb detonated in my brain and all my blood had leached from my body, leaving me cold to the bone. Damien was dead and no one had told me? It was a testament to how far the relationship with my bandmates had deteriorated. I was sadder about that demise than I was of my ex-boyfriend's.

"H-h-how did it happen?" I asked.

"Erik Schafnitz a.k.a. Damien Diamond was brutally beaten before he was shot point blank. The authorities think Deacon Bradley killed him after he attacked you."

I inhaled so fast that I choked. Bevan got up and filled a glass of water for me while Ben reached over and rubbed my back in soothing circles while I worked through my coughing fit. I sipped the cold water for a few minutes to soothe my raw throat.

"Jesus, Bevan, try for some fucking tact next time!" Ben's outrage on my behalf helped to settle my shattered mind.

"The perpetrator was obviously looking for something because the entire apartment had been tossed, and Deacon's fingerprints were everywhere. The police found evidence that Damien had been taking pictures of people in compromising situations and using them as blackmail, so the suspect pool is very large, but Deacon is the only one directly tied to the crime scene."

Damien was dead. Deacon had murdered him because of me. If I had been stronger and had stayed away from LA, then Damien would be alive, and Deacon wouldn't have his blood on his hands. I closed my eyes to block out the pitying looks on Bevan's and Ben's faces. My lungs started to seize up as panic gripped me. I let go of Ben's hand and wrapped my arms around myself and began to rock back and forth.

"My fault. All of it." I didn't recognize the desolate voice as my own. "Damien was an absolute slime, but nobody deserves to die like that. Deacon is a g-good man, and I've ruined his life." The St. Claires began speaking at the same time, trying to calm me down and assure me that none of it was my fault, but I knew better. I had done this. I might as well have pulled the trigger myself.

"Xavier, this isn't your fault. To be honest, it was only a matter of time before someone shot Erik. He was bound to pick the wrong person to black-mail and pay the ultimate price."

"Van." Ben practically growled his brother's name before he focused his attention back on me. "Babe, look at me, please. Don't do this to yourself, Xavier." I heard the fear in his voice that I might relapse, and he had every right to be fearful. I had never wanted to get high as much as I did right then.

"I, uh, I just need some time to myself to process everything you told me." I rose from my seat without looking at either of them. "I'm just going to change my clothes and go for a run. It always helps clear my head." I gripped my hands together so they couldn't see how badly they were shaking.

"I'll go with you," Ben offered.

"No!" I finally looked at Ben and saw how my harsh rejection had hurt him. I softened my voice and said, "Thank you for the offer, but I really need to be by myself while I work this out. You just go ahead with whatever plans you had, and I'll call you later."

I didn't wait around for his response. I ran up the stairs, changed into my running gear, and left the house without a goodbye to either of them. I had hoped I could outrun my demons like I had in the past, but it was wish-ful thinking. Guilt, regret, and self-loathing followed me and nipped at my heels, threatening to suck me into a dark abyss of despair I knew I'd never recover from.

CHAPTER
Twenty-Four

Ben

I SAT IN THE KITCHEN IN A STUNNED STUPOR AND STARED AT MY brother. I wondered if I looked as utterly helpless as I felt.

"What are you going to do?" Bevan had asked me.

I shrugged as if I didn't have a care in the world. "What can I do but wait for him to call me?"

"That's it?" Bevan seemed disappointed in my answer, but I didn't know what else he expected.

"That's it," I said.

But seven long and torturous days passed with no word from Xavier. I had sent him two texts and left one voicemail. All of them went unanswered. On the seventh day, I realized that whatever I had hoped for between us would never happen. The tentative relationship we had started to build was over. I just hoped at some point I could look back on the one special night we'd shared with fond memories and not the resentment that had begun to grow.

I understood that Xavier needed time to regroup and come to terms with what he had learned about his ex-manager and his friend. I wasn't an insensitive bastard who only cared about myself, but what I couldn't comprehend was the selfish behavior that made Xavier think it was okay to ignore me when it was so obvious in my messages that I was worried about him. How freaking hard would it have been to send me one short text to let me know he was okay?

None of it mattered anymore. I was done. Relationships weren't for the St. Claires. I'd known it my entire life, but when it came to Xavier, I wanted to believe differently. My family was only good at fucking, and it was time I remembered that and gave up my pie-in-the-sky hopes that I'd be any different.

Needless to say, I was in a really shitty mood when I picked Beverly up for the charity dinner like the dutiful son I was, even though she neither wanted nor deserved me. She actually seemed glad to see me, which made me suspicious right from the start. Beverly didn't care about anything but herself, therefore my required presence meant she was up to something. I couldn't dig up the energy to care at that particular moment. I tuned her out when she started up a steady stream of mindless chatter until we arrived at the convention center.

"Your morose attitude is both unwelcome and intolerable, Bennett." Beverly's narrowed eyes and pinched mouth hardly registered on my give-a-shit meter. "Snap out of your mood! It's no wonder you haven't landed a husband. Your people can marry in every state now. What's your holdup?"

"My people, Mother? Do you have any idea how offensive that statement is?"

"Don't be so sensitive, Bennett. You were always too emotional. It was the reason you got so fat." Her tone was both superior and dismissive, and it grated on my last damn nerve.

Why was I there? Why did I even bother? I was no longer a sad, lonely little boy who only wanted to be loved by his parents. I was a grown man capable of choosing who I let into my life, and for the life of me I couldn't figure out why I still tolerated my parents and their poison.

"Let's just get this over with," I said tersely, my tone going right over her head.

I escorted Beverly toward a person with a clipboard who could validate our tickets. Once inside the event, she began looking around and prattling quietly about this couple and that couple, whispering all about their personal lives as if I gave a shit.

"Oh, there he is." Beverly's excited voice made the hair on the back of my neck stand up. She dug her claws into my bicep and practically dragged me over to where a group of men stood. "Jagger," she exclaimed excitedly. I about crapped my pants when JJ turned around and smirked in my direction. I had forgotten his first name was Jagger until my mom said it like they were the best of friends.

"Ben," JJ said smoothly. "How's life been treating you?"

"Not bad. How about you?"

"Can't complain," JJ replied.

"Wait!" Beverly exclaimed. "You two already know each other?" My mother sounded gleeful as she directed her appraising gaze at JJ. "I didn't know you'd had the pleasure of meeting Bennett."

"I've not had all the pleasure he has to offer yet, but we have been acquaintances for over a year." I didn't miss how JJ's voice lowered several sexy notches when he mentioned pleasure.

"Well," Beverly said with a giggle, "I'll just let you two talk."

"What was all that about?" JJ asked me as soon as Beverly walked away.

"It's her pitiful attempt at matchmaking."

"Me? Why? I'd make a horrible husband. I couldn't be faithful if you paid me. I'd gladly fuck you, though." I watched as JJ's face went from shocked that my mom would think he was husband material to leering at the thought of a quick, dirty screw.

"She's not concerned about your fidelity or if you'd be a good husband to me. It's all about what you could do for Beverly's reputation." I chose to ignore his comment about fucking.

"So, how are things with you and the rocker?" JJ asked, changing the subject. Normally, I would've been grateful, but we jumped from one fire into another. "It looked like the two of you were all hot and heavy at the wedding reception. The way you moved together was like watching two men having sex with their clothes on. It was pretty hot."

His comment rubbed an already raw nerve. I'd had all I could take from people. "I'm surprised you noticed with all the drinking you were doing. Must've been pure misery watching the man you love marry someone else." JJ flinched, and I immediately regretted the hateful words. How would I feel if Xavier started dating someone else and all I could do was watch him move on without me? "Sorry, man. That was a low blow, and you didn't deserve it. Fuck! I can't stand myself right now."

JJ slapped me on the shoulder and chuckled. "Don't waste your time worrying about my nonexistent feelings, Ben. You'd be better off worrying about that." He nodded to something behind me, and I turned to follow his line of sight.

Xavier was at the benefit, and it was obvious he'd come with Miller Bexler, Gray's best friend and JJ's manwhore equal. I watched in dazed silence as Miller handed Xavier a bottle of water. I was overwhelmed with jealousy and disillusionment so fierce that it eviscerated me, leaving me in a bloody heap of heartbreak on the ground. *Fuck me!* Apparently, I wasn't over his abrupt exit from my life. One look at him and I recalled every lonely minute while I'd waited for one simple word from him.

"That should be your focus, buddy. Miller has wanted that guy from the moment he laid eyes on him. What Miller wants, he gets. Always."

I was fully aware of Miller's persuasiveness, but I chose to keep that tidbit to myself. I thought I detected a tiny hint of bitterness in JJ's voice, but I was too interested in self-survival to pay him much attention. "It's none of my business." It hurt to speak those words, but they were true. Xavier had chosen to exclude me from his life, and there wasn't a damn thing I could do about it, except make a quick exit before he realized I was there. I refused to cause a scene and embarrass myself. I left JJ standing there staring at the two handsome men across the room and went in search of my mother. I found her gossiping with the nest of pit vipers she called her friends.

"Mother, I'm leaving. You'll need to call your driver for a ride home." My goodbye was abrupt, and I offered no explanation. She followed after me, bitching about my poor attitude, lack of respect, and how I had once again embarrassed her with my behavior.

"Are you listening to me, Bennett?" she snarled as we reached the door.

"I've heard every hateful thing you've said to me since the day I was born. I'm going to do us both a favor and permanently remove myself from your life and my father's. Lose my number, Beverly." I left her gawping at the door.

It felt liberating to be free of her. I ripped my tie off as I made my way to my car. My blood pulsed and throbbed in my veins, and I had two choices: I could go find a man to screw or I could go home and box. I chose the latter, but I refused to acknowledge that Xavier played a role in my choice.

I made it across town in record time and was lucky I didn't get pulled over. I changed into a loose pair of shorts and headed to my garage where I kept my exercise equipment and punching bag. I tuned my radio to a heavy rock station, grabbed my jump rope off the hook, and began my warm-up routine of stretching and jumping rope. Once finished, I taped up my hands and set to work on my arms and shoulders with jabs, crosses, hooks, and uppercuts. I went through the circuit three times before moving on to my legs with front kicks, side kicks, and roundhouses.

I was dripping with sweat by the time I was finished, but I was too freaking exhausted to think about my misery, which was my intended goal. I tidied up my space and shut off my radio, and that was when I saw the ten texts and five missed calls from Xavier. I told myself to delete his messages without reading them, but I was a damn glutton for punishment.

JJ said you saw me with Miller at the benefit. I'd like to explain. Can I call you?

Ben, I'm sorry I didn't return your calls or texts last week. I wasn't ready to talk yet. I am now.

Come on, Ben. Talk to me!

I'm sorry about the way I treated you. Truly!

All the texts followed the same pattern of apologizing or pleading until I got to the final one.

OPEN YOUR DAMN DOOR!

CHAPTER
Twenty-Five

Xavier

MY FIRST REACTION WHEN I SAW BEN STANDING IN HIS DOORWAY dripping with sweat was unbridled lust. I wanted to catch the salty rivulet of sweat that was making a fast path down to the elastic waistband of his shorts. Of course, I noticed he was once again without underwear, and that did nothing to slake my thirst for him. Then I looked into his eyes and saw the raw hurt and disappointment, and I was ashamed because I had put it there.

"You don't owe me an explanation of where you were or who you were with." But the betrayal in his gaze said differently.

"Chase and Gray bought the tickets before they picked a wedding date. They'd forgotten about it until the tickets arrived in the mail. They asked Miller and me to go in their place, and we agreed to go. Separately. I wouldn't…"

"Why not? He's exactly what you need. Sexual relief without any emotional entanglement." There was so much hurt in Ben's voice, and it made my stomach ache.

"I thought you said it was overrated?" I asked. *Was I too late? Had I pushed him too far?* God, I hoped not, but I was scared I had ruined something full of promise and hope that had been building between us, but I wasn't giving up without trying.

"I was mistaken." Ben was kind enough to leave out the *because of you* part, but I knew I was the source behind the reversal of his opinion. Ben blew out a frustrated breath. "Are you okay, Xavier? That's all I needed to hear from you last week."

"I'm getting there." I ran a hand through my hair while I worked up the courage to ask for something I had no right to. "Can I please come in?" I saw the hesitation and wariness in his beautiful gray eyes before he stepped aside to allow me to pass.

"I'm going to take a quick shower, so go ahead and make yourself comfortable. There are plenty of soft drinks and juice in the refrigerator."

"Thank you," I replied to his retreating back.

I looked at Ben's vinyl record collection while he showered upstairs. I closed my eyes and wished I could curl up on his couch and burrow into him while we listened to albums. God, I missed him so fucking much, but I wasn't sure I had the right to say that to him.

Ben returned several minutes later and situated himself in the chair across from me instead of sitting beside me on the couch. The few feet between us seemed like an unsurmountable chasm made worse by the wall Ben had erected while he was upstairs. Damn if I didn't want to kick that wall down and crawl into his lap where I belonged. I wasn't sure where to start, so I chose to go with brutal honesty.

"This has been the hardest seven days of my life. The urge to use was the strongest I've faced since I quit. At one point, I got into my car and went to a club so I could find a dealer and buy some E. I sat in the parking lot and fought the biggest battle of my life, Ben, but I won in the end. I drove back home and called the Narcotics Anonymous hotline and talked to a counselor because I can't do this alone. I went to three meetings in seven days, and I'm feeling stronger now, but it will always be a battle for me." Ben's expressionless face told me nothing about how he was feeling. I took a deep breath for courage and soldiered on. No guts, no glory.

"I've missed you so damn much, Ben. There wasn't a day that passed that I didn't want to call you to hear your voice and let you assure me that everything would be okay. I wanted to lay my head on your broad shoulders and let you help me forget that my ex-boyfriend had been killed. I wanted you to tell me it was okay that I wasn't sad about Damien's death. I hurt you and I'm so sorry." Ben made a scoffing sound like he wasn't hurt. "I *did* hurt you, and I am sorry."

"What do you want from me, Xavier?" he asked. I wasn't the only one going straight to the crux of the problem.

"Right now or long-term?"

"Both. I made a really big move tonight, saying goodbye to my parents and my toxic relationship with them. I also learned this past week that I will no longer pursue a man who doesn't want my attention. I'm not the kind of guy who wants or needs a challenge in his personal life. I'm not asking for a declaration of your affections, Xavier, but I need to know what you want for us now and down the road. If you just want to be friends, then I will do that for you. I will find a way to push the crazy chemistry and my feelings aside and focus on being your friend. I can't be your fuck buddy and keep my heart intact, though." His honesty and vulnerability gave me the courage to be the same for him.

"Right now, I want to curl up with you on your couch and snuggle while we listen to some of the amazing records in your collection. Later, if you'll have me, I'd like to spend the night in your arms and wake up to your face in the morning." I took a shaky breath before I continued. "My long-term goal is to earn your trust again and give in to my heart when it screams at me to hold on to you and never let go."

Ben swallowed audibly. "I've missed you, Xavier. My world felt dull and out of focus without you in it."

He stood up and walked to me. I rose to my feet and Ben immediately wrapped his arms around me, holding on as if I were the most precious thing in the world to him. It felt like coming home. We stayed that way for several minutes, just breathing each other in.

"Don't disappear on me again, Xavier." Ben ran his nose along the outer shell of my ear, making me shiver. "My heart can't take it."

"I want to be the one you finally give your heart to for safekeeping, Ben."

"You terrify me." He placed a soft kiss on my lips. "Pick out the music, and I'll grab us some drinks."

Snuggling on the couch led to slow dancing, which turned into lazy kisses. The caresses got steamy as we slowly peeled off each other's clothes and tossed them on the couch. Our soft sighs soon turned into hungry kisses that threatened to scorch us both.

"I want to lay you down on my bed and love you, Xavier. Then I want you to ride me slowly and drive me wild with your hips. Damn, I've imagined nothing else since I saw you perform at Bottoms Up." Ben cupped my face in his strong hands. "I'm brave enough to give you all that I am, but are you brave enough to accept it?"

"Yes," I whispered through tears.

We showed each other how we felt with our bodies when words weren't enough. Ben laid me down and loved me so slowly, never letting his adoring gaze drift from mine. Then I rolled him over and rode him with everything I had. Ben caressed my body as I moved my hips to the beat of the song like I had at the bar. When Ben got close, I reached behind me and squeezed his balls to stop him from coming. I knew it would make his orgasm even more powerful when he finally came. I rode him to the edge and held him back time after time, ignoring his pleas to let him come. He was a lot stronger than me and could have easily rolled me over and fucked me into the mattress, but he loved receiving the sensual torture as much as I loved doling it out.

We came together, and it was magnificent, poignant, and loud, then we collapsed in a heap in the middle of his bed and held each other tight.

Ben rubbed his hand up and down my back soothingly while I nuzzled my nose against his chest. I wanted to stay just like that for the rest of my life, but Ben's growling stomach negated that idea.

"Let's go downstairs, and *I* will cook for *you* this time," I told him.

"You cook?"

I narrowed my eyes. Was that surprise I detected? "A little, but nothing near your level."

"I haven't eaten since breakfast, and I'm starving. I'd probably eat cardboard at this point."

"Good to know," I said with a chuckle.

We didn't bother getting dressed before we walked downstairs to his kitchen. I opened the refrigerator to see what I had to work with. Ben came up behind me as I was bending over to check his crisper drawer and began to caress my ass and nibble on the back of my neck.

"I changed my mind about food," he said huskily. "The only thing I want to eat is your…"

"Jesus Christ," a deep voice growled. "Haven't you two had enough of each other yet?"

The unexpected presence of a third person startled the hell out of us both causing us to jump and spin around. Ben pushed me behind him in a protective move, but not before I got a look at the man who stood in the kitchen, not that I needed to see him to know who our intruder was.

"Hi, Deac," I said from behind Ben. I realized Ben was naked and reached around with both hands to shield his cock and balls from Deacon's view. "A simple phone call would have sufficed."

Maybe I should have been afraid that Deacon was in Ben's house, after all he was wanted by the police for questioning in the murder of my ex-boyfriend, but even though I didn't know Deacon well, I knew down to the marrow of my bones that this man was not a ruthless killer. In my heart, I knew there was a lot more to the story than the black-and-white report Bevan had received, and I was glad I was getting the opportunity to hear Deac out and ask the questions that had been floating around in my mind since I'd heard the news.

CHAPTER
Twenty-Six

Ben

I LOOKED DOWN AT XAVIER'S HANDS SHIELDING MY MAN PARTS FROM Deacon's eyes. It thrilled me that Xavier didn't want anyone seeing my cock and balls but him. The big man standing in my house was intimidating, but he didn't have a crazed look in his eye like he was about to take a knife to my nuts. However, he cared enough about Xavier to potentially kill for him, and that alone had me a bit on edge. "Babe, you might want to keep still because your hand on my dick has the same outcome every time, unless you want to give your friend a show."

Deacon grinned good-naturedly, and I relaxed. "I just came to talk. It was bad enough listening to you torture the big guy, Xavier. I didn't know you had such a mean streak."

Xavier pressed his forehead between my shoulder blades and groaned.

I wasn't embarrassed about begging to come. It had been so sexy watching Xavier ride me slowly and taking control of our pleasure.

"No one forced you to listen to us having sex," I pointed out dryly. "Why don't Xavier and I get dressed, then you guys can talk."

"You want me to hide my eyes?" Deacon had a sarcastic sense of humor. I liked it.

"You go into the living room and wait while we go upstairs," Xavier said.

"Fine." Deacon huffed teasingly and exited the kitchen.

"I'm going to stay up here to let you guys have some privacy," I told Xavier once we were in my room. I pulled a pair of sweats out of my drawer and walked them over to him.

Xavier watched me closely as if that wasn't the reaction he expected. I had to remind myself that he'd spent a year or longer in a very abusive relationship. "You can come down, Ben. I have no secrets from—"

I cut him off with a soft kiss. I squatted down and held the sweats out for Xavier to step into, then I slowly pulled them up his legs. I kissed both of his leanly muscled thighs before covering them. I rose to my feet and tied the strings at his waist before rolling the waistband a few times to keep them up.

"Can I borrow a shirt too?"

"No."

"No?" he asked incredulously.

I lowered my mouth and sucked the skin directly above his heart into my mouth. I used my teeth, tongue, and lips to mark him as mine. Xavier ran his fingers through my hair and made a soft mewling sound in the back of his throat. I released his skin with a wet plop and licked over the red mark to sooth the angry-looking flesh. I leaned back to check my handiwork.

"One day, this heart will be mine, and I want him to know it."

Xavier affectionately traced my love bite with his finger and then pulled me down for a sweet kiss, which turned hot pretty quickly. We were breathing harshly into one another's mouths, and our hands began to roam.

"Both of you get down here already," Deacon hollered from the bottom of the stairs. "I have limited time and want to speak to both of you at once. You guys can kiss and fuck *after* I leave."

I was totally confused about why Deacon wanted to include me in the conversation, but the pleading look on Xavier's face won out. We finished dressing and headed down to the living room hand in hand. I sat on my cozy couch and Xavier leaned into me, so I wrapped my arms around him. It should have felt awkward with the could-be killer sitting on the loveseat across from us, but I had Xavier in my arms, and that made everything right.

"Where do you want me to begin?" Deacon's voice was calm, certain, and controlled. I understood why he'd earned his nickname.

"I'd like to go back to what happened to you after I left LA the first time, but you said you were in a hurry," Xavier replied, equally calm. *Shouldn't one of us be freaking out?*

"About that," Deacon said with an ornery smile, "I just said that to get you guys down here." Deacon leaned forward and placed his elbows on his knees. His face became serious as did his voice when he said, "I did not kill Damien, so let's just get that out of the way. After I leave here, I'm boarding a plane for LA and turning myself over to the authorities. I have absolutely nothing to hide, Xavier. I'll tell you what happened the night Damien died, and if we still have time, we can work our way backward, okay?" Xavier and I nodded in unison. "I got a voicemail from Pax about what Damien had done to you, and yes, I went to his home to beat the motherfucking shit out of him, but I promise I *did not* kill him. I was the one who tossed his place because I was looking for the shit he had on you and the rest of the band." Deacon took a deep breath and scrubbed his hands over his face.

"What shit?" Xavier asked.

"I saw evidence of his blackmail scheme on his coffee table and figured he had similar documents on you and the rest of the band. I tossed his shithole apartment until I found what I was looking for, then I got the hell out of there. I destroyed every photo, Xavier, so you don't have to worry about any of this getting traced back to you." Deacon leaned back in his seat, looking relieved to have told us his account of the night Damien had been killed.

Xavier and I sat quietly for a few moments, letting everything sink in. I can't say for sure what Xavier was thinking, but his body tensed and I figured it had to do with whatever Deacon had found and later destroyed. I ran my hand up and down his back, giving Xavier comfort as he worked things out in his head.

"What did Damien have on me, Deac?" Xavier broke the silence, and the shame I heard in his voice had all my protective instincts rising to the surface.

On one hand, Xavier had the right to know what Deacon had found, but I was afraid it would set him back. He'd come so damn far in his recovery, and I didn't want anything to jeopardize it, not even for something he was entitled to know. My eyes locked on Deacon's and what I saw there said he would willingly take that information to the grave with him. Xavier must have seen the truth too because he let out a frustrated sigh.

"I have the right to know," he said. "I can handle it. I'm much stronger now, and knowledge is power. I promise you both that I won't let this cause a setback." I heard the sincerity along with the strength in Xavier's voice. "Please, Deac."

Deacon took a deep breath, then nodded. I held Xavier tighter against my side to soften the blow. "It appeared he had taken intimate photographs of you while you were too stoned to care. He had similar photos of your bandmates along with some arrest records and evidence that two of them were in debt up to their eyeballs with a loan shark." I saw Deacon trying to implore Xavier with his eyes to not let this hurt his recovery. "Damien Diamond was a bad dude, Xavier. I won't say his ending was justified—because that was a prison sentence, not being shot in cold blood in his home—but I'm not sorry he's gone. Life doesn't always give us what we deserve, but we have to take the hand we're dealt and make the best of it." Deacon's voice sounded choked with emotion, and he cleared his throat before continuing. "You've been given a second chance with a good man, and you should run with it. Don't look back on your time in LA as anything other than a life lesson. Don't let one man's rottenness eat away at your happiness."

"Deac." Xavier sounded equally emotional. "I don't know how to feel right now or even what to say, except thank you for looking out for me. Again." Xavier looked down at his lap, and his voice was reduced to barely a whisper when he said, "I thought you were angry with me when I went back to LA. You wouldn't return my calls, and I was worried about you. What happened to you after Damien fired you? Were you okay?" I leaned over and kissed Xavier's temple to remind him I was there and would be whenever and however he needed me. He looked up at me and gave me an appreciative smile.

"Xavier, I was never angry with you for returning to LA." Deacon's voice was soft yet firm. "I took a job working private security for Heston's CEO, Mitch Heston. I've known him since we were kids, and it felt like fate when he called me out of the blue looking to hire me for his security team. Everything worked out well for me. I'm sorry if I gave you the impression that I was mad at you. I knew Damien would make your life miserable if he found out we'd kept in contact, even though we were never more than friends, so I stayed away." I heard the regret in Deacon's voice and wondered if he might be blaming himself for Xavier's downward spiral.

"I'm glad to know Damien didn't destroy your life like he threatened to, but I didn't know about your badass military career, or I would've laughed at him with you." Xavier was trying to lighten the mood so Deacon could see he was well and truly okay.

"Skills that include breaking and entering," I added wryly.

"I didn't *break* anything. I just entered," Deacon corrected. He looked down at his large watch with a grimace. "I seriously need to head to the airport to catch my plane." All three of us stood up at the same time.

"Won't you be arrested at the airport?" I asked.

"I'm just a person of interest at this point, and a warrant hasn't been issued for my arrest," Deacon explained. "I made arrangements through my lawyer to turn myself in, making it very clear I have nothing to hide. I will confess to beating the shit out of Damien but nothing more. They won't know about your photos, Xavier."

"Thanks, Deac." Xavier gave him a brief hug, and I shook his hand before we walked him to the door. "Stay in touch, okay?"

"Sure thing," the big man agreed. "You guys can go back to your regularly scheduled screwing now," he said, mimicking the recorded voice that followed an emergency broadcast. He gave us a small wave and disappeared into the dark night.

I shut the door, and we just stood there in silence for a few minutes. My earlier thoughts of food disappeared under the weight of all the information I had learned from Deacon. The guy had gone to a lot of trouble to tell Xavier he was okay, innocent of a crime, and would be turning himself in. He could have easily done that over the phone. It was obvious to me that Deacon truly cared about Xavier's well-being, and perhaps he needed to see for himself that Xavier was doing okay. He probably wanted to size me up and judge my worthiness, and that might be why he'd insisted I join the conversation. I reached out and pulled Xavier into my arms, holding him tight against my chest.

"Let me fix you something to eat, and we'll head up to bed. I'm ready to be held in your arms all night long." His hot breath against my neck stirred up a different kind of hunger—one farther south than my stomach.

"Let's just skip the food and go straight to bed," I replied huskily. "Morning will be here in just a few hours, and we'll go out for breakfast."

"Can we go to Spanky's, or is that too unhealthy for you?" I didn't miss the hopefulness in his voice.

"I've missed you so much, and I'd love to treat you to Spanky's. On one condition."

Xavier pulled back and looked at me suspiciously. "What?"

"You agree to come to my softball game tomorrow afternoon." I wanted everyone to see Xavier belonged to me and I belonged to him.

"I'll agree to go to your game. On one condition," he countered with a quirky smile.

"You're already getting Spanky's pancakes. What more do you want?" I was so happy to see the carefree smile on his face and the sparkle in his eyes that I would've agreed to anything.

"You come to family dinner with me at Gram's tomorrow night. I'd like to introduce you to my family as my boyfriend." He cocked his brow playfully.

"Deal." We sealed our negotiations with a kiss, then headed up to bed.

"How are you feeling?" I asked once he was snuggled against my chest under the covers.

Xavier cuddled closer and sighed. "Blissful. You feel so perfect, Ben."

"We feel perfect," I corrected. I blinked my eyes a few times, trying to stay awake. I had my guy back where I wanted him, and I didn't want to miss a minute. Xavier placed his hand over my heart, and I started to tell him my heart belonged to him, but his soft even breaths against my chest told me he had already fallen asleep. I whispered the words to him anyway and smiled when he burrowed even closer to me under the blankets. His heart had heard me, and that was good enough for now. I closed my eyes and let myself fall into a deep, much-needed sleep, content that all was finally right in my world.

It amazed me how natural it felt to hold Xavier's hand in public, give him a victory kiss after the game, and use the word boyfriend when I introduced him to my teammates. I was thirty years old and finally had my first boyfriend.

Even more amazing was the hand job Xavier had given me on the drive back to my house. I knew he was up to no good when he asked me to leave my cup on after the game. I could tell he wanted to be the one to remove it, but I wasn't expecting him to do it while I was driving the damn car. But I didn't try to stop him when he unbuckled my baseball pants, reached his hand inside, and pulled my cup out of my jock strap and tossed it into the back seat. I could've asked Xavier to wait when he pushed my jersey up and out of the way, but nah. I begged and pleaded all right, but it wasn't for him to stop. It was a miracle we made it back to my house alive and in one piece, especially when he started licking my release off his fingers before wiping off my stomach with a towel from my bag.

"What are we going to do about that?" I asked, pointing to Xavier's erection when I put my car in park in my driveway.

"I plan to bury it in your ass while you're still wearing your jock strap."

Goose bumps dotted my skin and a tremor skipped down my spine. "Can we at least go inside so we have more room?" I spotted Mrs. Hernandez loitering on her porch like she was waiting for me. "And privacy?" I nodded in her direction and made sure Xavier was aware of her presence.

Xavier untucked his T-shirt, trying to cover up his excitement the best he could. I reached for his hand once we both exited the car and rounded the hood. The devilish look in his eyes promised that I was in for a treat.

"Bennett, why didn't you just tell me you were gay?" Mrs. H had her hands on her hips and a wry smile on her face as she yelled across the yard. "You could've saved us both the embarrassment of me trying to foist my granddaughter off on you." Mrs. Hernandez looked Xavier up and down, then smiled at me. "He's smoking hot. Don't strain yourself." She gave us a wink and went back inside her house.

Xavier was on me the minute my front door was closed and locked. "Don't you want me to take a shower first? I could put on a clean jock for you. I have a variety of colors."

"No. Right here. Right now." Xavier fished a condom and a packet of lube from his wallet. *Whoa! Someone was prepared.* "I've been planning this since I watched you get dressed before the game. I'm going to take you right there on the stairs."

"Those?" I pointed my thumb over my shoulder. I was amazed I could even speak at that point. I started stripping out of my sweaty uniform until only my jock strap remained. I walked over to the staircase, bent over, and braced my hands on a step. I eagerly offered up my ass to Xavier and couldn't wait to experience my personal stairway to heaven. "I'm all yours, baby."

CHAPTER
Twenty-Seven

Xavier

"**D**O YOU MIND TELLING ME WHAT HAPPENED WITH YOUR MOM last night at the charity event?" I hummed "Over the River and Through the Woods" as I drove us to Gram's for dinner. Ben burst into laughter, and I glanced over at him. He was grinning like a loon. "What?"

"Get this! She tried to fix me up with JJ." This time we laughed together.

"Why the hell would she do that?" I asked. "What made her think he'd make a decent son-in-law?"

"His name," Ben answered simply. "JJ has become quite the power player in DC." Ben sighed deeply before he continued. "I'm done with my parents' passive-aggressive behavior, though. I'm through with them implying that I was lucky to be loved by them. Ha! Loved. They barely tolerated me, and I'm no longer willing to accept it. All I've heard from them my entire life is what a disappointment I am. I was the fat kid no one wanted to befriend. I was the overly emotional gay kid with a chip on my shoulder. I failed to follow the career path they set out for me." Ben's emotional outburst was followed by a frustrated breath. "Bevan is my family, and he's all I need."

"You have me and my family too." It was pretty much an acknowledgment of how deep my feelings went and how strong our brewing connection was.

"That means the world to me, Xavier. Thank you."

I reached over and entwined our hands together. "Yeah, you might want to hold out on thanking me just yet."

I showed Ben around Autumn Years, and he was impressed with how lovely the grounds were with the beautiful ponds, landscaping, and paved trails so the residents that used mobility aids could still get out and enjoy nature. We entered the dining room, and the first thing I saw was Gram's boyfriend, Lennie, circling a man half his size with his fists up like they were about to go a few rounds.

"Awesome! Rocky 98," Ben joked.

"Lennie, knock it off," Gram said casually from her designated dining table. Her calmness implied that Lennie's fighting was a recurring event.

"I'm going to kick your ass this time, you horny old bastard." *Whoa.* Lennie wasn't playing around.

"Jesus Christ." I jumped into the fray to keep the fight from escalating further. I wrapped my arms around Lennie and began walking him backward.

"It's okay, kid," the horny old bastard said. "I can take his ass. She's probably let all the air out of his muscles and he's ripe for a beat down."

"That's enough talk out of you, Edmond." Gram's authoritative tone echoed through the room as she rose to her feet. "I'll whip your ass myself."

I looked over at Ben and was ready to apologize, but I found him grinning from ear to ear. He was clearly enjoying the show. I guessed my crazy family didn't offend him after all. Three of Edmond's friends dragged him from the dining room, warning that he better settle down before he got tossed out for good.

"I love this place." Ben smiled and wrapped an arm around my shoulders, pulling me close and kissing my temple.

Gram's shrewd eyes took it all in, not missing an expression or movement. "You boys look exhausted but sated. I knew the moment I saw you two together that you'd be tearing up the sheets."

"Be nice, Gram." She waved off my lightly spoken warning. "My boyfriend isn't used to all this drama yet. I mean, I bring him home to meet my family for the first time and it's an all-out brawl for your affection."

"Not for long," Lennie said, wrapping an arm around Gram. "I'm going to make an honest woman out of her."

"Boyfriend!" I didn't miss the fact that Gram had deliberately ignored Lennie's declaration. "I'm so happy for you both. You make such a beautiful couple." She went to Ben first, hugging him and kissing his cheek before turning to me and doing the same. "I don't think I've ever seen your eyes sparkle that much. It goes beyond the physical, am I right?" The last part was whispered in my ear.

"Way beyond," I whispered in return. I caught Ben watching us, and I gave him a reassuring smile.

Ellie showed up a few minutes later. She looked so much better since she'd entered the second trimester of her pregnancy. Gram and Lennie fussed over her and asked how she was feeling. Everyone was getting excited that we'd have a new baby in our family by Christmas. I'd never told Ellie about the stakeout. She had come to terms with being a single mom, and I didn't want to stir up any pain. I was sure she had an inkling of just how bad Drake was and didn't need me to confirm.

"El, I believe you're already acquainted with my boyfriend."

Ellie knew how much I'd missed Ben during the week we didn't speak. I came clean to her about everything one night after I started going to NA meetings. She sat on the guest bed at the Wrights' house and cried with me as I fought to reconcile the mistakes in my past with a chance with Ben as my shiny, promising future.

"Welcome to the family." Ellie gave Ben a tight squeeze.

Dinner was served, and I spent most of the meal telling hilarious stories from my childhood. Ben fit right in, and it made me so happy. There were many times that our hands connected beneath the table. It just felt right to have him be there sharing a meal and breathing the same air as my family. I hoped he would join us every Sunday and planned to ask him on the way home.

An awkward silence settled over us once we'd said our goodbyes and were back in my car. I figured it was because neither of us was ready for the weekend to be over or wanted to say goodbye, but we weren't sure how to broach the topic of sleeping arrangements for that night. Ben had to work the next day, and I couldn't leave Oliver alone for a second night. He had plenty of food and water, but I had promised to take good care of him, which included human interaction. If he was alone for too long, he would act up, which I learned firsthand when Gray left him in my care for a few days while he wooed Chase back after a misunderstanding.

I pulled up in front of Ben's house but left the car running. Ben looked over at me with an unspoken invitation in his eyes.

"If I go inside with you now, I won't want to leave. I have to get back to Oliver. He's probably destroyed their house by now."

"I can pack a bag and stay with you. I hate to be presumptuous, but damn, I'm not ready to turn you loose yet."

"I'd love to have you stay over with us." Another night in his arms sounded like pure heaven to me. "Are you sure it's not too much of an inconvenience since you have to work?"

"Not at all. I'll just run into my house and pack a few things. I'll drive separately so I can go straight to the office in the morning. Their house is actually closer to work than mine. I get another night with you, and I can leave for work later. It's a win-win for me."

I let us inside Gray and Chase's home fifteen minutes later. I flicked on the light and found Oliver sitting midway up the staircase. He was giving me an evil "where the fuck have you been" kitty glare and swishing his tail like he meant serious business. I half expected to find a pile of poop on my bed. Oliver stood up, turned around, and haughtily walked up the steps.

"We better sleep with one eye open tonight," Ben whispered in my ear, and I couldn't agree with him more.

CHAPTER
Twenty-Eight

Ben

XAVIER AND I WERE INVITED TO CELEBRATE THE FOURTH OF JULY AT the Wrights' house. They were hosting their first pool party and barbeque as a married couple. Gray told me we'd have a great view of the fireworks being set off at a park a few miles from their house. I really liked the idea of holding Xavier in my arms while watching fireworks explode across the night sky. I was starting to turn into a big sap, and I loved every minute of it.

The usual suspects were present with a few surprises thrown in. Liam, the cute bartender from Bottoms Up, was there, but without hulking Jack Murphy to keep an eye on him. Liam told me that the Fourth was usually a slow night, so Jack had closed the bar.

"Jack didn't feel like coming?" I asked Liam.

"Fireworks and explosions probably aren't his thing after all of his tours of duty in Iraq and Afghanistan," Liam replied solemnly.

"I'm sure you're right," I said. "I'm glad you get the holiday off to spend with some friends."

Liam looked around the growing crowd. "I really don't know that many people here, but I *am* grateful to have been invited."

Gray told me I could invite Bevan to the party, and I did, but I didn't expect him to show up. It was a welcome surprise when I heard him introducing himself to people. I gave him a big hug with a hearty slap to his back. We'd talked several times since the night of the benefit and had gotten even closer. He was really happy I'd found Xavier but had made me promise not to try to fix him up with anyone.

"Ellie, it's good to see you again," he said. *Had his voice dropped an octave or two?* "Pregnancy really suits you." I had forgotten Ellie had met Bevan when he'd gone to her house looking for Xavier the morning after Chase and Gray's wedding.

"Thanks," she replied shyly. I took in Ellie's pink cheeks and Van's shy smile and my wheels started turning, but I stopped myself before I got too carried away. After all, a promise was a promise.

JJ and Miller were both at the party, which I found kind of strange. I would have thought the two tomcats would have been somewhere else, picking up their next conquests instead of attending a family-friendly barbecue. Maybe those two were outgrowing all the screwing around like I had. Then I caught JJ and Miller both sizing up Liam like he was a tasty treat. Nope, they were happy just the way they were, and that was just fine too, but not with Liam. There was something about the younger guy that brought out big-brother feelings in me. Jack wasn't there to look out for him, so I did the honors, glaring at JJ and Miller until they looked at me. I shook my head, and they both threw up their hands in surrender.

It was hard to believe I had been like them not so long ago. I looked over at where Xavier sat next to his sister at a table beneath a large rainbow-colored umbrella. He sensed he was being watched and looked up, and our eyes met and held. I wouldn't trade what I was building with him for a meaningless night of debauchery with a stranger. JJ and Miller could keep their lonely nights because I knew how right it felt to hold the man I loved in my arms.

Love? Yes, love.

"I no longer want to hear a single snarky comment out of you." Gray had come over to stand beside me, and I hadn't even noticed. "No more re-marks about lovesick fools or telling me I'm whipped. Do you hear me?" Gray's good-natured admonishment made me smile.

"Yes, sir," I said contritely. I really did tease him endlessly about his sappy love affair with Chase, but that was before I'd known what it was like to need someone else in order to breathe.

"Welcome to the club, my friend." Gray held out his fist, and I bumped it. "Say, are you any good at water volleyball or polo?"

"I've never tried water polo, but I'm pretty decent at volleyball. Please tell me you're not thinking of Wright versus Wright matches." I groaned at the possibility. "This is supposed to be relaxing and fun for *all* of us, not just feisty foreplay for you two," I said with a laugh.

We ended up drawing colored straws out of a paper bag for teams, which would have made it less stressful for everyone if Gray and Chase had both drawn the same color, but fate was not smiling down upon us. Gray drew a red straw, and Chase drew blue. Xavier and I both drew blue straws, and I chose to focus on that positive.

I found every opportunity to touch my boyfriend, whether it be a simple touch beneath the water or an all-out kiss and hug after we won a game. Our team ended up winning the best of three matches in volleyball but lost our asses in water polo. We were like ravenous wolves by the time we climbed out of the pool. Luckily, Lennie and Gram had manned the grill while Gray's parents had laid out all the condiments and side dishes.

"Are you done in the pool for the night?" I asked Xavier when we'd finished eating. He nodded and leaned in for a kiss. "Let's go put on some dry clothes."

I snagged our bag on our way through the kitchen with the intention of using the small half bath down the hall to get dressed. The door opened just as we approached, and JJ stepped out followed by Miller. Both men were straightening their clothes and hair, but it was the surprised looks on their faces that really gave them away.

"I'll be damned." I couldn't let the moment go without some sort of remark.

"Shut up," JJ snarled.

Miller looked embarrassed at being caught and made a hasty retreat without saying a word. JJ watched him walk away and looked like he wanted to call out but held back. I thought back to the night of the charity benefit and the comment JJ had made about Miller getting whatever he wanted. I had to wonder if there had been more to that seemingly innocent statement.

JJ walked away without another word, and Xavier and I grinned at one another. The bathroom was vacant, and being the chivalrous guy I was, I wanted to make sure Xavier got out of his wet things and into dry clothes. It was the only considerate thing to do. Too bad my gallantry stayed on the other side of the door.

"I have an announcement to make," Gram said once we returned to the party. Xavier and Chase groaned, but I just smiled. I loved every crazy thing that came out of the woman's mouth. "Lennie and I are getting married."

The announcement was met with cheers and applause. Xavier and Chase leaped from their chairs and hugged her within an inch of her life before they hugged Lennie. Ava and Ellie followed at a slower pace due to the precious cargo they carried.

"We haven't set a date yet," Gram announced. "I'm still not convinced why we"—she gestured back and forth between Lennie and herself—"need to get married at seventy years old. I resisted for as long as I could, but he threatened to start withholding sex, so I caved."

There was the Gram I had come to know and love.

"Aggie," Lennie playfully admonished. "The kids don't want to hear about our personal relations."

"As if they're not all screwing like monkeys every damn chance they get. Don't think I didn't notice how long it took some of you to *change* into dry clothes."

Van guffawed beside me, and I forgot this was his first time around Gram. "She's really something, isn't she?" I asked.

"She's freaking awesome! Man, Chase and Xavier were lucky to be raised by her," Van replied in awe.

Gram came to our table after the excitement wore off. She placed her hand over mine, leaned in, and kissed me on the cheek. "I thank God for you daily, Ben." No one had ever told me they were thankful for me, and I wasn't sure how to respond. "I do!" She clearly read the skepticism in my eyes.

I swallowed hard around the lump of jumbled emotions in my throat. I didn't quite know how to respond to a statement like that. "Thank you, Gram." It wasn't a very savvy response, but it was all I could muster.

"You're welcome, sugar. You just keep that sparkle in my boy's eyes, and that will be thanks enough. You know, I give Lennie a hard time about the marriage stuff, but it feels really good to belong to someone again." Tears welled in her eyes. "I never thought I'd love again, but look at me now."

"Congratulations. You're going to make a beautiful bride."

"What kind of dress are you going to wear?" Ellie asked.

"Oh, something classy and timeless," Gram replied.

"Classy and timeless? I miss the wild outfits you used to wear," Ellie confessed with a pout. "Are you toning it down because of Lennie?"

"In part," Gram said softly. "Mostly, I realized that sexiness is a state of mind and not an outfit choice. I feel just as beautiful in this sleeveless top and capris as I would in a halter dress. There is no shame in dressing sexy, and there is no expiration date on feeling sexy. Lennie has helped me see that I don't need risqué outfits to be hot. I just need to feel it inside." Gram reached over and patted Ellie's arm. "Don't worry, baby girl, I'm not toning down my mouth one bit." Gram winked at us and stood to go find Lennie. "I've had a beautiful time, but I'm ready to go home. Lennie is all the fireworks I need tonight."

I commandeered a lounge chair as the night sky turned darker. I sat down, and Xavier nestled in between my legs and lay back against me. I wrapped my arms around him, forming an X over his chest. Xavier placed his hands around my wrists and sighed in contentment like he'd wanted to be right there in my arms all day long. I knew just how he felt because it was exactly what I had been craving too.

The first firework exploded, jolting me out of my thoughts. Several more colorful bursts lit up the dark sky.

"That's how you make me feel inside, Xavier. You bring vibrant color into my life and light up my world." He rolled over so he was lying on top of me. The magical lights were bursting overhead as he looked down at me. I knew I wasn't going to find a better moment to tell him how I felt. "I love you, Xavier."

His eyes widened in surprise, then his lips moved as if he were trying to speak, but no sound came out. I hadn't said the words to him with the expectation that he would return them. I'd just needed him to know. He closed his eyes briefly, and when he reopened them, I clearly saw what my words meant to him in his radiant gaze. Xavier lowered his mouth to mine and kissed me with all the emotion he was unable to express with words, and that was all the response I needed.

CHAPTER
Twenty-Nine

Xavier

AUGUST BROUGHT SOME EXCITING CHANGES IN MY LIFE. I SOLD AN-other original score to Ryan Productions and received my royalties from the first sale. Ben agreed to help me look for a house, and I hoped to find one we both loved because I wanted it to be *our* home someday.

Things were great between us, and I fell deeper in love with him every single day. I just wished I could tell him all the things he stirred inside me. I could write a song about how he made me feel, but I couldn't make my mouth form the three little but very important words. I had tried to tell him the night of the Fourth of July celebration when the fireworks reflected in his eyes. I saw his love for me in their depths before he said the words. I opened my mouth to say it back to him, but nothing had come out.

"It's okay, Xavier. There's no pressure for you to say it back. I just wanted you to know how I feel," Ben had said after I kissed him following his dec-laration. I had poured my whole heart into that one embrace, and I hoped he'd recognized it.

I knew how Ben felt because the amazing man told me every day since and showed me in every possible way. Ben never let on if he was upset I still hadn't said the words to him. He smiled his same brilliant smile and loved me with all that he had—heart, body, and soul.

My own insecurities were what held me back from telling Ben I was in love with him too. As much as I had grown these last few months—and it had been by leaps and bounds—I still found myself thinking I didn't deserve Ben. There was a small part of me that feared he would wake up someday and realize he could do better, and that tiny molecule of doubt was what held me back.

Ben once confessed his parents had never told him they loved him. Van was even more emotionally damaged than Ben, so it was unlikely they'd ex-pressed their affection for one another. If I said the words *I love you* to Ben, would I be the first? If so, I worried he would tie himself to me for the rest of his life out of obligation. I wanted Ben forever but not at the cost of his own happiness.

Maybe my fear was unfounded and irrational, but that didn't make it any less real or scary. Van had been right when he'd said people threw the L word around like it meant nothing, but to Ben it would mean *everything*. It took me a month to come to terms with my fears and to be ready for the next step. I was ready to bare my soul to Ben and speak the words out loud. Ben—we—deserved it.

Ben had been out of town for four days, which was longer than nor-mal for him, but the trip had included visits to three different accounts on the West Coast. I had missed him like crazy and told him so every night. Ben ended each call with those three magic words that always brought me comfort. I loved him with every fiber of my being, and I couldn't wait to tell him as soon as he got home. No more living in fear. I was going to blurt it out the minute I saw his face so I wouldn't work myself up over trying to find the perfect moment.

I was just about to put a frozen pizza into the oven when Chase called me and said Ava had gone into labor. Chase sounded frantic, so I headed to the hospital to help Gray keep him calm for Ava's sake. The last thing she needed was a wound-up Chase riling her up while she was trying to bring her baby into the world. I turned off the oven and headed straight over. I sent a quick text to Ben to let him know what was going on, even though he was on a plane on his way home to me and wouldn't get the message until he landed. *Home to me.* I loved the sound of that.

The labor and delivery waiting room was already packed by the time I arrived. Most of the guys were lounging in uncomfortable chairs, but the ladies and Chase were noticeably absent. I said hello to everyone and walked over to Gray, who informed me my brother and the ladies had gone to the vending machines to get snacks and drinks for everyone.

"How is Chase?" I asked.

"He's a hot damn mess." Gray snorted, then covered his mouth. "What's he going to be like when we have our own kids? He'll have to be medicated." Gray grabbed my elbow and moved me out of hearing range. "Chase demanded to see the doctor's credentials after Ava introduced them. He insisted she was barely old enough to have completed college let alone medical school and surgical rotations. You have no idea how glad I am to see you. I'd bet your left nut Chase has snuck back to Ava's room."

I grimaced and resisted the urge to cover myself. "I'll do my best, buddy, but I make no promises." I patted Gray on the back, giving him a wink.

"That's all I ask, Xavier. Let's go see the little mama."

Ava's calm voice floated out into the hallway as we approached her room. "Chase, come sit by me and hold my hand."

"Are you hurting?" he asked. "Do you want me to page the nurse?" I heard the panic in Chase's voice and had to stifle a laugh.

"I'm fine, honey, but I could just use an extra hand to hold."

"She's got this under control," I told Gray. We walked into the room, and Ava was propped up in bed with Brandon on one side and Chase on the other. "Hi, gorgeous."

"Uncle Xavier is here," Ava said to her belly. "He'll be singing you beautiful lullabies as soon as he gets to hold you."

I dropped a kiss on her head and patted Chase's shoulder. "Has the doctor said how long she thinks you'll be in labor?"

"I'll be lucky to have this baby tonight," Ava replied. "I guess she'll get here when she's ready."

"It might be a boy, my love," Brandon interjected. We all laughed at the byplay between the two lovebirds.

An hour or so passed, and not much progress had occurred with Ava's labor. The nurse asked us all to leave the room except Brandon so she could get some rest. It was apparent it would be many hours before the little guy or gal made an appearance.

Ben was due home soon, and I wanted to be the first thing he saw when he crossed the threshold. I was going to tell him I loved him as soon as he opened the door. Maybe I'd say it while wearing nothing at all. I figured I'd hang around for a while longer, then head on home to meet my guy.

"I'm going down to the cafeteria to get you guys some good coffee," I said to Gray and Chase after a half hour passed. We'd already sampled the shit from the vending machine, and I'd never risk their health by bringing them a second cup. I was glad to get up and get my blood flowing. The TV in the waiting room wasn't working, and the time just seemed to drag.

"Hazelnut for Gray," Chase called to me as I walked away.

When I returned from the cafeteria, I saw anxiety was riding Chase hard again. I put surprising Ben with my love declaration on the back burner to focus on calming my brother. Eventually, his tension eased and he fell asleep leaning against Gray. I lowered myself in my chair, tipped my head back against the wall, and closed my eyes. I thought of Ben—his smile, his voice, and the way he made me feel safe and cherished—and let the rhythm of us sweep me away.

CHAPTER
Thirty

Ben

XAVIER LOOKED SO PEACEFUL ALL CURLED UP ASLEEP IN A CHAIR IN the hospital waiting room. I hated to wake him up, but Ava had just delivered a baby boy, and he'd want to know. I kneeled down in front of him, and that was when I noticed the dried tears on his face. I hated the thought of him in any pain—even in his sleep.

Xavier had told me about the nightmares he'd had almost on a nightly basis after he was attacked by Damien, but that had been before we met. *I brought back his music,* I thought smugly to myself. He hadn't said the *L* word back to me, but he showed me his feelings in so many other ways, so the sight of his tear-streaked face was like a punch to the gut.

I hated Damien Diamond with a fucking passion. If Deacon *had* killed the slimy bastard, I would have gladly shaken his hand and bought him a beer. Knowing that the little weasel had taken pictures of the man I love when he was vulnerable to use against him made me want to dig his carcass up and kill him all over again. The level of hatred I felt toward Damien was almost frightening.

Xavier whimpered, pulling me away from my morose thoughts. "I love you, Ben." Xavier's words were merely a whisper, but I heard them all the same.

My heart hammered in my chest, sending my blood zinging through my veins. I leaned forward and kissed his cheeks while brushing my thumb across his full lips. "Wake up, love, and say those sweet words to me with your gorgeous eyes open. You know how much I love them."

"Ben?" Xavier's eyes slowly fluttered open, and he blinked several times while trying to wake from what appeared to be a very deep sleep. He looked around, trying to orient himself. "Why are we at the hospital?"

"Ava just gave birth to a baby boy about twenty minutes ago. Everyone is at the nursery window waiting for baby Jacob to be brought in for them to see. Gray and Chase said you had fallen asleep, and they didn't want to disturb you." I kissed his soft lips a few times and wished I could linger for a longer embrace. I had missed him so damn much while I was away. "I came to the hospital as soon as my plane landed."

Xavier jerked up in his seat like a volt of electricity had zapped him. "I had a nightmare that your plane crashed. You died Ben, and you left me all alone." His lips trembled. "And I never got to tell you—"

I silenced him with a kiss. I wanted the words but not like this. "I haven't left you, Xavier. I'm right here." His tears made sense to me now. I opened my arms, and Xavier launched himself at me, wrapping his arms around me and holding me close.

"It was so real, Ben." His voice broke, and more tears threatened. "But you're here."

"I am, and there's no place I'd rather be."

Xavier sucked in a shaky breath, then said, "Ben, I—"

"There you two are!" Chase exclaimed, his voice a few decibels above enthusiastic. "You're going to miss baby Jacob."

"Babe, they'll have him in the nursery for more than five minutes," Gray calmly said. "Ava is exhausted, and it sounds like Jacob is spending the night in the nursery so she can get some uninterrupted sleep." Gray, as usual, was the voice of reason.

"Xavier, were you crying?" Chase asked him, then turned to me. "What the hell did you do to him?"

"Me?" I might have sounded a little defensive. "I didn't do anything. He just had a really vivid dream that shook him up."

"A dream?" Chase's voice was full of disbelief.

"You were there and you were there," Xavier said, not missing a beat as he pointed at Chase and then Gray.

"Very funny, Dorothy." Chase playfully punched Xavier in the arm.

"That's my guy," I said lovingly. I leaned in and kissed his lips once, twice, and then lingered on the third time. "When we get home, you're going to tell me *the words* while you're awake. You said them in your sleep, but I need to hear them again." I held out my hand and pulled him to his feet after he placed his hand in mine.

We followed Gray and Chase through the hospital corridors. We were just a few feet away from the nursery when Xavier halted abruptly and tugged my hand so I would stop too.

"I don't want to wait another second." Xavier lightly shoved me up against the wall and pressed his body against mine. "I love you, Ben. I crazy love you. I'm going to say it until you're sick of hearing it."

"That's never going to happen, babe."

Xavier stood up on his toes and pressed his mouth to mine.

"It's been four days since I've been inside you," I growled. "I'm not willing to wait much longer, so you might want to back up a bit unless you want me to drag you into the nearest bathroom to remedy the situation right now. I had hoped for something a little more romantic."

"Not to mention more hygienic," Xavier added with disgust. "With my luck, I'd end up with a staph infection." Xavier backed away slowly and patted my arm as if he was trying to soothe the beast inside us both.

"Ten minutes of *ooh*ing and *ahh*ing, then we're out of here." I swatted him playfully on the ass as we joined the crowd gathering to look at baby Jacob. "He's a cute little guy," I said, peering down at his pink face. He was wearing a blue knit hat and little blue mittens. I had the sudden urge to see his tiny fingers and toes. "Shit, I'm turning into one of them," I said, nodding toward Gray and Chase who practically had their noses pressed to the window. "We should place a bet on how long it takes them to adopt or find a surrogate. What do you think? A year?"

Xavier scoffed. "Nine months max." He turned and looked at me with serious eyes. "Do you want kids?"

"Gray, I really want a baby," Chase said softly before I could answer.

Xavier and I exchanged a smug smile. All joking aside, Gray and Chase were going to be amazing parents.

"I've never given much thought to kids," I admitted. "But then again, I never imagined myself falling in love with someone either. What about you?"

"Same here." Xavier reached over and placed his hand around the back of my neck. "Take me home, Ben."

We said goodbye to everyone and left the hospital hand in hand until we reached his car. I pushed him against the driver's side door and lowered my head until my mouth was just a hair's breadth away from his lips. "My home is wherever you are, Xavier." I kissed him like I had wanted to since I'd seen him sleeping in the chair. Our kiss turned insanely hot in a matter of seconds, and I didn't want to start something we couldn't finish. "We need to find you a house with a garage so I can fuck you over Mistress's hood like I wanted to the first night I saw her."

"Okay," Xavier said shakily.

That night I made love to Xavier slowly and completely, not letting him goad me into screwing him into the mattress. I loved taking him like that, but tonight, I needed a more emotional joining. I'd never known I could make love until meeting Xavier, and I needed that closer connection with him after being away for a few days. Especially after he'd said those three amazing words. The same ones I made him say repeatedly before I let him come.

Later, after Xavier fell asleep in my arms, I lay in bed thinking about the changes I needed to make in my life. First, I needed to tell Bevan I loved him. Although I didn't feel like Xavier's dream had been an omen, I needed to make sure Bevan knew how I felt about him. He was my big brother, my dragon slayer, and my hero. It was past time he knew how much he meant to me.

Second, I decided I would not try to reconnect with Beverly or Daniel. I had spoken the words to Beverly already, but I knew I'd probably have to make myself clear again. My parents didn't want the same type of relationship I had dreamed of having with them, and it was a complete waste of time to get my hopes up only to have them shit upon time and time again. I had Bevan, Xavier, and his family, and I had friends I loved as much as a family. That was enough.

Last, I decided to do everything in my power to hold on to the man lying in my arms. I wouldn't hold him back or behave like a possessive fool. I'd never abuse him or his precious trust. I wouldn't try to hold him down with my hands or any other type of restraints. I would love him with everything I had inside me and burrow myself so deep in his heart that he couldn't remember a day without me in his life. Falling in love with Xavier was the scariest thing that ever happened to me, but I wouldn't change a single thing.

"Love you," Xavier whispered in his sleep and nestled closer.

He was so worth the risk.

CHAPTER
Thirty-One

Ben

"HONEY, I'M HOME!" XAVIER AND I WEREN'T OFFICIALLY LIVING together, but he was at my house more often than not. I started to loosen my tie but froze when Xavier walked into my line of sight. He stopped halfway down the stairs, and it was all I could do to stay still and wait for him to descend them all the way. "Damn, baby."

Xavier did a slow turn in front of me. "Are these the black jeans you wanted to slowly peel off my body with your teeth?" I nodded. "Is this the black leather jacket you like so much? I believe you mentioned you wanted to fuck me while I wore nothing else."

"Over the hood of Mistress," I added, "but my garage isn't big enough for her with all my workout gear in there. How upset do you think the neighbors will be if we do it anyway?" I wiggled my eyebrows for emphasis.

"We'll save that part of the fantasy for another time." Xavier wrapped his arms around my waist and leaned in for a kiss. I think he meant it to be a short peck, but I had other ideas. I savored every part of his mouth until he pulled free with a teasing glint in his eye. "Are you ready to eat dinner?"

"Not at all. I want my dessert first." I nibbled on his neck and began to tug down the zipper on his jacket. I wanted to see his beautiful bronze skin and feel his lean muscles beneath my hands. Xavier stopped me when I got the zipper down to his belly button. "I need you."

"You have me, Ben."

Xavier took my hand and led me into the living room where he gestured for me to sit on the couch. I noticed he'd moved the coffee table and placed lit candles all around the room. Xavier pulled the curtains closed and turned off the lights so the only light in the room was the glow from the candles. He sauntered over to the record player and moved the needle into position but looked over his shoulder before he lowered it.

"What's your other fantasy?"

"I have so many when it comes to you, Xavier. It's a miracle I accomplish anything at work."

Xavier gently placed the needle on the record, and I heard the soulful cry of Led Zeppelin's "I Can't Quit You Baby" begin. He kept his back toward me and began to sway to the sultry, bluesy song, and I knew I was about to experience the sexiest four minutes of my life. Xavier turned and walked to me, hips swaying, as he sang the words of the song to me. My dick began to throb to the beat of the drums.

Xavier leaned over and removed my tie, tossed it aside, and unbuttoned my shirt. His lower body kept perfect rhythm with the music, and he sang breathily in my ear. Xavier trailed his hands up and down my chest, teasing my flesh until I was quivering.

Xavier teased my lips with his tongue while he worked my belt loose and opened my pants. "He's going to need some room to breathe," he whispered in my ear. I was prepared to stand up and strip naked, but Xavier stopped me with a firm hand on my chest and a shake of his head. "Sit back, relax, and enjoy the show."

He stood up and turned so I got a great view of his tight ass moving in his sinful jeans. Realistically, they were probably too tight to remove with my teeth, but I was willing to give it my all. Xavier lowered his gorgeous ass until it hovered just above my erection. He imitated a slow grind, and it was all I could do to not pull him down onto my lap.

Xavier turned and repeated his moves, but this time I looked into his sultry eyes while he drove me wild. I tried to pull him down for a kiss, but he evaded my grasp. I groaned, and he laughed seductively, letting me know he was having a lot of fun tormenting me. Xavier raised his arms over his head and undulated his hips, placing his amazing ass directly in front of me.

He kept up the slow roll of his hips while he pivoted to face me. I watched in complete awe as he slowly unbuttoned his fly, giving me a peek at the sexy black underwear beneath. My mouth went bone dry as I watched him remove his jeans, too mesmerized to feel cheated that he'd done it without me. The jacket went next, and that was when I noticed the new ink peeking out of the waistband of his underwear. It was a curving bar of music that flowed along the sexy vee of his hips. I couldn't wait to see how far the tattoo went beneath his briefs and trace it with my tongue.

Xavier turned and lowered his body until his ass was pressed firmly against my straining erection. Oh fuck! I fisted my hands next to my thighs to keep from grabbing him, which only got harder when he pressed his back against my chest. The combined heat rolling off our bodies threatened to burn me alive.

"Your new tattoo looks sexy, baby. I can't wait to get a closer look and run my tongue all over it." Unable to be good any longer, I grabbed his hips and moved his ass up and down my erection, making us both growl.

"You're supposed to keep your hands to yourself, sir." His rebuke was weak at best. Xavier kept grinding until the song played its very last note. I slid my hands up and pinched both his nipples, and his protests died. "You're going to take me just like this, Ben."

Xavier stood up, and I turned him around by his hips. I loved what he was promising to do to me, but first, I wanted to inspect his new ink and take a little taste of him. I removed his underwear slowly and discovered the music started a few inches beneath his belly button, then curled up and along the indent of his hip on one side.

"It's sexy and beautiful just like you," I told him. "What song did you choose?"

"It's our song, 'Rhythm of Us.' This is the opening line that came to me the first night I came here." His voice was soft as he lovingly traced his finger over the notes. "Someday soon I'll play it for you."

He'd permanently inked us on his body, and I found myself tearing up a bit. God, the things he made me feel. I traced my tongue along the curving line of notes and kissed each one that represented the connection we had shared from the very beginning. I tried to take his weeping cock into my mouth, but he pushed me back against the couch.

"I want this to last," he said playfully.

"You think I can hold out much longer after all your teasing?" I hoped I didn't embarrass myself by ending the party too soon.

Xavier helped me get undressed and straddled my legs, kissing me while I got him ready for penetration. I caught a pearl of his precum with a finger and licked it clean. I wanted him to see what he was missing. I could tell by the look in his eyes and his sharp intake of breath that he knew.

Once he was stretched and pliant, Xavier stood up, turned around so he was facing away from me, and straddled my thighs. I placed my hands on his hips and lowered him until my condom-covered erection nudged up against his puckered entrance, then I let Xavier take the lead. I held my dick steady so he could lower himself at his own pace, which was sinfully slow.

I bit my lip hard, hoping to get my attention away from my cock and the burning need to press him down until I was completely sheathed by his body. Instead, I leaned back against the sofa cushions and watched as my dick disappeared inside him, inch by achingly hard inch.

Once he was fully seated on my cock, he moved his hips to a rhythm that was uniquely us. Holy fuck, I was a goner. Xavier owned me, and not just because of the sex. I could have gotten that anywhere, but what we shared was so much more—a beautiful and rare gift.

Xavier raised his arms above his head, which signaled he was really lost in our lovemaking. He arched his back and a shiver worked its way down his spine, kicking off a matching shudder in me. I ran my hands up and down his sides, then teased and pinched his pierced nipples.

"Your heat is burning me alive, Xavier." My hands roamed lower until I wrapped one around his cock and used the other to cup his firm sac. Xavier whimpered and picked up his rhythm, chasing his climax. "I could spend the rest of my days right here inside you, baby."

"Ben." My name was a whispered plea, and I knew just what my man needed. I stroked his dick with long, slow pulls until he begged. "Yes, Ben. Please."

He collapsed against my chest, and I took over, thrusting my hips up into him while I continued to jack him. I was so close. My balls retracted, and I felt the familiar hum along my spine telling me my climax was imminent. "Xavier."

"I'm right here with you, baby."

Xavier angled his head and sought my lips, and I met him halfway. I felt his hot release on my hand, and his ass clamped harder around my cock when he came. I relaxed my body and let my orgasm power through me as I pistoned my hips into him.

I wrapped my arms around Xavier's chest and held him tight to my body once the last tremor left me. Our kiss turned from searing to languid and sweet as we floated back down from heaven. I never wanted to turn him loose or end our kiss, but my stomach chose that moment to interrupt us with a growl.

Xavier smiled against my lips. "Let's take a quick shower, then I'll feed you. Ellie gave me some new recipes to try out."

"They'll be amazing, love."

Our shower was much quicker than I wanted, but I was starving. Xavier gave me a rundown on the menu, and I couldn't wait to eat. I offered to help cook but he refused. He had marinated the skirt steak for a few hours and had already cut and prepped the vegetables. I watched as he prepared corn, black bean, and tomato salsa.

"Let me at least fire up the grill for you," I said.

"Okay, but then I want to hear about your day."

I went outside, turned on the gas grill, and cleaned it with the wire brush. I hung up the tool and walked back into the kitchen, and all of my good humor vanished when I saw we had company. *How long had I been outside?*

"Bennett," my father said. Here was the man I'd wanted to love me unconditionally, but I'd concluded years ago that resigned tolerance would be the best I could hope for out of him. Yet there was something different in his eyes when he stood in my kitchen that night.

"Daniel." I stared at him in shock for a few seconds until the awkward silence of the moment registered. Thankfully, years of good etiquette kicked in to help me out. "Xavier, this is my father, Daniel St. Claire." I pulled Xavier against me, and the heat of him melted my tension. "Daniel, this is my boyfriend, Xavier Cruz."

Xavier stepped forward and held out his hand for my father to shake. I expected Daniel to sneer at him and ignore the gesture, but instead, he shook Xavier's hand. "It's nice to meet you, Xavier."

"Likewise," Xavier replied politely. He turned to me with an encouraging smile. "I'm going to turn off the grill and head upstairs to give you two some privacy."

"You don't have to do that, babe." I wanted—needed—his warmth to help get me through this confrontation. I wouldn't say those things in front of my father because he'd see me as weak, and that wouldn't help when I tried to take a stand. But I saw the situation was making Xavier uncomfortable, so I held back the plea for him to stay. Xavier went outside briefly to turn off the grill, then he stood on his tiptoes and gave me a reassuring kiss and gently squeezed my hand before he went upstairs. I missed his presence immediately.

I turned to face my father when Xavier was out of sight. "If you're here to lecture me over some assumed transgression, you can save yourself the energy and walk right back out the door."

"That's not why I came, Bennett." He swallowed hard, then cleared his throat as if what he had to say was lodged there. "I'm here to apologize for the way I've treated you and to tell you that someday I hope you can forgive me."

I didn't know exactly what I had expected Daniel to say, but that hadn't been it. I would have been less surprised if he had pulled a gun on me. Truly, I wasn't sure I wanted his apology after all this time, nor did I know if I could forgive him for the things he'd said and his past behavior.

"Will you at least hear me out?" Daniel's tone was one I had never heard before. It was softer than usual and full of pleading.

I could send his sorry ass packing—no one would blame me—or I could hear what he had to say. I chose the latter because at the minimum the bastard owed me an apology, and I was going to get it. I silently gestured to the kitchen table, indicating Daniel should have a seat. There was no mistaking the relief in his features over the small victory.

"Thank you, Bennett."

"Don't thank me yet, Daniel. I'll hear what you have to say, but you can bet your ass I'll have the final word when you're done." I sat down across the table from my father, afraid to hope this would be the first step toward reconciliation with him.

CHAPTER
Thirty-Two

Xavier

"N ATALIE, COULD YOU GIVE BEN AND ME A FEW MINUTES TO LOOK around privately?"

"Sure, Xavier," the realtor said with a smile. "I'll just step out onto the front porch and return some phone calls. Let me know if you have any questions."

"Will do. Thanks."

What Ben didn't know was that Chase and I had already looked at the house last week when Ben had been in Tampa. I'd found it online, and the moment I saw it, I swear I could imagine us in every room. I saw Ben leaning against the kitchen cabinet while he drank coffee out of his favorite cup and pictured his robe hanging on the hook in the master bathroom. I called Natalie and requested a showing, and she promised to keep it a secret. This house felt like home to me the minute I crossed the threshold, and I just wanted to make sure Ben felt the same way.

"What do you think about this one?" Ben asked after we toured the Cape Cod style house with four bedrooms, three bathrooms, a spectacular great room, and a finished walkout basement. "I know it seems like too much space, but maybe you could put a studio in the basement someday instead of renting one to record your music." What he didn't say was how disappointed he was that I hadn't played our song for him yet, but I had to make it perfect, and I wanted the moment to be just right.

I truly wanted to do something special for him, especially after the showdown with his father. It had been almost a month since his dad had come over, and Ben still hadn't said much about it. Maybe it was because he had recognized there was no future relationship for them or maybe it was because he didn't want to burden me with his problems. I was afraid it was the latter, and it upset me that he didn't think I was strong enough to support him in his time of need. If we didn't learn to lean on one another, then we were doomed to fall apart.

My heart ached at the thought of Ben not being in my life. I mean, I was looking at houses with the hope that he'd someday live with me. I needed to make sure we were on the same page, or I risked emotional wreckage that could be dangerous to my recovery. Sweeping my concerns under a rug didn't make them go away; it just temporarily hid them so they festered and became larger and more worrisome when I revisited them later.

We were standing in the basement looking out the wall of windows when Ben rested his chin on my shoulder and wrapped his arms around me. He started nibbling at the bottom of my neck, which always led to other things.

"Ben?"

"Hmmm?" He kissed a path up to my ear and sucked the lobe into his mouth.

"No, babe. Wait!" Ben stiffened in surprise and stood back. "I need to talk to you, and I can't think when your lips are on my body. I need to talk about us."

"Us?" Ben sounded nervous, and that was the last thing I wanted. I turned around and met his stormy gray eyes. He was assuming the worst. I saw it both in his posture and the wall he was erecting right before my eyes.

I reached over and grabbed his hands and lifted them so I could kiss each one. "Don't do that, Ben. Don't assume the worst when I want to have a serious discussion." I lowered our joined hands and leaned forward, pressing my lips to his. I pecked him a few times before I spoke again. "You're not the only one in love for the first time, and I'm stumbling through this the best I can." A sudden case of nerves gripped me, and I wondered if I'd be drinking the sparkling cider Natalie had hidden in the fridge by myself.

"Xavier, what's wrong?" He read me so well. "Have I done something to upset you, babe?" I swallowed hard and nodded. "Please tell me what I did so I don't do it again."

"Okay, here goes." *Deep breath, Xavier.* "It's about your dad's visit."

"Daniel." Ben corrected before I could blink an eye. "Why do you want to talk about him, and what does he have to do with us?"

"I want to talk to you about everything, Ben, and I want you to be able to do the same with me. I don't want you holding back, fearing you'll send me to the nearest street corner in search of a drug dealer. I need to know that you think I'm strong enough to face the bullshit life throws at us. I want *all* of you, not just the bits and pieces you think I'm strong enough to handle. You're the one who told me I wasn't broken, and I need you to show me you believe it."

"I don't think you're weak or broken, love. If you recall, I told you that you didn't have to leave Daniel and me to talk in private. I was perfectly fine with you overhearing everything that was said between us. In fact, I really needed you there with me." Ben placed his hands on my neck in a loving, nonthreatening way. I loved the comforting weight of his hands on my body. "You didn't stay when I said you could, and you didn't ask me any questions after he left, so I didn't think you wanted to know. Has this been on your mind this whole time?"

I nodded. Ben did tell me I could stay when his dad arrived, but it didn't feel right to stay and listen. There had been so much tension between them that it made me feel uncomfortable. Ben had introduced me to his dad as his boyfriend, and Daniel had politely shaken my hand. He didn't even flinch when Ben said I could stay. I thought Ben was trying to spare my feelings with his offer. I had no idea he'd needed me there. *Shit!*

"I thought you were just being polite when you said I could stay. You seemed lost in thought afterward, and I didn't want to cause you any more stress by rehashing the visit. I just assumed you'd tell me about the conversation the next day or soon after, but you didn't bring it up, so I didn't either. I'm sorry I let you down. I promise I will be there for you next time."

"You didn't let me down, Xavier." Ben growled in frustration. "I—*we*— just need to communicate better. Should we come up with some sort of hand signal or code word for when the situation is awkward, kind of like a safe word, to stop me from making a fool of myself or upsetting you?"

"No." A laugh bubbled out of me as I thought of him blurting out some absurd word to get my attention. "Perhaps you could just reach for my hand or wrap your arm around me and pull me in tight. That's just a suggestion, but maybe you'd rather blurt out a random word in the middle of a conversation."

"SQUIRREL!" His yell echoed around the basement, and once I quit laughing, I remembered the reason I had cornered him.

"We'll figure out signals later." I gave Ben a grin. "So, the basement would need some modification if I wanted a studio down here. I mean, I would love to put a baby grand piano right in front of this window. The sun and the view would be so inspiring, but you can tell by the echo that it wouldn't work for recording music. But there is this nifty little feature I wanted to show you."

I walked behind the custom bar and plugged my phone into the auxiliary cord that was connected to the sound system. I pulled up the file I was looking for and hit Play. I turned and looked at him as our song began. This was a part of me I showed no one. They all knew I was an accomplished musician, but I'd never shared one of my original scores until this moment. It was the most important piece of music I'd ever written because it was for Ben. I had recorded my piano, acoustic guitar, and violin parts separately, then engineered it all together when I got the individual elements just right.

"This is our song." Ben didn't ask because he instinctively knew.

He closed his eyes, and I watched as the music moved through him. The opening was soft and tentative, then it gradually picked up in intensity just as our relationship did. Then came the part I wrote while we were apart. The music became turbulent to express how I was feeling during that time. Ben opened his eyes and reached for me. I saw the mood of the music reflected on his face.

We swayed together in a slow dance as the turbulent notes turned to a seductive harmony of renewal and devotion. My favorite part was fast approaching, and I saw recognition in Ben's eyes as the music imitated the colorful explosions in the night sky as he'd told me he loved me for the first time. Ben pressed his lips to mine when the final sweet note ended.

"I do love you, Xavier. I know they're just simple words and nothing nearly as grand as the song you composed for us, but I mean them sincerely."

"There is nothing simple about the words or the way you say them to me. They're spoken from your heart, and they're very meaningful. I love you, Ben."

"This place is beautiful, babe. Are you going to make an offer?"

"That depends."

"On?"

"You. Can you imagine yourself living here with me someday? I can picture you in every room, but I need to know if you see that too."

"Is this you asking me to move in with you?" A joyful smile spread across his face.

"This is me asking you to move in with me whenever you're ready. We haven't known each other very long, and—"

Firm lips pressed to mine, cutting off the rest of my sentence. That was okay because I had the answer I needed. This was going to be our home together, whether it be in a few weeks, a month, or a year; it didn't matter to me how long it took, just that we would someday be together in this house. Our home.

CHAPTER
Thirty-Three

Ben

"**Y**OU LOOK RIDICULOUSLY HAPPY, BRO." BEVAN CLAPPED ME ON the shoulder as our waiter placed platters of fish and chips on the table. "And I'm glad you included me in on your diet cheat day. Where's lover boy?"

"He and Chase went to pick out some linens and things for the house. I may be a besotted fool but not enough to go shopping for sheets and crap."

"You don't care about the bedding? What if he picks out something with fluffy kitties on it?" Bevan laughed at his own joke.

"Nah, I already have that bed set. He wouldn't waste money buying something we already have. Besides, I don't care what's printed on the sheets as long as he is lying between them with me, or beneath me, or on top of me."

"Yeah, I get it," Van said, cutting me off with an exaggerated roll of his eyes. "You're getting laid nightly, I know. It's meaningful and beautiful, and you pity poor saps like me who haven't found their soul mate yet. Save me the sermon."

"I didn't say it, you did, and I think you're protesting just a little bit too much." The truth was, I saw the wistfulness in Bevan's eyes when he thought I wasn't looking. I'd caught him studying Xavier and me with a curious expression.

"You don't have to say it, Ben. It's a way you have of looking at me." Van pointed to my face. "That's the look right there! You smug little prick." I threw back my head and laughed, while Van rolled his eyes. "Seriously, I'm very happy for you, Ben. I'm also proud you didn't let Beverly and Daniel scar you for life…"

"But?" I knew it was coming, so I helped him out just a little.

Van grinned at the way I read his mind. "Aren't you afraid you're moving just a little too fast? I mean, you've only known each other for a few months and you're getting ready to play house with him. Why not wait a few more months, or a year, before you move in together?"

"First, I'm not *playing* at anything, Van. I. Love. Him. I need him just like I need food, air, and water." I closed my eyes briefly and laughed. "I used to think Gray was an idiot for the way he went gaga over Chase, but damn do I get it now."

My eyes lost focus as I thought about the way Xavier sought me out in the middle of the night to cuddle or how he looked sleeping on the pillow beside mine each morning. I loved the way we worked together in the kitchen, moving like a synchronized unit as we prepared meals. He knew just what to say or do to bring me peace after a hectic day or a long business trip. No matter what life threw at me, I got to go home to him, and it made everything better. I hoped I brought him the same happiness.

The sex between us was incredible because it wasn't just sex. Making love couldn't even describe what happened when our bodies connected. It was like we were bonded on a molecular level, and even then, I couldn't get close enough.

"Van, I've slept beside him almost every night for the last month except when I've traveled for work. We've shared meals, done laundry together, fought over which TV shows to watch, and every morning I wake up thankful I get to do it all over again. I've done the bachelor thing for a very long time, and it doesn't come close to the feeling I get from just sitting beside him on the couch and holding his hand. So, no, I don't think we're rushing anything."

"Fair enough," Van conceded with grace and a good-natured grin. "Have you talked to Dad since he showed up at your house last month?"

"No."

"I still can't believe he asked for your forgiveness." Van shook his head just like I'd done every night since I turned and found Daniel in my kitchen.

"Bennett, I know I've been a bastard of a father to you boys, but I never, ever wished you hadn't been born. Lord knows we've had many arguments over the years, but I hate that you think I never wanted you. I hated that I followed the path my father set for me, and I resented your mother for my own unhappiness, but I never really wished you or Bevan away.

"I'm proud you forged your own path, even though I led you to believe otherwise. You've grown stronger and more confident these last several years, and I've envied the fact that you were man enough to do something I never could. I hope someday you can forgive me and perhaps we can forge a new relationship."

It was everything I had ever hoped to hear from my father, but it felt like it was a bit too little too late for me. He asked me if I would give it some thought and if he could call sometime. I had agreed. So far, I hadn't heard a peep from him, and quite frankly, it stung a little. I thought he had been sincere, and I'd foolishly gotten my hopes up. Again.

"Well, I'm not sure why he showed up like he did, asked for forgiveness and permission to call, and then hasn't. Xavier thinks I should reach out to him since he took the first step but hell if I'll do that. I need him to be the one to make the move."

"The road runs both ways," Van said. "Dad took a really big step, and he's probably afraid of rejection. I would be if I were in his shoes." Van was always the voice of reason, which I sometimes hated and loved. The only time

Van couldn't be objective was when it came to love and relationships, but I figured someday he'd find a person who made him reconsider everything.

"I know, Van, and I'll give it some thought." He nodded as if mollified. I watched as he began to fidget a bit, shoving his food around his plate rather than eating it. "Your turn to spill."

"God, this is awkward." Van ran his hands through his hair, and I stared at him. I'd never seen him look so uncertain. "I'm just going to say it. No beating around the bush." He looked at me with uncertainty in his eyes. I couldn't imagine what he was about to say. "I'm thinking about asking Ellie on a date."

"Ellie, as in Xavier's sister?" Well, I certainly hadn't expected that, and I think both of my eyebrows disappeared into my hairline in surprise.

"Yes, Xavier's sister. Do you think he'd be upset if I asked her out?"

I tried to think about how Xavier would feel, but all I could think about was the fact that Bevan wanted to go on a *date*. A real date. Had that even happened since college? "Why Ellie? You know she's due to have a baby soon and that her life is really complicated right now. I don't want to see her get hurt." I was pretty sure that was what Xavier would say.

Van began bouncing his legs beneath the table. "Of course. I know all about her situation. I remember that disastrous make out slash stakeout that you and lover boy tried to conduct like a bunch of amateurs." Van grinned at the memory, but I bet he was smiling over something completely different than I was. "Anyway, I've been helping El draw up legal papers to protect her and her unborn baby. It seems Drake is perfectly happy signing over his parental rights as soon as she provides a DNA test that proves he's the father. No child support and no obligations."

"What a dick."

"You have no idea how bad I want to smash that guy's face in, Ben. He's a freaking sleaze, and I can't believe someone as beautiful, smart, and kind as Ellie Cruz fell for his shit."

"What about making sure she doesn't get hurt? How are you planning to approach this? A dinner between friends or what?"

"Yes, probably. I just want to keep it light and see what happens."

"I hate to keep pointing out the obvious here, Bevan, but she's pregnant. I know you're just talking dinner, but you're a guy, and she's an attractive woman. Are you planning to take this to a physical level?"

"Jesus, Ben," Van whispered harshly. I couldn't help but notice the blush that spread across his cheeks. "Of course I find her physically attractive, but I haven't let myself go there. Damn, I just planned to ask her to dinner."

I couldn't help but laugh at his discomfort. "I don't think Xavier will have a problem with it. Ellie is almost forty. She's been on her own for a very long time. If he thinks you'll make her happy, then he'll be all for it. He just wouldn't want her to get hurt."

"Maybe I should talk to Xavier first. I don't want to mess things up between the two of you."

"We're having our first cookout at our new house on Sunday," I said. "You can talk to him then and see how he feels about it. Ellie will be there, and you can spend time with her in a pressure-free environment to see how things feel."

"Sounds perfect. Thank you." Bevan's expression spread into a shit-eating grin. "So, what do I buy two guys as a housewarming gift?"

CHAPTER
Thirty-Four

Xavier

"So"—I leaned close to Chase so I wouldn't be over-heard—"guess who we saw coming out of your bathroom together while readjusting their clothes at your Fourth of July party?"

"Gram and Lennie?" Chase asked, then laughed at his joke. "Who? And why are you just telling me now? We already had the Labor Day pool party, and you didn't say anything then." Chase was helping me load various cheeses and sandwich toppings onto a large platter but stopped to put his hands on his hips in exasperation. I glanced back outside to see Gray and Ben were still manning the grill and quickly looked around to make sure no one else was listening in.

"JJ and Miller." I knew I'd delivered the names with a gossipy gleam in my eyes.

"Shut. The. Fuck. Up!" Chase said.

We both turned and looked out the French doors at the same time. JJ and Miller were sitting at a table by themselves talking and drinking beers. They looked a lot more relaxed since I last saw them coming out of the bathroom. I hadn't forgotten the look on JJ's face when Miller had walked away without a backward glance. Ben and I both believed something more was going on between them.

"I'm serious. There was no mistaking what JJ and Miller had been doing in your bathroom. Ben and I got the impression this wasn't the first time. JJ made a comment to Ben at the charity event about Miller wanting me and always getting everything he wanted. It was said as if JJ had personal knowledge of just how convincing Miller could be."

"Ben ought to know," Chase said with a smirk. His eyes bulged out of his head, and he covered his mouth with both hands when he realized what he'd blurted out.

I laughed hysterically at his horrified expression but quickly took pity on him. "I know all about Ben and Miller hooking up a few years ago. It doesn't bother me. It was long before we met and meant nothing. I get to see a side of Ben no one else gets to, and it's amazing."

"That's beautiful, Xavier." Chase, my champion, my brother, and my best friend teared up as he looked around my first home—the home I shared with the man I loved. "To say I'm happy for you isn't enough. I don't think ecstatic even works. Gah! I'm so excited to see the sparkle back in your eyes, but they've never sparkled like this." He pointed at my eyes for emphasis. "Miller and JJ, huh? Well, they have gotten closer since Gray and I met. They're kind of thrown together at these things since they're the only bachelors left. Do you get the impression they've been screwing each other for a long time?" Chase and I turned to look at them again but found empty chairs instead.

"Where'd they go?" I looked around the backyard but didn't see them anywhere. "Oh man. I bet they're in here screwing." A loud thump and muffled laugh came from somewhere in the house. "I think they're in the hallway bathroom. What is it with them and bathrooms? They better not leave spunk all over my damn floor."

"It's better than your bedroom. Let's confront them," Chase said with a look of pure mischief in his eyes. "Those two are constantly ragging on us about our sappy relationships. It's only fair we give some of that back. They're lucky I don't call our men in here to witness this with us." *Our men. I liked it.*

"Let's do it."

Chase and I tiptoed down the hallway, probably looking like a bad imitation of Shaggy and Scooby. I was obviously Scooby Doo. As we approached the door, blatant sex sounds echoed into the hallway.

"Ohhh," Miller moaned. "God that feels so good."

JJ made a purring sound. "You like that? Right there?"

"Fuck yes," Miller replied breathlessly, "but harder, J. I need it harder."

Two bodies slammed together repeatedly on the other side of the door.

"J. Oh, fuck! More, baby."

"Baby," Chase and I mouthed at each other.

JJ let out a long groan, and our eyes bugged out of our heads as we fought not to laugh and give ourselves away. The bathroom door opened suddenly, and two fully dressed grown men caught us with our heads practically pressed to the door.

"Caught you didn't we, you little assholes," Miller said playfully and jabbed at Chase's stomach with his fists.

"You little gossip gays were so busy yapping you didn't hear us walk in. We stood there listening to you talking about us having sex." JJ looked over at Miller, then back to us. "What we are or aren't doing is our business."

JJ wrapped his arm around my neck in a headlock so fast that I didn't have time to prepare myself. As soon as his arm hooked around me, I started to squirm and panic.

"What's going on in here?" Gray's voice was full of mischief.

"JJ and Miller are trying to talk us into a foursome," Chase lied. "See? J is trying to pull X into the bathroom."

Black dots danced across my vision, and a full-on panic attack loomed. I tried to remind myself it was JJ, who cared about me and would never hurt me, but my brain screamed *danger*. I fought to take air into my lungs, but it felt like they had seized up.

"Let go of him, JJ." Ben's authoritative voice had JJ releasing me immediately. I gasped as soon as I was free from him, but I still struggled to pull air into my lungs. Ben immediately wrapped me in his arms. "Can we have a moment please?" Ben didn't wait for a response before he pulled me into the bathroom and shut the door. "You're okay, love. Breathe with me." He placed my hand over his chest so I could feel the steady rhythm of his lungs working, moving air in and out, in and out. It didn't take me long to calm down and breathe with him. Ben placed his hands gently on my neck, knowing how much I loved for his touch to chase away the bad memories.

"Ben," I whispered brokenly. "I'm such a damn mess." I felt hot tears of humiliation burning the back of my eyes. "JJ was only playing around with me, and look what happened."

"Stop being so hard on yourself, Xavier. You survived a very abusive relationship, and you're bound to have triggers." Ben had read a lot about drug addiction and domestic abuse recovery. It was one of the many reasons why I loved him so much. "I'll go with you if you want to talk to a professional." And he would, just like he had gone to quite a few of my NA meetings. "Anything you want, but please don't put yourself down."

"I love you so much, Ben." I didn't always feel deserving of his love, but I was getting better.

"And I love you." He held me close and kissed my face sweetly. "Are you ready to return to the party?"

I nodded, and we opened up the bathroom door to find JJ pacing the hallway. I was shocked at the level of concern I saw in his eyes. I'd never told him about my abusive relationship, and I was certain no one else had either. The expression in his eyes gave away a secret from his past that I'd bet not even Chase knew.

JJ knew what it was like to suffer abuse. He must have recognized the signs in me and had to feel horrible about triggering a response. "Xavier, I would never hurt you. I am so sorry."

"It's okay, J. It wasn't your fault. You were only playing around and had no idea that would happen. Hell, I didn't know it would either. I'm sorry I scared you."

JJ pulled me into a gentle hug. "Don't let the memories of the past ruin your future. Take it from someone who lives with regret daily. Fight for what you have because it's worth it." He dropped an innocent kiss on my forehead and walked away. His shoulders sagged with whatever was weighing down his heart.

I knew he was talking about Chase, and my heart broke for him. How freaking hard must it have been for him to watch Chase fall in love and marry Gray? It astonished me that he kept accepting invites to spend time with them because it had to be emotional torture. But Chase would be hurt if he didn't show up, and it was now crystal clear to me that JJ would do anything to make Chase happy, even at the expense of his own sanity.

"Wow," Ben said. He pulled me into a hug because it was what the moment called for. We were both grateful we had found each other and weren't members of the lonely hearts club. "I'm going to battle for us every damn day. I'll fight to the finish to keep you in my life."

"Me too, Ben. Sometimes I'll be combatting myself, but I'll give you everything I am—the good, the bad, and the downright ugly." I looked up at Ben and said, "I need a kiss." He gladly obliged and kissed me until I was ready to send everyone home so we could be alone together. Ben pulled back, and I could tell he felt the same. "Let's go feed them, then maybe they'll leave faster."

"Good idea."

We rounded the corner into the kitchen, and I came to a screeching halt. Bevan and Ellie were deep in a conversation as they leaned against the kitchen counter. They looked like they were in their own little world. I recognized those expressions for what they were—blossoming feelings.

"Hi, gorgeous," I said. "Are you ready to eat?" I wrapped my arms around my sister and placed a kiss on the top of her head.

"I'm starving, hot stuff," Bevan replied with a laugh.

"Me too." Ellie rubbed her baby bump. "We're starving," she amended.

I watched Bevan's expression as Ellie brought up her pregnancy. I wanted to see if it was a problem for him. He kept his gaze steadily on mine and didn't flinch at the reference to her unborn child. I felt like there was more in his look as if he was seeking something from me, and then it dawned on me. He was asking for my approval. *Oh, how the mighty have fallen,* I thought to myself with a smug smile. I gave him a playful wink over Ellie's head and saw him visibly relax.

"I'm going to relieve Lennie from grill duty," Ben said. "I'll let you know how much longer it will be." He dropped a kiss on my cheek before he left.

I felt bad for intruding on their moment, but I needed to talk to Van about the birthday party I wanted to plan for Ben. Chase and Gray entered the kitchen a minute later, and I was glad I could get their input.

"I want to plan a birthday party for Ben, and I need your help," I told them. "I was thinking something really casual at Bottoms Up. We could play darts and pool, do karaoke, and eat cake. What do you think? Is that too lame?"

"It sounds perfect to me," Gray said. "I don't think he'd like us to make a big fuss, but he'd enjoy a casual gathering at the bar."

"I agree," Ellie said.

"Sounds good to me," Chase replied.

"Are you talking about a surprise birthday party?" Bevan asked.

"Nooooo," Ellie, Gray, Chase, and I all said at the same time.

"Okaaaaay," Bevan said, not understanding our vehement response, so we enlightened him. "Jesus," Bevan said when we were through, then turned to Gray. "You met when your ex brought Chase home to fuck when he thought you were out of town? The lights get flipped on and there stands Chase with your boyfriend at his feet ready to blow him?" We all nodded. He turned to Chase and asked, "Then you show up at your new job a few days later and learn Gray is your boss?" We all nodded again. We were starting to look like bobbleheads. "Holy shit! No wonder you all are such believers in fate. Hell, you and my brother might not have happened if not for Chase and Gray's fated encounter. Huh?"

"It's possible I would've met Ben through Ellie but doubtful," I agreed. "We owe it all to Devon Bellows." A chorus of groans and laughter followed my declaration. "Van, I really could use your help on two things. Your dad and the birthday cake."

"You want my dad to pop out of the birthday cake?"

I laughed. "Not exactly..."

CHAPTER
Thirty-Five

Ben

I T WAS A TOUCHING MOMENT WHEN I LOOKED AROUND AT ALL THE people who had shown up to celebrate my birthday with me. My co-workers, my brother, my closest friends, and my amazing boyfriend all gathered in one place to wish me well. I'd never had a birthday party before, and the fact that Xavier had put so much thought into it drove home how blessed I was to have him in my life.

The door to Bottoms Up opened, and my dad walked into the bar with a wrapped gift tucked under his arm. He looked around for someone famil-iar, and I saw a friendly smile split his face when Xavier approached him. They shook hands and Xavier gestured to where I was standing.

Daniel's eyes met mine, and he smiled tentatively at me. I tried to re-turn the gesture, but the truth was that I was too emotional to do anything but stare. I was in real jeopardy of losing my shit and crying like a little boy because there stood my father making the move I needed him to make. I knew Xavier and Van were behind his invitation, but he was the one who had accepted it and shown up.

This was the moment I'd wanted my whole life. I could be a dick and reject his gesture, but I'd regret it for the rest of my life. I decided to meet him in the middle, both literally and figuratively.

"Happy birthday, Ben." I felt his nervousness rolling off him in waves.

"Thanks, D-Dad." I had started to say Daniel, but if I was going to take this leap, I needed to give it my all—no matter how scary.

"You think we could find a quiet corner and chat for a minute?" His smile was hopeful after I'd called him Dad for the first time in probably twenty years.

"Sure." I found us a table in the back corner and took a seat. "Thanks for coming to my party."

"I'm glad I was invited. Listen, I want to tell you that I think Xavier is a wonderful young man. He has a pure heart, and that's really rare." My dad waved at someone behind me, and I turned to see who. Ian waved awkwardly at my dad, then offered me an encouraging smile.

"Are you in love with Ian's mom?" I asked once I'd turned back around to face him.

"Cassandra," he corrected, "and, yes, I am in love with her."

"Dad, you're trying to do right by me, and I truly appreciate it. I think it's also time to do right by Beverly, Cassandra, and yourself. Life is too short to live in misery, and you don't owe your parents jack shit." I looked my father straight in the eye while I searched for the right words to say. This whole thing was new to us, and I didn't want to do or say something that would ruin our tentative truce, but I had to be completely honest with him. His cheating really rubbed me the wrong way, even if my mom was a heartless bitch. "You took over a fairly successful law firm and made it one of the top ten in DC. What's the worst that will happen if you divorce Beverly? You'll give up half your wealth, which will still leave you with a stupid amount of money. If you get ousted from the firm, then you can take Cassandra on a very long vacation and be happy for once in your life. Dad, you have to look yourself in the mirror every day, and I don't see how you can possibly like what you see, knowing that you're married to one woman and in love with another." I blew out a nervous breath.

"I've thought about it, Ben. A lot," he confessed. "I'm not proud of the way I've lived my life, and blaming my parents and Beverly is getting really old. *I'm* getting old, and I just want some peace and tranquility for the rest of my time. And, yes, I want to be able to look in the mirror and see someone I actually like. Thank you, son."

"There's your answer, then. Divorce Beverly, resign from the firm, and sail off into the sunset."

"I'm just getting to know my sons, and I don't want to disappear. I want it all." It was the first time I'd heard excitement in my dad's voice over anything other than landing a large client.

"Then have it all. You can build a relationship with us while you discover who you really are. Those two things don't have to be mutually exclusive. I'm not saying you sail off and never return." The thought of him leaving bothered me more than I would have thought. I looked for Xavier because the sight of him always brought me comfort. I found him talking and smiling with Chase and Gray by the bar. I felt my heart swell with love at seeing my lover looking so whole and happy. I turned my attention back to my dad and said, "That beautiful man over there is going to be your son-in-law someday, and you won't want to miss it."

"You're absolutely right." He cleared his throat, then said, "You're wise beyond your years, Ben. Thank you for giving me another chance. I'm going to work hard as hell not to blow it, and if nothing else, I am a damn hard worker. Here." He slid my present across the table. "I hope you like it." I slowly unwrapped the gift, and what I found inside made me tear up. "It was the only thing you wanted for Christmas when you were ten, and I always regretted not getting it for you."

I ran my hand over the *Jumanji* board game. Bevan had taken me to see the movie for my tenth birthday, and I'd loved it. The only thing I'd wanted for Christmas that year was the board game I held in my hands. The St. Claire boys weren't given frivolous toys as gifts. All our rarely permitted toys were for learning and development, not fun.

I looked up at my dad but could hardly see through the tears in my eyes. The fact that he'd remembered how badly I'd wanted this game was more important than receiving it as a gift. "It's perfect, and I love it." A lone tear escaped my eye and slid down my face. I wiped it away quickly. "Thank you."

"You're very welcome." My dad's voice was also choked with emotion.

I felt Xavier's presence before he even spoke. "Oh, wow! I haven't played that game in years."

"Let's play it now," my dad suggested.

"Really?" I looked around at the party guests and felt torn. I wanted to play the game, but I didn't want to ignore my guests.

"Definitely." My dad nodded.

Bevan came over as we began to unpack all the pieces. "Can I get in on the action too?"

"Hell yeah." We bumped fists.

I lost track of how long we played, and I ashamedly forgot about my party and the people who had come to celebrate with me. We laughed and teased each other mercilessly, and I learned my dad had a wicked sense of humor. Xavier reached for my hand beneath the table, wanting to feel our connection but unsure how he should behave in front of my dad. I loved Xavier with everything I had, and I wasn't hiding it from anyone. If my dad wanted a relationship with me, then seeing me show my love for Xavier was part of it. I pulled Xavier to me for a short but sweet kiss.

We eventually put the game away after Dad beat us twice. Xavier had ordered my favorite cake, red velvet, and wanted to serve it. He gave me a quick kiss and said he had another surprise for me before he left to deal with the cake. I was certain that whatever he had planned couldn't top what he'd already given me, but I was wrong.

Xavier took his trusted guitar, Bess, and climbed the stage. The lights of the bar dimmed, and my beautiful man stood in front of the microphone with a spotlight shining on him. His eyes met mine and held while he sang Richard Marx's "Now and Forever," and I cried.

"That was a beautiful gift," I told him once he finished singing and exited the stage. "I loved it, and I love you."

"I'm so glad you did. I was afraid it was too mushy to sing in front of our family and friends."

"It was perfect just like this party and your gifts."

"I'm not done with your surprises yet," Xavier said with a leering smile. "We have yet to properly anoint our new garage. I believe you mentioned something about me bending over Mistress's hood."

"It's time to go home," I said in a rush, reaching for his hand. "I'm older now, and I need to stop staying out so late. Let's try not to be obvious that I'm about to make it less than comfortable for you to walk tomorrow, okay?"

"Too late," Gray said from behind me before Xavier could answer my question. Xavier and I moaned in unison.

I turned to find Gray and Chase standing behind us wearing matching grins. Xavier told me what Van had said about Chase and Gray's fated encounter leading to our relationship. I had never really thought about it quite like that, but Van was right. Their love had brought Xavier into my life like some amazing ripple effect. I looked around the bar and wondered which one of our friends might be next. I shared my musings with Chase, Gray, and Xavier, who also began looking around and speculating.

I saw Jack leaning awfully close to Liam as they talked behind the bar. Of course, he could've been doing that to be heard over the music. JJ and Miller appeared to be having a good time playing pool against a couple of guys I didn't recognize. It was hard to imagine those two ever settling down—especially with each other—but who knew?

"Oh, the possibilities," Xavier said with glee. "It's sure as hell going to be fun to kick back and watch now that we've found our happily ever after."

Happily ever after. Three words I'd only read about in books or saw in movies or television shows. I thought they were fabled things that didn't happen in real life, but I was wrong. So wrong. I would be taking my happily ever after home with me, and I would spend that night, and every night after, grateful for the blessing that was Xavier Cruz.

Epilogue

Xavier

A FEW WEEKS LATER, JACK CALLED CHASE AND TOLD HIM THAT HE had a family emergency and asked if Chase could help out for a few weeks while he was gone. Jack wasn't the kind of guy who asked anyone for anything, so Chase was happy to help.

One Friday night while Jack was away, Ben and I went to keep Gray company while he stared down any man who even thought about hitting on Chase while he tended bar. It was the funniest damn thing Ben and I had ever seen.

I watched Chase and Liam behind the bar and noticed how well they worked together as if they'd done it for years instead of just a few days. They laughed and seemed to be having a great time. Once again, I was struck by a nagging feeling that there was something familiar about Liam. It wasn't so much his looks but his mannerisms. Then it hit me how I knew those expressions and gestures.

I sat speechless on the stool for a long time while Gray and Ben chatted about work. They eventually went to play pool or darts, but I wasn't listening. I waived Liam over to get a refill on my Coke and told myself to keep my mouth shut. But I didn't listen.

I leaned forward and crooked my finger for him to come closer. "When are you going to tell Chase you're his half brother?" I watched all the color leech from Liam's face, and I knew I had guessed correctly. The trouble was, what the hell was I going to do with the knowledge?

The End

Want to be the first to know about my book releases and have access to extra content? You can sign up for my newsletter here: http://eepurl.com/dlhPYj

My favorite place to hang out and chat with my readers is my Facebook group. Would you like to be a member of Aimee's Dye Hards? We'd love to have you! Go here: www.facebook.com/groups/AimeesDyeHards

Other Books by
AIMEE NICOLE WALKER

Curl Up and Dye Mysteries
Dyeing to be Loved
Something to Dye For
Dyed and Gone to Heaven
I Do, or Dye Trying
A Dye Hard Holiday
Ride or Dye

Road to Blissville Series
Unscripted Love
Someone to Call My Own
Nobody's Prince Charming
This Time Around
Smoke in the Mirror
Inside Out
Prescription for Love

Welcome to Blissville Collection (Both M/M Blissville series)
Volume One
Volume Two

The Lady is Mine Series
The Lady is a Thief
The Lady Stole My Heart

Queen City Rogue Series
Broken Halos
Wicked Games
Beautiful Trauma

Zero Hour Series
Ground Zero
Devil's Hour
Zero Divergence

Matrimony and Mayhem (Continuation of Zero Hour)
The Magnolia Murders

Sinister in Savannah Series
Ride the Lightning
Mr. Perfect
Pretty Poison

Savannah Standalone Books
Invisible Strings

Fated Hearts Series (Second Edition)
Chasing Mr. Wright

Standalone Novels
Second Wind

Coauthored with Nicholas Bella
Undisputed
Circle of Darkness (Genesis Circle, Book 1)
Circle of Trust (Genesis Circle, Book 2)

Acknowledgments

I must give a huge shoutout to my editing team, Susie Selva and Lori Parks, for tackling this rehab project with so much gusto and passion. If not for their guidance and cheerleading, the Fated Hearts series probably would've stayed in the vault. Thank you so very much, ladies.

I've been so fortunate to work with Stacey Blake of Champagne Book Designs since virtually the dawn of my career. In fact, *Chasing Mr. Wright* was the first book she formatted for me, so it only seemed right that I tapped her to work on the covers for the second editions. Stacey is a brilliant artist, and I'm always so thrilled to show off her pretties.

And I'm sending so much love to the fans who've waited for the Fated Hearts gang to return.

xoxoxo

About

AIMEE NICOLE WALKER

Ever since she was a little girl, Aimee Nicole Walker entertained herself with stories that popped into her head. Now she gets paid to tell those stories to other people. She wears many titles—wife, mom, and animal lover are just a few of them. Her absolute favorite title is champion of the happily ever after. Love inspires everything she does, music keeps her sane, and coffee is the magic elixir that fuels her day.

She'd love to hear from you.

Want to connect? All her links are in one nifty location. Click here: linktr.ee/AimeeNicoleWalker